THE BOFFIN

What chemistry, we are often asked, takes place in the succulent bosom of the sherry casks where The Macallan lies slumbering for a decade (at least) before it is allowed out to meet the bottle?

The fact is, we do not know.

It is a _matter of history_, of course, that someone in the last century discovered that whisky ages best in oaken casks which have previously contained sherry (and that today The Macallan is the _last malt whisky_ exclusively to be so matured).

And it is a _matter of fact_ that in goes the translucent stripling spirit. And out comes amber-gold nectar positively _billowing_ with flavour.

But let us take our cue from a party of scientists whom we once invited to explore the matter. '_Magic!_' they exclaimed, swigging their drams in a most unboffinly manner. 'But magic is merely undiscovered science and we'd like to take some home _for further investigation_.'

THE MACALLAN. THE SINGLE MALT SCOTCH.

Sole U.S.A. Distributor, Remy Amerique, Inc., NY, NY Scotch Whisky 86 Proof, 43% Alc./Vol. © 1995

The Paris Review

Founded in 1953.

The Paris Review is published quarterly by The Paris Review, Inc. Vol. 37, No. 134, Spring 1995. Business Office: 45–39 171 Place, Flushing, New York 11358 (ISSN #0031-2037). Paris Office: Harry Matthews, 67 rue de Grenelle, Paris 75007 France. London Office: Shusha Guppy, 8 Shawfield St., London, SW3. US distributors: Random House, Inc. 1(800)733-3000. Typeset and printed in USA by Capital City Press, Montpelier, VT. Price for single issue in USA: $10.00. $14.00 in Canada. Post-paid subscription for four issues $34.00, lifetime subscription $1000. Postal surcharge of $7.00 per four issues outside USA (excluding life subscriptions). Subscription card is bound within magazine. Please give six weeks notice of change of address using subscription card. *While The Paris Review welcomes the submission of unsolicited manuscripts, it cannot accept responsibility for their loss or delay, or engage in related correspondence. Manuscripts will not be returned or responded to unless accompanied by self-addressed, stamped envelope. Fiction manuscripts should be submitted to George Plimpton, poetry to Richard Howard, The Paris Review, 541 East 72nd Street, New York, N.Y. 10021.* Charter member of the Council of Literary Magazines and Presses. This publication is made possible, in part, with public funds from the New York State Council on the Arts and the National Endowment for the Arts. Second Class postage paid at Flushing, New York, and at additional mailing offices. **Postmaster:** Please send address changes to 45-39 171st Place, Flushing, N.Y. 11358.

Flaubert compared losing oneself in literature to perpetual orgy.

Here's your invitation to the party.

The Paris Review. It's the kind of writing that gives you goosebumps. That sends a shiver down your spine. That makes your hair stand on end. It's the kind of writing that's the result of a longstanding commitment to literature. A commitment The Paris Review has made for more than 40 years.

Whether you want short stories, poetry, photography, art or our renowned interviews, call (718) 539-7085 to subscribe and you'll get a better understanding of the place where Flaubert found his passion.

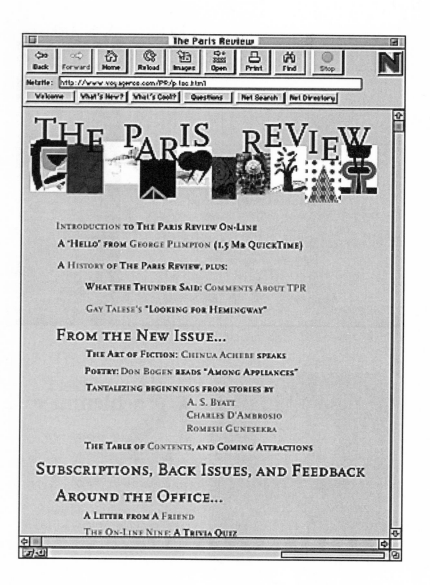

on the internet...

HTTP://WWW.VOYAGERCO.COM

The
Paris
Review

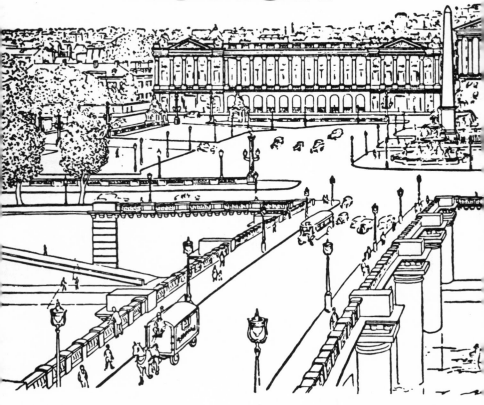

Editorial Office:
541 East 72 Street
New York, New York 10021

Business & Circulation:
45-39 171 Place
Flushing, New York 11358

Distributed by Random House
201 East 50 Street
New York, N.Y. 10022
(800) 733-3000

Number 134

Rhett Arens, "Pigeon House.".
Frontispiece by William Pène duBois.

NOTICE

Sharp-eyed subscribers will note that the last issue (winter 1994–1995), and indeed this one, enjoy a new look — a clearer, more distinct typeface on the cover which itself has been redesigned. For the first time the featured contents are listed on the spine. Also on the spine is the Paris Review bird, designed by the magazine's first art editor, William Pène du Bois, and which reappears after an absence of thirty-three years. An American eagle astride a pen and wearing a Phrygian cap to denote the French connection, it perched in the top-left quadrant of the cover until the spring of 1962 when the artist Larry Rivers displaced it with a design of a winged helmet which took up the entire cover.

Readers of this issue may also note that a theme seems to run throughout much of the content — namely one of self-destruction. This is, in fact, a coincidence, though it is indeed becoming increasingly common in literary magazine circles to focus on a single topic. *Granta* is an obvious example with its pronounced policy of labelling each number — "Sex," "Money," and so on. This autumn we are falling into line, at least temporarily, with an entire issue devoted to the subject of humor — perhaps because it seems such a rare if desired element in what is sent us. Subscribers will recall that in the past we have tried to chivvy humorous or witty pieces out of our contributors by offering a humor prize — first the Gertrude Vanderbilt, then the John Train Humor Prizes, this last finally discontinued because (1) of the uncertain quality of the works submitted, and (2) the editors and John Train, a former managing editor and bestower of the prize money, could never agree on what was worthy of recognition. All of this has suggested that an issue devoted to the subject would be of considerable interest. The contents will include interviews with Garrison Keillor, T. Coraghessan Boyle and Calvin Trillin.

Also in coming issues we intend to open a letters column — so that in the future readers can reach us with their opinions, comments, outrage, whatever. We have published letters as content material in the past (the Delmore Schwartz–James Laughlin correspondence, for example) but only a few letters to the editors. One instance was an exchange between J. P.

Donleavy and John Irving on whether the former had insulted John Cheever at the Iowa Writers' Workshop. Odd, this lack, because the first issue of *The Paris Review* was introduced by a letter from William Styron setting forth the magazine's editorial aims.

Other developments. Last month *The Paris Review* arrived "on-line" — that is to say we are to be found on the information superhighway. In collaboration with Voyager, a publisher specializing in new media forms, we are on the Internet not only with excerpts from the contents of the last issue (snippets of fiction, poets reading their work, segments from the interviews with Chinua Achebe and Czeslaw Milosz), but also with access to work from the past, dating as far back as the first issue, published in 1953. This present issue will be edited for viewing on-line by the time you read this. *The Paris Review* and the Voyager site can be accessed through the World Wide Web by typing our address which is: http://www.voyagerco.com on any Internet provider, Prodigy, Compuserve or America On-line.

Also, in recent months *The Paris Review* has affiliated itself with the American Poetry and Literacy Project, a national non-profit organization founded by Andrew Carroll and the Nobel laureate Joseph Brodsky to encourage people to read more poetry. Several thousand back issues were donated which the Project then distributed to various four-star hotels to be placed on bedside tables. One hotel returned a shipment of the winter 1991 number because guests were startled, if not upset, by the cover — a pair of intertwined snakes. It was not what they expected to find nestled next to the Gideon Bible at bedside! We will have to be more careful with future donations — perhaps our first concession to public taste since we got going over four decades ago!

One last note. This year *The Paris Review* was a finalist in the annual National Magazine Awards fiction category for the fifth time — quite an achievement since the annual competition sponsered by the American Society of Magazine editors includes mass circulation magazines like *Esquire* and *The New Yorker*. We did not win, alas. The prior week *The New York Observer* predicted as much, though they thought we were the strongest competitor. Our taking home the award, an odd-looking stabile called "The Elephant," was billed as unlikely because "snowy-haired, party-throwing, bicycle-riding George Plimpton still puzzles the AMSE."

Whether the undersigned will make a concession in *this* case is another matter . . .

— G.A.P.

In Memoriam: James Merrill

In issue #131 (summer 1994), we printed a poem by James Merrill about the death by AIDS of one of his friends. These prescient lines occur:

"See," breathed the mirror, "who's alive,
Who hasn't forfeited the common touch,

The longing to lead everybody's life"
—Lifelong daydream of precisely those
Whom privilege or talent set apart:
How to atone for the achieved uniqueness?
By dying everybody's death, dear heart—
Saint, terrorist, fishwife. Stench that appals.
Famines, machine guns, the Great Plague (your sickness),
Rending of garments, cries, mass burials.

I'd watched my beard sprout in the mirror's grave.
Mirrors are graves, as all can see:
Knew this emerging mask would outlast me,
Just as the life outlasts us, that we live . . .

How characteristic of him, to have spoken more suitably on this occasion than any grieving sentences of ours at his sudden death. But not loss—we cannot lose such a poet ("achieved uniqueness") when he dies, only something of ourselves. James went out to life (explored), and his work invited us in (implored), the systole and diastole of genius. We are proud of his writings that appeared in the *Review*, and prize the entire oeuvre, a growing triumph. I found these words with which to say good-bye, by his beloved Cavafy:

. . . They're asking for a few lines
as an epitaph for the poet, something
very tasteful and polished. You can do it,
you're the one to write something suitable
for the poet, for our poet . . .
Of course you'll speak about his poems—
but say something too about his beauty,
about that subtle beauty we loved.
. . . Your verses, you know, should be written
so they contain something of our life within them,
so the rhythm, so every phrase clearly shows
that an Alexandrian is writing about an Alexandrian.

—Richard Howard

The Revisionist

Helen Schulman

It had been a hundred years since Hershleder had taken in a late afternoon movie, a hundred years since he had gone to the movies by himself. It was 5:45. There was a 6:15 train Hershleder could still make. But why give in, why not not do something as inevitable as being home on time for dinner? At heart he was a rebel. Hershleder walked up the avenue to Kips Bay. There, there was a movie house. He could enter the theater in daylight. When was the last time he had done that — gone from a dazzling summer afternoon, when the air was visible and everything looked like it was in a comic book, only magnified, broken down into a sea of shimmering dots — into the dark, cool mouth of a movie theater? It was a dry July day. It was hot out. Who cared what was playing? Porno. Action. Comedy. All Hershleder wanted was to give himself over to something.

He was drawn to the box office as if the gum-chewing bored girl behind the counter was dispensing pharmaceutical cocaine and he was still a young and reckless intern — the kind he had always planned on being, the kind Hershleder was only in his dreams. She had big hair. Brown hair, sprayed and teased

into wings. She had a dark mole beneath her pink lips on the
left-hand side of her face. It looked like the period that marks
a dotted quarter in musical notation. She was a beautiful girl
in an interesting way. Which means if the light were right
(which it wasn't quite then), if she held her chin at a particular
angle (which she didn't, her chin was in a constant seesaw on
account of the gum) when she laughed or when she forgot
about pulling her lips over her teeth (which were long and
fine and, at the most reductive — canine) she was a lovely,
cubist vision.

Hershleder bought two tickets from this young girl. He
bought two tickets out of force of habit. He entered the building, passed the two tickets toward the ticket taker and realized
that he was alone.

Back at the box office, the girl wouldn't grant Hershleder
a refund. She said: "It's a done deal, doll." But she smiled
at him.

Hershleder gave the extra ticket to a bag lady who sat under
the marquee where the sidewalk was slightly more shaded
than the street, where the open and close of the glass doors
to the air-conditioned theater provided the nearest thing to
an ocean breeze that she would feel on this, her final face.

Hershleder the blind, Hershleder the dumb — oblivious to
the thrill of a beautiful big-haired girl's lyrical smile, a smile
a musician could sight-read and play. Blind and stuck with
an extra ticket, Hershleder gave it away to the old lady. He
wasn't a bad guy, really. Hadn't the old woman once been
somebody's baby? Wasn't it possible, also, that she was still
somebody's mother? Were there ever two more exalted roles
in this human theater? This woman had risen to the pinnacle
of her being; and she'd fallen. She suffered from La Tourrette.
Hershleder held the glass door open for her; he'd been well
raised by his own mother, a woman with a deep residing respect
for the elderly.

"Bastard," said the old lady, smiling shyly. "Cocksucker."

Hershleder smiled back at her. Here was someone who spoke
his language. Hadn't he seen a thousand and one patients
like her before?

"Fucking Nazi prick," the woman said, her voice trailing low as she struggled to gain control of herself. Her face screwed up in concentration; she wrestled with her inner, truer self. "Faggot," she said through clenched teeth; she bowed her head now, trying to direct her voice back into her chest. The next word came out like an exhalation of smoke, in a puff, a whisper: "Motherfucker."

The old lady looked up at Hershleder from beneath hooded lids—in her eyes was a lifetime of expressions unfortunately not held back, of words unleashed, epithets unfettered—there was a locker room of vile language in her head, but her face seemed apologetic. When Hershleder met her gaze, she fluttered her lashes, morse-coding like the quadriplegic on Ward A, then turned and shuffled away from him.

•

It was delicious inside the theater. Cold enough for Hershleder to take off his jacket and lay it flat like a blanket across his chest. His hand wandered across his crotch, stroked his belly. In the flirtation of film light, Hershleder felt himself up under the curtain of his jacket. There were a couple of teenagers in the back of the house who talked throughout the movie, but what did Hershleder care? It was dark, there was music. Stray popcorn crunched beneath his feet. A side door opened, and he got high off the smell of marijuana wafting on a cross breeze. An old man dozed in an end seat across the aisle. A beautiful girl on screen displayed a beautiful private birthmark. A bare-chested man rolled on top of her, drowning Hershleder's view. Above war planes flew, bombs dropped, the girl moaned, fire fire fire. Something was burning On screen? Off screen? The exit sign was the reddest thing he'd ever seen. It glowed on the outskirts of his peripheral vision. Time passed in a solid leap, as in sleep, as in coma. When the lights came up, Hershleder was drowsily aware that much had happened to him—but what? Couldn't the real world have jumped forward at the rate of onscreen time in quantum

leaps of event and tragedy and years? The movies. Like rockets
hurtling a guy through space.

It was a way to make the hours pass, that's for sure, thought
Hershleder. For a moment he had no clue as to what day it was.

•

Grand Central Station.

Hershleder waited for information. On the south wall was
a huge photo essay, Kodak's, presenting the glories of India.
A half-naked child, his brown outstretched hand, an empty
bowl, his smile radiant. A bony cow. A swirl of sari, a lovely
face, a red dot like a jewel amidst the light filigree of a happy
forehead. A blown-up piece of poori: a bread cloud. The Taj
Mahal. . . *In All Its Splendor.*

The lobby of Bellevue looked something like this. The
women in their saris, the homeless beggars, the drug addicts
that punctuated the station like restless exclamation marks.
Inge, his chief lab technician, had told him that at the hospital,
in the ground floor women's bathrooms, mothers bathed their
babies in the sinks. Hershleder could believe this. There, like
here, was a place to come in out of the cold, the rain, the
heat.

The signboard fluttered its black lids, each train announcement inched its way up another slot. Hershleder's would de-
part from Track 11. There was time for half a dozen oysters
at the Oyster Bar. He headed out past Zaro's Bakery, the
bagels and the brioche, the pies of mile-high lemon frosting.
Cholesterol — how it could slather the arteries with silken ecs-
tacy! (Hershleder had to watch himself. Oysters would do the
trick — in more ways than one. What was that old joke . . .
the rules of turning forty: never waste an erection, never trust
a fart.) He hung a left, down the curved, close passageway —
the tunnel that felt like an inner tube, an underground track
without the track, an alimentary canal, a cool stone vagina.
Vagrants sagged against the walls, sprawled beneath the arch-
ways. There was a souvenir stand. A book store. A florist!

Daisies, bright white for Itty, beckoned from earthenware vases. This was a must-stop on his future trek to Track 11. The passageway smelled like a pet store. The horrible inevitable decay of everything biological, the waste, the waste! Hershleder did a little shocked pas de bourrée over a pretzel of human shit, three toe-steps, as lacy as a dancer's.

•

They slid down easy, those Wellfleets, Blue Points. Hershleder leaned against the polished wood and ordered another half dozen. Not liquid, not solid—a fixed transitional state. A second beer. So what if he missed his train? There would always be another. Death and taxes. Conrail and the Erie Lackawanna. The fact that oysters made him horny.

They slid down cold and wet. Peppery. Hershleder wasn't one to skimp on hot sauce. The shell against his upper lip was blue and smooth, his lower lip touched lichen or was it coral? Pinstripes made up his panorama. The other slurpers were all like him. Commuters. Men who traveled to and from their wives, their children, "the Office." Men with secret lives in a foreign land: the city. Men who got off on eating oysters, who delayed going home by having yet another round of drinks. They all stood in a row at the bar the way they would stand at a row of urinals. Each in his private world. "Aaach," said Hershleder, and tipped another briny shell to his lips. His mouth was flooded by ocean.

Delays, delays. A lifetime full of delays. Hershleder the procrastinator, the putter-offer. Hershleder of the term papers started the night before, the grant proposals typed once into the computer, the postmarks fudged by the hospital's friendly postmaster. He was the kind of man to leave things to the last minute, to torture himself every moment that he did not attend to what needed attending to, his tasks, but also the type always to get them done. While in his heart he lusted after irresponsibility, he was never bad enough. Chicken-shit. A loser.

Hershleder's neighbor at the bar was reading *The New York Times*.

"Hey, Mister," said Hershleder, sounding like he was seven. "Would you mind letting me look at the C section?" Now he spoke like a gynecologist.

The neighbor slid the paper over without even glancing up. Hershleder turned to the book review.

David Josephson. His old pal from college. A picture of the sucker. A picture; why a picture? Hershleder thought. It wasn't even Josephson's book. He was just a translator, that schlep was.

Josephson had not fared well over time, although to be fair, the reproduction was kind of grainy. A hook nose. A high forehead. He still looked brainy. That forehead hung over his eyes like an awning at a fancy club. Hershleder read the article for himself.

A 1,032-page study of the Nazi gas chambers has been published. . . . The study is by Jacques LeClerc, a chemist who began his work doubting that the Holocaust even took place. . . . The book, written in French, (translated by that bald rat Josephson!) . . . presents as proof, based entirely on technical analysis of the camps, that the Holocaust was every bit as monstrous and sweeping as survivors have said. . . . It is also a personal story of a scientific discovery during which, as Mr. LeClerc writes in a postscript, he was converted from "revisionist" to "exterminationist."

Exterminationist. What a hell of an appellative. Hershleder shook his head, in public, at the Oyster Bar, at no one in particular. Exterminationist. Is that what he himself was? His beloved mother, Adela Hershleder, just a child, along with her sister and her mother, her father recently dead of typhus, smuggled out of Germany on Kristallnacht. His mother's mother lost six brothers and sisters in Hitler's crematoria. And the friends, the extended family, even the neighbors they didn't like — all gone, gone. Hershleder's grandfather Chaim and his grandfather's brother, Abe, came to this country from Austria as refugees after World War I, the sole survivors of the sweeping tragedies of Europe that did away with their entire extended family.

And *heerre* . . . was Hershleder, the beneficiary of all that compounded survival; Hershleder the educated, the privileged, the beloved, the doctor! Hershleder the first generation New York Jew, Hershleder the bar mitzvahed, the assimilated, Hershleder with the shiksa wife, the children raised on Christmas, bacon in their breakfast, mayonnaise spread across their Wonder Bread, the daughter who once asked him if calling a person a Jew was really just another way to insult him.

He was lucky; his ancestors were not. What could you do? Isn't this the crux of it all (the history of civilization): those of us who are lucky juxtaposed against those of us who are not?

Mindy and Lori, his sisters, married with children, each active in her own temple, one out on Long Island, one on the Upper West Side. Irv, his father, retired now, remarried now, donating his time to the Jewish Home for the Blind. Were they any more Jewish than he was? Wasn't it true, what his own mother had told him, that what mattered in life was not religion per se, but that one strived to be a good person? Wasn't he, Hershleder — the researcher and, on Tuesdays and Thursdays, the healer (albeit a reluctant one), the father, the husband, the lawn mower, the moviegoer (he did show that bag lady a good time), the friend to Josephson (at least in theory) — a good person?

My God, thought Hershleder, just imagine being this chemist, this LeClerc, having the courage to disprove the very tenets upon which you've built your life. But Hershleder knew this kind, he had seen them before: LeClerc's accomplishments were probably less about bravery than they were about obsessive compulsion: LeClerc was probably a man who practiced a strict adherence to facts, to science. After all, Hershleder had spent much of his adult life doing research. You let the data make the decisions for you. You record what you observe. You synthesize, yes, you interpret; but you don't theorize, create out of your own imagination needs and desires. He knew him, LeClerc, LeClerc the compulsive, the truth-teller. They were alike these two men, rational, exact, methodical. Science was their true religion. Not the ephemeral mumbo jumbo of politicians, philosophers, poets.

Hershleder and LeClerc: they told the truth, when they were able, when it stared them in the face.

Hershleder folded up the paper and left it on the counter, its owner, his neighbor, having vanished in the direction of the New Haven Line some time ago. Paid up and exited the comforts of the Oyster Bar and headed out into the festering subterranean world. He stopped at the florist to pick up those daisies, two dozen, a field of them, a free-floating urban meadow. He held the bouquet like a cheerleader's pom-pom in his hands.

"Daisies are wildflowers," said the florist when he wrapped them up, those hothouse posies, in a crinkly paper cone. What did he think, that Hershleder was a poster child? He'd been to summer camp, away to college. Didn't he live in the suburbs and have a wife who cultivated daisies of her own? Daisies smell awful, but their faces are so sunny and bright, so fresh, so clean, petals as white as laundry detergent.

As he made his way to Track 11, Hershleder had a musical association: "Daisy, Daisy, give me your answer true." He had a poetic association: "She loves me, she loves me not." He had a visual association: the daisy stickers on the leaded glass windows that faced his yard, the plastic daisy treads that his mother had stuck to the bottom of his bathtub so that he, Hershleder, her precious boy-child, the third born and most prized, wouldn't slip, hit his head and drown. The big bright patent-leather daisies that dressed the thongs of his own daughter's dress-up sandals. The golden yolk, the pinky white of Itty's eyes when she'd been crying.

Hershleder walked through the vaulted, starred, amphitheater of Grand Central Station with a sensual garden, his human history, flowering bitterly in his hands.

•

"Smoke," hissed a young man in a black concert T-shirt. "Thai stick, dust, coke." The young man stood outside Track 11. Hershleder saw this dealer there, this corrupter of the young and not so young, this drug pusher, almost every day for months and months. Hershleder nodded at him, started down the ramp to the train tracks, then stopped. He had been a good boy. At Bronx Science he had smoked pot, at Cornell he'd done magic mushrooms once in awhile at a Dead show — then usually spent the rest of the night in the bathroom throwing up. For the most part, he'd played it safe; a little blow on a prom night or some graduation, but no acid, no ups, no downs, (well, that wasn't true, there were bennies in med school, valiums after), no needles in the arm, no track marks. No long velvety nights of swirling hazy rock songs. Drugwise, he was practically a virgin. Hadn't this gone on long enough?

Hershleder backtracked up the ramp.

"How much?" asked Hershleder.

"For what?" said Mr. Black Concert T-shirt.

For what? For what?

"Heroin?" asked Hershleder, with hope.

Mr. Black Concert T-shirt looked away in disgust.

"Pot?" asked Hershleder, humbly, in his place.

"Smoke," hissed the young man, "Thai stick, dust, coke."

"Thai stick," said Hershleder. Decisively. "Thai fucking stick," said Hershleder the reckless, the bon vivant.

And then, even though he was in danger of missing his train (again) Hershleder went back into the lobby of the station and officially bought cigarettes. He bought Merit Ultra Lights, thought better of it, backtracked to the kiosk and traded in the Merits for a pack of Salems.

•

The john was small enough that if you were to sit your knees would be in your armpits and your elbows in your ears.

Hershleder and his daisies floated in a cloud of smoke, men-
tholated, asiatic (the Thai stick). The chemical smell of toilets
on trains and airplanes permeated all that steam. The resultant
odor was strong enough to etherize an elephant, but Hershleder the rebel was nose-blind to it. He was wasted.

The MetroNorth rumbled through the tunnel. Outside the
scenery was so familiar Hershleder had it memorized. First
the rude surprise of 125th Street, all those broken windows,
empty eye holes, the flash of grafitti, of murals, loud paint.
The decals of curtains and cozy cats curled up on cheery sills
pasted to crumbling bricked-up tenements, the urban renewal. Then onward, the Bronx, Riverdale, Spuyten Duyvil.
The scramble of weedy green, the lumber yards, factories,
houses that line the train tracks in the suburbs. At night,
all of this would be in shadow; what he'd see would be the
advertisements for *Cats*, for Big Mac attacks, for Newport cigarettes: usually of a man gleefully dumping a bucket of something over an equally gleeful woman's head. The lonely maid
still in uniform waiting for the train to carry her home two
towns away. A couple of emasculated teenagers without driver's licenses. A spaced-out commuter who had stumbled off
at the wrong station. Hershleder knew this route by heart.

In the train car itself, there was always the risk of running
into one of his neighbors, or worse yet the aging parents of
a chum from college. Better to hang out in that safe smoky
toilet pondering the meaning of life, his humble existence.
He was stoned for the first time in years. Drunken synapse
fired awkwardly to drunken synapse. His edges were rounded,
his reflexes dulled. The ghosts that lived inside him spiraled
around in concentric circles. Hershleder's interior buzzed. His
head hung heavy off his neck, rested in the field of daises. A
petal went up his nose, pollen dusted his mouth. He couldn't
really think at all — he was full to the brim with nothing.

It was perfect.

"Laaarchmont," cried the lock-jawed conductor. "Laaarchmont," ruining everything.

•

Hershleder lit up a cigarette and coughed up a chunk of lung. Larchmont. The Station. A mile and a half from Casa Hershleder, a mile and a half from Itty and the kids, a mile and a half from his home and future heart failures. His eyes roved the Park and Ride. Had he driven his car this morning or had Itty dropped him off at the train? Had he called for a cab, hitched a ride with a neighbor? Where was that beat-up Mazda? His most recent history dissolved like a photograph in water, a dream upon awakening, a computer screen when the power suddenly shuts down. It receded from his inner vision. Must have been the weed . . . It really knocked him out.

Good shit, thought Hershleder.

He decided to walk. What was a mile and a half? He was in the prime of his life. Besides, Hershleder couldn't arrive home like this, stoned, in front of his innocent children, his loving wife. A long stroll would surely be enought to sober him; it would be a head-clearing, emotional cup of coffee.

Larchmont. Westchester, New York. One curvy road segueing into another. A dearth of street lights. The Tudor houses loomed like haunted mansions. They sat so large on their tiny lots, they swelled over their property lines the way a stout man's waist swells above his belt. A yuppie dog, a dalmatian, nosed its way across a lawn and accompanied Hershleder's shuffling gait. Hershleder would have reached down to pat its spotty head if he could have, but his arms were too full of daisies. He made a mental note to give in to Itty; she'd been begging him to agree to get a pup for the kids. There had been dogs when Hershleder was a child. Three of them. At different times. He had had a mother who couldn't say no to anything. He had had a mother who was completely overwhelmed. The longest a dog had lasted in their home had been about a year; Mrs. Hershleder kept giving those dogs away. Three dogs, three children. Was there some wish fulfillment involved in her casting them aside? His favorite

one had been called Snoopy. A beagle. His sister Mindy, that
original thinker, had been the one to name her.

Hershleder remembered coming home from camp one summer to find that Snoopy was missing. His mother had sworn
up and down that she had given the dog to a farm, a farm
in western Pennsylvania. Much better for the dog, said Mrs.
Hershleder, than being cooped up in some tiny apartment.
Better for the dog, thought Hershleder now, some twenty-
eight years later, better for the dog! What about me, a dogless
boy cooped up in some tiny apartment! But his mother was
dead, she was dead; there was no use in raging at a dead
mother. Hershleder the motherless, the dogless, walked the
streets of Larchmont. His buzz was beginning to wear off.

Why neurology? Mrs. Hershleder had asked. How about a
little pediatrics? Gynecology? Family practice? Dovidil, don't
make the same mistakes I made, a life devoted to half-lives,
a life frozen in motion. But Hershleder had been drawn to
the chronic ward. Paralysis, coma. He could not stand to watch
a patient suffer, the kick and sweat, the scream of life battling
stupidly for continuation. If he had to deal with people—and
wasn't that what a doctor does, a doctor deals with people—
he preferred people in a vegetative state, he preferred them
non-cognizant. What had attracted him in the first place had
been the literature, the questions: what was death? What
was life, after all? Did the answers to these lie, as Hershleder
believed, not in the heart but in the brain? He liked to deal
in inquiries; he didn't like to deal in statements. It was natural
then that he'd be turned on by research. Books and libraries,
the heady smell of ink on paper. He'd been the kind of boy
who had always volunteered in school to run off things for the
teacher. He'd stand close to the Rexograph machine, getting
giddy, greedily inhaling those toxic vapors. He'd walk back
slowly to his classroom, his nose buried deep in a pile of freshly
printed pages.

Hershleder was not taken with the delivering of babies,
the spreading of legs, the searching speculum, the bloody
afterbirth like a display of raw ground meat. But the brain,
the brain, that fluted, folded mushroom, that lovely intricate

web of thought and tissue and talent and dysfunction, of
arteries and order. The delicate weave of neurons, that thrilling
spinal cord. All that communication, all those nerves sending
and receiving orders. A regular switchboard. Music for his
mind.

A jogger passed him on the right, his gait strong and steady.
Hershleder's dalmatian abandoned him for the runner.

Hershleder turned down Fairweather Drive. He stepped
over a discarded red tricycle. He noticed that the Fishmans
had a blue Jag in their carport. The Fishman boy was his own
boy's nemesis. Charlie Fishman could run faster, hit harder.
No matter that Hershleder's own boy could speak in numbers—a = 1 b = 2, for example, when Hershleder arrived home
at night the kid said: "8-9 4-1-4" (translation: Hi Dad!)—the
kid was practically a savant, a genius! So what, the Fishman
boy could kick harder, draw blood faster in a fight. Could
Charlie Fishman bring tears to his own father's eyes by saying,
"9 12-15-22-5 25-15-21" when Fishman's father tucked him
in at night? (Even though it had taken Hershleder seven minutes and a pad and pencil to decode the obvious.) Charlie
Fishman had just beaten out Hershleder's Jonathan for the lead
in the second-grade play. The Fishman father was a famous
nephrologist. He commuted to New Haven every morning on
the highway, shooting like a star in that blue Jag out of the
neighborhood, against the traffic, in the opposite direction.
Hershleder admired the Jag from afar. It was a blue blue. It
glowed royally against the darkness.

The jogger passed him again, on the right. The dalmatian
loped after the runner, his spotted tongue hanging from his
mouth. The jogger must have circled around the long circu-
itous block in record time. A powerful mother-fucker.
Bearded. And young. Younger than Hershleder. The jogger
had a ponytail. It sailed in the current of his own making.
His legs were strong and bare. Ropey, tendoned. From where
he stood, Hershleder admired them. Then he moved himself
up the block to his own stone Tudor.

Casa Hershleder. It was written in fake Spanish tile on the
front walk, a gift from his sisters. Hershleder walked up the

slate steps and hesitated on his own front porch. Sometimes
it felt like only an act of courage could get him to turn the knob
and go inside. So much tumult awaited. Various children: on
their marks, getting set, ready to run, to hurl themselves into
his arms. Itty, in this weather all soft and steamed and
plumped — dressed in an undulation of circling Indian shma-
tas — hungry for connection, attention, the conversation of a
living, breathing adult. Itty, with tiny clumps of clay still
lodged like bird eggs in the curly red nest of her hair. Itty
with the silt on her arms, the gray slip-like slippers on her
bare feet. Itty, his wife, the potter.

By this point, the daisies were half-dead. They'd wilted in
the heat. Hershleder lay them in a pile on his front shrub
then lowered himself onto a slate step seat. If he angled his
vision past the O'Keefe's mock turret, he would surely see
some stars.

The steam of summer nights, the sticky breath of the trees
and their exhalation of oxygen, the buzz of the mosquitos
and the cicadas, the sweaty breeze, the rubbing of his suit
legs against his thighs. The moon above the O'Keefe's turret
was high, high, high.

The jogger came around again. Angled right and headed
up the Hershleder walk. His face was flushed with all that good
clean high-octane blood that is the result of honest American
exertion. He looked young — far younger than Hershleder, but
hadn't Hershleder noted this before? Must be wanting to know
the time, or in need of a glass of water, a bathroom, a phone,
Hershleder thought. The jogger was jogging right towards
him.

In a leap of blind and indiscriminate affection the dalmatian
bounded past the runner and collided with Hershleder's head,
his body, his lap. David was stunned for a second, then revived
by the wet slap of the dog's tongue. He was showered with
love and saliva. "Hey," said Hershleder. "Hey there, Buster.
Watch it." Hershleder fended off the beast by petting him,
by bowing under to all that animal emotion. The dalmatian
wagged the bottom half of his spinal column like a dissected
worm would, it had a life all its own. His tail beat the air like

a wire whisk. His tongue was as soft and moist as an internal organ. "Hey, Buster, down." Hershleder's arms were full of dog.

The jogger jogged right past them. He wiped his feet on Hershleder's welcome mat. He opened Hershleder's door and entered Hershleder's house. He closed Hershleder's door behind him. There was the click of the lock Hershleder had installed himself. That old bolt sliding into that old socket. What was going on? What was going on around here?

Buster was in love. He took to Hershleder like a bitch in heat, this same fancy mutt that had abandoned him earlier for the runner. A fickle fellow, thought Hershleder, a familiar fickle fellow.

"Hey," said Hershleder. "Hey," he called out. But it was too late. The runner had already disappeared inside his house.

The night was blue. The lawns deep blue-green, the asphalt blue-black, the trees almost purple. Jaundiced yellow light, like flames on an electric menorah, glowed from the Teretsky's leaded windows. At the Coen's, from the second floor family room, a T.V. flickered like a weak pulse. Most of the neighborhood was dark. Dark, hot, blue and yellow. Throbbing like a bruise.

A car backfired in the distance. Buster took off like a shot.

Hershleder sat on his front step feeling used. He was like a college girl left in the middle of a one-night stand. The dog's breath was still hot upon his face. His clothes were damp and wrinkled. The smell of faded passion clung to him. His hair—what was left of it—felt matted. He'd been discarded. Thrown-over. What could he do?

Stand up, storm into the house, demand: What's the meaning of this intrusion? Call the cops? Were Itty and the kids safe inside, locked up with that handsome, half-crazed stranger? Was it a local boy, home on vacation from college, an art student perhaps, hanging around to glean some of his wife's infinite and irresistible knowledge? The possibilities were endless. Hershleder contemplated the endless possibilities for a while.

Surely, he should right himself, climb his own steps, turn

his key in his lock, at least ring his own bell, as it were. Surely,
Hershleder should do something to claim what was his: "If I
am not for me, who will be for me? If I am not for mine,
who will be for mine?" Surely, he should stop quoting, stop
questioning, and get on with the messy thrill of homeown-
ership. After all, his wife, his children were inside.

The jogger was inside.

Hershleder and LeClerc, they told the truth when it stared
them in the face. In the face! Which was almost enough but
wasn't enough, right then at that exact and awful moment
to stop him, the truth wasn't, not from taking his old key out
of his pocket and jamming it again and again at a lock it could
not possibly ever fit. Which wasn't enough, this unyielding
frustration, to stop him from ringing the bell, again and again,
waking his children, disturbing his neighbors. Which wasn't
enough to stop him, the confusion, the shouting that ensued,
that led Itty *his wife* to say: "Please, Sweetheart," to the jogger
(Please, Sweetheart!) and usher him aside, that pony-tailed
bearded athlete who was far, far younger than Hershleder had
ever been, younger than was biologically possible.

She sat on the slate steps, Itty, her knees spread, the Indian
shmata pulled discreetly down between them. She ran her
silt-stained hands through her dusty strawberry cloud of hair.
There were dark, dirty half-moons beneath her broken finger-
nails. She was golden eyed and frustrated and terribly pained.
She was beautiful, Itty, at her best really when she was most
perplexed, her expression forming and reforming like a ka-
leidescope of puzzled and passionate emotion, when she patiently and for the thousandth time explained to him, Dr.
David Hershleder, M.D., that this was no longer his home,
that the locks had been changed for this very reason. He had
to stop coming around here, upsetting her, upsetting the children, that it was time, it was time, Dave, to take a good look
at himself; when all Hershleder was capable of looking at was
her, was Itty, dusty, plump and sweaty, sexy-sexy Itty, his
wife, his wife, sitting with him on the stoop of his house in
his neighborhood, while his children cowered inside.

Until finally, exhausted, (Hershleder had exhausted her)

Itty threatened to call the police if he did not move, and it was her tiredness, her sheer collapsibility that forced Hershleder to his feet — for wasn't being tired one thing Itty went on and on about that Hershleder could finally relate to — that pushed him to see the truth, to assess the available data and to head out alone and ashamed and apologetic to his suburban slip of a sidewalk, down the mile and a half back to the station to catch the commuter rail that would take him to the city and to the medical student housing he'd wrangled out of the hospital, away from everything he'd built, everything he knew and could count on, out into everything unknown, unreliable and yet to be invented.

Carolyn Kizer

Halation

A phenomenon . . . which caused an ambiguous
shimmering brightness to appear on the print
where sunlight and foliage came into contiguity.
—Janet Malcolm

My dear, you moved so rapidly through my life
I see you as a ghostly blur;
You are the subject, I the ornament
Eternally crossing some cobbles on some *rue*,
Where a covey of pearl umbrellas glistens
And ladies pause—courtesy of Caillebotte—though
This is of an era before we were born.
But the impression is emotionally true:
A sheen of rain, a gray noncommital sky;
Limp banners cling to window frames (Monet);
And the bonnet, shovel-shaped with a crimson brim,
Casts a becoming glow over my face,
No longer young, ambiguous, shimmering.
A bunch of violets tucked at the waist, the figure
Navigates curb and puddle, assisted by
A gentleman in black, a courtly crook of arm:
Poseur and posed, the painter and the painted
Doubly exposed. Now I am reminded

Of a woodland picnic slightly earlier,
You almost fully dressed, I not quite naked;
You in the serge of your reserve
And I as bare as in those disturbing dreams
That reveal our vast uncertainties, including
Those of Giorgione and Manet.

Background figures (us, in fair disguises)
Haunt the middle distance, bosky, green,
Stand witness, even when reclining . . .
But I am no *Cherie* but *Liebchen. Liebchen.*
Our expeditions did not end in halcyon places.
Instead, all roads led to a sanitary fill
In full sunlight. Nothing ambiguous about that.
We raise champagne in paper cups, toast one another,
Perched on the tailgate of an ugly car.
But the shutter snaps, and we slip into art,
Its negative image: sister into brother.

Once a little coarse, a trifle epicene
(a little too Rouault, whom you admired),
You've silvered over through the passing years.
Now, like a platinum plate, imagination,
That elusive lustre, may transform
A row of poplars to the filaments of desire;
An alley, lit by one gas lamp, the path
To Charon's boat, that ultimate black stream.
This fluid which develops and embalms
Beyond the possibility of alteration,
Is cropped by us, to suit perversities
Of taste and time. Your sinewy arm (Cezanne's)
Seemed to wrap twice around my waist.
Dreamer and dream, in close up confrontation,
The pair emerged as Bonnard's moving blurs.

Touch now, O author of my authorhood,
Your peer at last in contiguity
Before we went our ways and broke the frame.
What happened to us friend? You saw the light,
Not that of haloed streetlamps. Halogen
Impersonally scanned us, banishing
All subtle shadows, a trace of leaves at night.
The hallowed moon, astigmatized before,
Is glowing with a brighter face than ours,
Scored by the years, focussed last, and free.

Greg Williamson

Up in the Air

Gin-weary, temple on the pane,
I watch the props begin to shake
The sunlight. As we climb, the plane
Trolls its crank bait shadow across a lake.

It drags an airy grappling hook
Over the churches of white towns
Tucked away in the hills that look,
For all their pleated folds, like dressing gowns

Where all the clouds are shaving cream
And powder, periwigs and lace,
The fragments of a lazy dream
That conjures up a ballroom in their place

And finds, across the dreamt parquet,
In a cirrus gown, a girl. Then all
At once this cloying matinee
Dissolves, as if the episodes I call

My life were just such masterstrokes
Of whimsy, false and protean,
And all I think I love a hoax
Invented by the shadow of a man

Muttering in a windowseat,
Watching a toothless anchor comb
A lake, fooled by his own conceit.
At most, from all of this, someone at home

May shake his head in a reading chair
Or glance up from a gin and lime
At this annoyance in the air,
A minor thing which happens all the time.

Rick Barot

Phantasmal Cities

Walter Benjamin, Paris, 1940

1

Flecked on a layer of mortar on the pillbox lid,
the tiles pieced together by some kindred myopic
have caught this much of Tuscany: hills worn down
and yellow as old teeth, a tweed-colored villa
rising above a scatter of olives, under which
two black dogs sleep through the afternoon heat.
The size of a silver dollar, that much of the world
seems dark and lost to him, and when the doors
of the museum have been shut, he will go outside
to the flaring of gaslights on the rue de Rivoli
and to the puddles of a January shower staring up
gray as fish eyes on the quays. The stone rail
of the Pont Neuf is cold, and it is that fragment
of feeling that now returns everything to him:
the glint of heavy doorknobs along Delbruckstraße,
the iron trelliswork bracing the dusty glass dome
of an arcade, above which utopias of stars shone.
Again he finds those huddled stalls in frozen Moscow:
the knife sharpener, the parrot seller, the soothsayer
whose divining letters, dense on a board, glittered
in his memory like the roads' bituminous gravel
sparkling on the snow. Even the improbable ravens,
tearing at the butcher's scraps, fly back now to mind,
embedding themselves there like glass in masonry.

2

A ribbon of sky roofs over the narrow street here.
The tilted buildings have the slack-faced weariness
of travelers who have been waiting much too long.
Like peelings of eucalyptus, bills posted on the trunks
of kiosks strip of themselves. Winter has cleared
the black clots of leaves and paper from the gutters;
each street's noise fades like ink dropped in water.
If he wonders now where these have drifted — the heady
cut-grass must of the carriage horses, the new dunes
of sidewalk snow — he knows he will have walked too far
from himself to ask. The city has rarefied down
to stone details, as imperceptibly as his solitude
thinned into a light-starved, muttering fever.
— Still, some nights it is enough that a sudden phrase
turns the mind towards a light of its own making,
until his words are like cobbles he can walk on
and the matrices of streets seem a believable order.
Then there is no ruin here, and memory is brief as day.
And the visible things remain as the only affections
he will answer for: the swept parks, and the river silver
as his room's mirror, the pearl-topped lamps lining
the bridges and boulevards, the high incurious windows
reflecting a sky he is suddenly quickened to look to.

3

From out of the fluorescent gutter-fog and mist
from the river, the blank avenues have turned
into stretches of London and Prague, whose tutelary
specters, like Baudelaire's solitary ragpickers,
he imagines with a flaneur's love. He is enchanted
by these fierce appearances: the razed *quartiers*
springing up to mock Haussmann's imperial vistas,
the barricades raised once again, the city won back—
even if only in his mind, pressed to find bearings
here in history's mire, in the stage-set loneliness
of empty benches and thin cats, alleyways haunted
by his childhood's laughing hunchback, a Falstaff
of cruel luck who has followed him this far, exiled
among remembered forms. It takes a hero's will to die
from one's own hand, he writes. It takes passion.
He knows that the border towns have fallen too late
to stop, and his papers have lapsed like outdated maps.
And in cool, gnomic lines noted down in his books,
the past keeps occurring, exact as a lock clicking
open, then shut. In Berlin, the fish brokers keep
shouting prices, the store dummies keep smiling
behind glass fronts. Dickens counts Holborn's lamps,
and Kafka coughs himself home—the morning arriving
slowly around them, the first pigeon song in earshot.

4

The hours turn like wheels grinding down bricks,
bottles, shoes. He is walking, breathing thickly
with his mouth open, past windows where the maps
of phantasmal cities spread as frost on the glass.
In real cities it has begun — the walls, like shale,
slipping around those who insist on silence as a right.
Paint burns like paper, clothes curl, while planes
cross overhead, grazing their shadows on rooftops,
cars, and squares bare as winter graveyards.
And the stunned phrasings of love the dead gasped
fill the archives of some other world, where the millions
are counted at last, and set down again to start
conversations where they stopped, to finish meals,
to listen to the noise of midday from the street.
To them, the city he is walking through has become
the past, whose wreckage he stumbles onto and sifts,
as if the charred shop-signs and cracked statues
still landmarked the place where he last knew
what could be saved and imagined, what was erased
but retrieved, as if he were the scribe cast out
to find the words lost in the rubble like gold rings
or combs. Ice stiffens on the river, chestnut boles
split with cold, the windows whiten into cities
he dreams to enter, his pockets heavy with spoons.

Three Poems by James Longenbach

The Grace of the Witch

The romance of the twelve-year-old who finds
Himself behind the school in a stingray,
How he's never the same. I had a friend

Whose father slipped a condom in his hand—
But make her swear, no witches' tricks—a rite
Of passage meaningless to us because

We understood it wasn't ours. One summer night
We found a woman at the playground, barefoot,
Floppy hat, her frayed jeans dragging

In the dust as she swung back and forth.
Block letters cut into her wrist spelled *Paul*.
There, on our bicycles, the streetlights

Signalling our time was up, we learned—
It wasn't obvious—she loved him then
And so it didn't hurt. I tossed the beads

And eagle feathers when she disappeared,
To where, we couldn't guess, since any house
We knew seemed impotent of breeding her.

In a movie she'd have been the Nazi wife
Who overwhelms the beautiful French soldier,
Underage, who's grateful anyway:

The woman in the woods, her long white hands,
The amber honey mixed with wine—*never*
A man that drank this cup but when it passed

His lips he had succumbed — and in her arms
A hairless torso heaving expertly.
We saw her at the beach, or someone like her,

Swimming in her clothes, no underwear,
A bottle hoisted to her lips each time
The water knocked her down. It seemed

Unfair — indecent — that your body would
Display, where everyone could see,
The name of someone whom you didn't love.

We asked her at the swings — it baffled me —
If she would scrape the scar away: she said,
I'd need a razor. Can you get me one?

The Origin of Angels

Everything we've heard of heaven is true:
Italian landscape hazy with the blush
That varnish takes above an egg-wash smear.
Except the faces. Not like Leonardo's
With the parted lips and golden hair

But like a child's face, still grimy from
The wagon train. In heaven everyone's
A reckless child: we choose the dead before
The living since their helplessness is ours,
And only by great effort do we raise

A voice above the dark Ohio's roar.
Each night, hovering above the shape
That heaves its perfect breaths, the hands
Unclenching from an object, hard or soft,
No less important for not being there,

I make some useless gesture, smooth a blanket,
Brush my lips against the dampened hair:
This is the origin of angels, all
Of providential history turning back
To our first parents, Adam's fingers twisted

In a knot of grief above the silver corpse
As in *The Death of Abel* by Bonnat,
Eve wondering, as I do every night,
How it could be, with everything we know
Of heaven, that our children understand

The means and ends of suffering before
Their parents do. It's when I'm on the verge
Of sleep myself that I can see the faces,
Hear their voices as they scamper through
A backlit meadow, unaware of me.

Letting Go

The highest point for miles but it's nothing
Like the natural world. Too steep for vistas
So it's valueless as real estate.
A rise of sumac, burning red. A scarecrow
Made of roots and mud collapsing slowly
On the last frontier of dense suburban sprawl.

There weren't tablets or a crater's rim
For Petrarch climbing Mount Ventou,
The only obstacle the nature of the place.
At the summit Augustine rebuked him:
Men admire high mountains and great floods,
Wide-rolling rivers and the ring of ocean
And the movement of the stars — forgetting
Nothing's admirable except the soul.

It's not the wild grape leaves or the figs
And alders on the slopes around you,
Not the chestnuts or the terraced rows
Of olives, bleached to silver, down below;
It's not the sumac's fire, the city's rise
Of glass and steel or the polished surface
Of Ontario, just visible in winter
When the sycamores have dropped their leaves.

It's bed springs, one shoe littering the trail,
A condom near the black char of a fire
Ringed with stones, the man who camped
One summer with a doberman that shared
His sleeping bag, or else a worn out book
You bring to scatter language at the top—
Anything to guarantee that there
Were never natural worlds the human soul
Kept alone.   It's like not being able
To let go. The downtown pigeon
Jerking pizza crust from side to side
Because at home, a hundred years ago
On Adriatic cliffs, it fed on seed pods,
Shaking nature's handouts free.

S.X. Rosenstock

Aubrey Beardsley on the Subject of His Own Willful Ignorance of the *Caprichos* of Francisco Goya

No one misunderstands my satieties
Once they have had at the *Caprichos*
Without knowing what they are, that they are,
That Goya existed.
        I do rest my long face on sheets
Of paper and the spirits of *the thing to be*
Release themselves into a kind of massage of me
That so incites and embarrasses my self-possession,
I draw
  —kings, queens; the designs are not preordained—
                           them out
As I have been found, drawn, out.
It *is* ordained that I sleep with my work
Ruined by my sleeping hacking.

Goya had Spanish ladies
Sit upon and—it can't be said otherwise—smudge,—
Sincerely!—*smudge* the living daylights
Out of his work. Chiaroscuro
Results from women making a tuffet of somebody's cartoon.

The diapering of natural children is done
Of cartoons which are later laundered
In a tincture of tears and set out
On a line near which a small boy is
Assigned the task of crying out, "Dry. As far as I can discern,
And I am a lonely, misused boy with no dog,
They're bloody well dry."

In my bones and in my sidesplitting
Lungs, I am not
Like other men; rather, I contain
A skeleton that is a liquid,
A brine, whippet-mix, *a real, artful* one.
It teethes on my work,
Evidence of which I try
To hide in some lines of a nervy
Opacity: I am exhumed
In ignorance.

Señor Goya permitted cosies
Made of his cartoons; I know.
And the milkmaid was forever
Lining her pail with his satires, and then hanging
Them out to dry in the merciless
Spanish midday sun where they would rot
Open some invective in their mildew
That spoke reams to the painter, and they would
Have to be both salvaged and redone.

When I was three I dreamed I was bleeding
Into the *Caprichos*. I dreamed I was not so much
Satiric as young. I bled a baby onto a pasty.
I kept fainting and fainting into vividness
In the dream. England was wordless and night
Was falling when I was three and I worked
Like a dog in the ensuing years to be
Ignorant of the *Caprichos*, in the dark
And perfectly clear.

Two Poems by Susan Mitchell

Venice

Furtive, that's the version I want.
With eyes averted. Downcast, a little sly.
It's where it's looking, that's
where I want us—
in a harbor where we in our gondola
stare up and up at the enormous
freighters rusting the Adriatic, the ocean
oiled and ropey, scary even,
the way the waters seem higher than
our boat, about to topple onto.
Did I forget to say it's night, we're
seeing by artificial light how small
fists of snow are falling from. So easy
to say *the sky*, but that
would be wrong. We could puzzle over
how to say this. Or we could kiss.
Let's kiss, standing up in
scary, its huge hood lowering,
cover of darkness down
which the crusaders with lances and crosses
high held in a once upon a time still
tarnishing, still audible version
of a version of a version.
There's a vertigo to history different
from the vertigo of sex.
The children sold into slavery, into brothels.
The sores. The futility of crying and the futility
of stories that gradually wash up
on other shores. To what purpose all this
telling, version by version
deteriorating like silk, the patterns

no longer recognizable: ripple by ripple, the lush
lappings as if certain words, *pietà*
or *sofferenza* were enough.
I had wanted to sightsee, to be taken slowly
by gondola, canal by canal where Byron
where shadows on stilts or like inverted
bells somberly under the arches
swaying and Goethe who stood on the foamy
crescendos and saw the *chiaro*
nell' chiaro and bibelots
of old and charming, the glimmers
well-worn where the moon
all its chandeliers and stairways let down
into the sea-black sea. To stand
on the outstretched lip of
what might be called a romantic evening,
though already that version is
starting to bore me. It's not a question
of what's true or not true, it's more
a matter of what I want to hear.
Which is why we are standing in a boat
perilously small and stiffening
our necks to size the hugeness
of prows — barnacle-studded, ironclad, steely
beaked, with involucral bracts, with
scale on scale, a rust of buds.
Yet, that's how I want us, our love
pressed mouth to mouth
with history, and if with a partition,
then something thin
as lingerie.
I don't want us anaesthetized, I want
us terrified and tied to it.
I used to think *it* was teeming, alive
with voices, flashings, with
music in which the dark lit candles.
I tried to reach any way
I could, rung by rung

or with sex shouldering me all the way.
Well, now I think otherwise.
More of a wall or impasse, more of — nothing.
Which isn't to say I'm not moved.
What tumbles through is icy and swift
and doesn't stop. I want us pressed
to that when you shove into me.
No candles. Not even darkness.

Girl Tearing up Her Face

Where it's rubbed out, start there, where it's torn
where something like a burn in cloth the hot
metal pressed too long, forgotten

in paper the worm-
hole, the eaten up, the petal frayed browning
at the edges the flower's
flesh like cigarette paper

consumed by the breath sucked back into
the body: yes, body, that's what
that is what — no, I'm not stalling   body

is what I mean to talk about, what I have
on my mind   in my mind   my mind
in the body   of the body

and what's disturbing, yes, that above all: the joy
right there in her face, the girl's, as if she
had been smacked with it, the big fish joy

a cold hard wet smack by something flailing out, this
joy thing throwing itself around

or as if someone had thrown a pudding, a thick batter
and now her face was trying to work its way
through that mess, yes, joy, the mess

the ugliness of it because it has not yet
been practiced, the mouth trying out
positions before the mirror   the mouth

performing little sounds up and down the scale
of pleasure   the joy not yet prepared
for anyone else to look at   the shock like

a flashbulb going off, a camera
pouncing before one is ready   before
one has run the tongue over   taken a bite

out of the smile   hands arranging the hair
the girl looks all doors open, the sheer
weight of her coming starting

to come and her body sucking it back
inhaling each tooth of bliss
running her fingers up and down the comb

It's that ugly I want to rub my face in, that
blossoming, as if a tree had suddenly—
the stamen pushing up out of

the petals, the throat of the apple, its
woods and the dark seeds
bursting the blossom, so I push

her back, I open her mouth right there
where she sits on the swing
a rage of delight shivering the tree's—

can I say flesh, can I say skin?—and
I can't bear to look at her
doing that, it seems too private, as if she

had been caught having a dream she
didn't know she was having
all her wings run over by pleasure, joy

having a tantrum all over her, this
limp rag of beaten down, and the photographer
thinking, Yeah, this is it, the moment

he wants to last and last—the forever: now with
the girl falling asleep on the swing,
her sleep in full view, its lids

pulled open so the deep anaesthesia
of her pleasure is suddenly visible, sucked
inside out so he can hear every sound

a face can make and it's those sounds
he wants to shudder down on, those
cries with the flesh still

attached to them and what they have
been pulled from gaping and
ragged and this is what will be handed

to the girl in black and white, this face
which in two seconds would have
changed and gone on changing, this face

she never suspected and of course, she'll have to
rip it into pieces and keep ripping
because even now I can't bear

to look at her suddenly awake, I want
her asleep again, unbegun, unstarted, the shades
drawn so I can float every which possible, all

manner of across her face accommodating
as a lap, and I don't think
For God's sake, she's only eleven, what does she

know or understand of anything? I'm—I'm flooding
even as she rips herself in two, even as
she vows never to be this person

I'm putting my head down in her lap, pushing
her back on the swing with so much force—
What could split open? What could eat her up?

43

When Crow was white he decided the sun was too white
He decided ... too white
He decided to attack it & defeat it

Crow got his strength flush & in full glitter.
He clawed & ... his rage up.
He aimed his beak direct at the sun's centre.

He ... his confidence, like a ...
He ... his determination, like a Gunsight.
He launched himself to the centre of ... himself
the attack.
At his battle cry trees grew suddenly old,
Shadows flattened.

But the sun, brightened grew ...
and Brightened
Crow returned back clawed black (or
Unrecognisable)

He opened his mouth but what came out was clawed black (or
Incomprehensible)

"Up there," he managed,
"Where white is black, and black is white, I won."

A manuscript page of a poem by Ted Hughes.

Ted Hughes
The Art of Poetry LXXI

Ted Hughes lives with his wife, Carol, on a farm in Devonshire. It is a working farm — sheep and cows — and the Hugheses are known to leave a party early to tend to them. "Carol's got to get the sheep in," Hughes will explain.

He came to London for the interview, which took place in the interviewer's dining room. The poet was wearing a tweed jacket, dark trousers and a tie whose predominantly blue color matched his eyes. His voice is commanding. He is often invited to read his work, the flow of his language enlivening the text.

In appearance, he is impressive, and yet there is very little aggression or intimidation in his look. Indeed, one admirer has said that her first thought sitting opposite him was that this was what God should look like "when you get there."

Born Edward James Hughes on August 17, 1930 in the small mill town of Mytholmroyd, he is the youngest of the three children of Edith Farrar Hughes and William Henry Hughes. The first seven years of his life were spent in West Yorkshire, on that area's barren windswept moors. Hughes once said that he could "never escape the impression that the whole region [was] in mourning for the First World War."

He began to write poetry at age seven, after his family moved to Mexborough. It was under the tutelage of his teacher at the town's only grammar school that Hughes began to mature — his work evolving into the rhythmic passionate poetry for which he has become known throughout the world.

Following two years of service in the Royal Air Force, Hughes enrolled at Pembroke College, Cambridge University. He had initially intended to study English literature, but found that department's curriculum too limited — archeology and anthropology proving to be areas of the academic arena more suited to his taste.

Two years after graduating, Hughes and a group of classmates founded the infamous literary magazine, St. Botolph's Review — known more for its inaugural party than its longevity (it lasted only one issue). It was at that party that Hughes met Sylvia Plath, an American student studying in England. Plath would recall the event in a journal entry: "I met the strongest man in the world, ex-Cambridge, brilliant poet whose work I loved before I met him, a large, hulky, healthy Adam, half French, half Irish, with a voice like the thunder of god — a singer, story-teller, lion and world wanderer, a vagabond who will never stop." They were wed on June 16, 1956 and remained married for six and a half years, having two children, Frieda and Nicholas. In the fall of 1962, they became estranged over Hughes's alleged infidelities. On February 11, 1963, while residing in a separate apartment, Plath placed towels under the door of the room where her children were napping, laid out a snack for them, turned on the gas jet of her kitchen stove and placed her head in the oven — asphyxiating herself. A few months after their marriage, Plath had entered a number of her husband's poems in a competition judged by W.H. Auden, among others. Hughes was awarded first prize for his collection Hawk in the Rain. It was published in 1957 by Faber & Faber in England and Harper & Row in America. With his next publication, Lupercal, in 1960, Hughes became recognized as one of the most significant English poets to emerge since World War II, winning the Somerset Maugham Award in 1960 and the Hawthornden Prize in 1961.

His next notable work was Wadwo, a compilation of five short stories, a radio play and some forty poems. Although it contained many of the violent animal images of Hughes's earlier work, it reflected the poet's growing enchantment with mythology. Wadwo led Hughes into an odd fascination with one of the most solitary and ominous images in folklore, the crow. While his aspiration to create an epic tale centering on this bird has not been fulfilled, he did publish Crow: From the Life and Songs of the Crow in 1970, sixty-six poems or "songs," as Hughes referred to them. The American version, published by Harper the following year, was well received. The New York Review of Books said that Crow was "Perhaps a more plausible explanation for the present condition of the world than the Christian sequence."

Still deeply interested in mythology and folklore, Hughes created Orghast, a play based largely on the Prometheus legend, in 1971, while he was in Iran with members of the International Center for Theater Research. He wrote most of the play's dialogue in an invented language to illustrate the theory that sound alone could express very complex human emotions. Hughes continued on this theme with his next work of poetry entitled Prometheus on His Crag, published in 1973 by Rainbow Press.

His next two works of note, Cave Birds and Gaudete, were predominantly based on the Gravesian concept that mankind has sinned by denying the "White Goddess," the natural, *primordial aspect of modern man, while choosing to nurture a conscious, almost sterile, intellectual humanism.*

Following the publication of his 1983 work, River, Ted Hughes was named Poet Laureate of Great Britain. His recent publications, Flowers and Insects (1987) and Wolfwatching (1991), show a return to his earlier nature-oriented work — possessing a raw force that evokes the physical immediacy of human experience.

Hughes has shown a great range in his work, and aside from his adult verse, he has written children's stories (Tales of the Early World), poetry (Under the North Star) and plays (The Coming of the Kings). Hughes has also edited selections of other writers' work, most notably, the late Plath's. The controversy surrounding Hughes's notorious editing and reordering of Plath's poetry and journals, the destruction of at least one volume of the latter, as well as the mysterious disappearance of her putative final novel have mythologized both poets and made it difficult for Hughes to live the anonymous life he has sought in rural Devonshire.

—A.B.

INTERVIEWER
Would you like to talk about your childhood? What shaped your work and contributed to your development as a poet?

TED HUGHES
Well, as far as my writing is concerned, maybe the crucial thing was that I spent my first years in a valley in West Yorkshire in the north of England, which was really a long street of industrial towns — textile mills, textile factories. The little village where I was born had quite a few; the next town fifty. And so on. These towns were surrounded by a very wide landscape of high moorland, in contrast to that industry into which everybody disappeared everyday. They just vanished. If you weren't at school you were alone in an empty wilderness.

When I came to consciousness, my whole interest was in wild animals. My earliest memories are of the lead animal toys you could buy in those days, wonderfully accurate models. Throughout my childhood I collected these. I had a brother, ten years older, whose passion was shooting. He wanted to be a big game hunter or a game warden in Africa—that was his dream. His compromise in West Yorkshire was to shoot over the hillsides and on the moor edge with a rifle. He would take me along. So my early memories of being three and four are of going off with him, being his retriever. I became completely preoccupied by his world of hunting. He was also a very imaginative fellow; he mythologized his hunting world as North American Indian—paleolithic. And I lived in his dream. Up to the age of seventeen or eighteen, shooting and fishing and my preoccupation with animals were pretty well my life, apart from books. That makes me sound like more of a loner than I was. Up to twelve or thirteen I also played with my town friends every evening, a little gang, the innocent stuff of those days, kicking about the neighborhood. But weekends I was off on my own. I had a double life.

The writing, the reading came up gradually behind that. From the age of about eight or nine I read just about every comic book available in England. At that time my parents owned a newsagent's shop. I took the comics from the shop, read them and put them back. That went on until I was twelve or thirteen. Then my mother brought in a sort of children's encyclopedia, which included sections of folklore. Little folktales. I remember the shock of reading those stories. I could not believe that such wonderful things existed. The only stories we'd had as younger children were ones our mother had told us—that she made up, mostly. In those early days ours wasn't a house full of books. My father knew quite long passages of "Hiawatha," which he used to recite, something he had from his school days. That had its effect. I remember I wrote a good deal of comic verse for classroom consumption in Hiawatha meter. But throughout your life you have certain literary shocks, and the folktales were my first. From then on I began to collect folklore, folk stories and mythology. That became my craze.

Can you remember when you first started writing?

HUGHES
I first started writing those comic verses when I was eleven, when I went to grammar school. I realized that certain things I wrote amused my teacher and my classmates. I began to regard myself as a writer, writing as my specialty. But nothing more than that until I was about fourteen when I discovered Kipling's poems. I was completely bowled over by the rhythm. Their rhythmical, mechanical drive got into me. So suddenly I began to write rhythmical poems, long sagas in Kiplingesque rhythms. I started showing them to my English teacher—at the time a young woman in her early twenties, very keen on poetry. I suppose I was fourteen, fifteen. I was sensitive, of course, to any bit of recognition of anything in my writing. I remember her—probably groping to say something encouraging—pointing to one phrase saying: "This is really . . . interesting." Then she said, "It's real poetry." It wasn't a phrase; it was a compound epithet concerning the hammer of a punt gun on an imaginary wildfowling hunt. I immediately pricked up my ears. That moment still seems the crucial one. Suddenly I became interested in producing more of that kind of thing. Her words somehow directed me to the main pleasure in my own life, the kind of experience I lived for. So I homed in. Then very quickly—you know how fast these things happen at that age—I began to think, Well, maybe this is what I want to do. And by the time I was sixteen that was all I wanted to do.

I equipped myself in the most obvious way: whatever I liked I tried to learn by heart. I imitated things. And I read a great deal aloud to myself. Reading verse aloud put me on a kind of high. Gradually, all this replaced shooting and fishing. When my shooting pal went off to do his national service, I used to sit around in the woods, muttering through my books. I read the whole of *The Faerie Queene* like that. All of Milton. Lots more. It became sort of a hobby-habit. I read a good deal else as well and was constantly trying to write something of course. That same teacher lent me her Eliot and introduced me to three or four of Hopkins's poems. Then I met Yeats. I was still preoccupied by Kipling when I met Yeats via the third part of his poem "The Wandering of Oisin," which was in the kind of meter I was looking for. Yeats sucked me in through the Irish folklore and myth and the occult business. My dominant passion in poetry up to and through university was Yeats, Yeats under the canopy of Shakespeare and Blake. By the time I got to university, at twenty-one, my sacred canon was fixed: Chaucer, Shakespeare, Marlowe, Blake, Words-worth, Keats, Coleridge, Hopkins, Yeats, Eliot. I knew no American poetry at all except Eliot. I had a complete Whit-man, but still didn't know how to read it. The only modern foreign poet I knew was Rilke in Spender's and Leishmann's translation. I was fascinated by Rilke. I had one or two collec-tions with me through my national service. I could see the huge worlds of other possibilities opening in there. But I couldn't see how to get into them. I also had my mother's Bible, a small book, with the psalms, Jeremiah, the Song of Songs, Proverbs, Job and other bits here and there, all set out as free verse. I read whatever contemporary verse I happened to come across, but apart from Dylan Thomas and Auden, I rejected it. It didn't give me any leads, somehow, or maybe I simply wasn't ready for it.

INTERVIEWER

Was it difficult to make a living when you started out? How did you do it?

HUGHES

I was ready to do anything, really. Any small job. I went to the U.S. and taught a little bit, though I didn't want to. I taught first in England in a secondary school, fourteen-year-old

boys. I experienced the terrific exhaustion of that profession.
I wanted to keep my energy for myself, as if I had the right.
I found teaching fascinating but wanted too much to do something else. Then I saw how much money could be made quite
quickly by writing children's books. A story—perhaps not
true—is that Maxine Kumin wrote fifteen children's stories
and made a thousand dollars for each. That seemed to me
preferable to attempting a big novel or a problematic play,
which would devour great stretches of time with doubtful
results in cash. Also, it seemed to me I had a knack of a kind
for inventing children's stories. So I did write quite a few.
But I didn't have Maxine Kumin's magic. I couldn't sell any
of them. I sold them only years later, after my verse had made
a reputation for me of a kind. So up to the age of thirty-three,
I was living on what one lives on: reviews, BBC work, little
radio plays, that sort of thing. Anything for immediate cash.
Then, when I was thirty-three, I suddenly received in the post
the news that the Abraham Woursell Foundation had given
me a lecturer's salary at the University of Vienna for five years.
I had no idea how I came to be awarded this. That salary took
me from thirty-four years old to thirty-eight, and by that time
I was earning my living by my writing. A critical five years.
That was when I had the children, and the money saved me
from looking for a job outside the house.

INTERVIEWER

Do you have a favorite place to write, or can you write
anywhere?

HUGHES

Hotel rooms are good. Railway compartments are good. I've
had several huts of one sort or another. Ever since I began to
write with a purpose I've been looking for the ideal place. I
think most writers go through it. I've known several who liked
to treat it as a job—writing in some office well away from home,
going there regular hours. Sylvia had a friend, a novelist, who
used to leave her grand house and go into downtown Boston

to a tiny room with a table and chair where she wrote facing a blank wall. Didn't Somerset Maugham also write facing a blank wall? Subtle distraction is the enemy—a big beautiful view, the tide going in and out. Of course, you think it oughtn't to matter, and sometimes it doesn't. Several of my favorite pieces in my book *Crow* I wrote traveling up and down Germany with a woman and small child—I just went on writing wherever we were. Enoch Powell claims that noise and bustle help him to concentrate. Then again, Goethe couldn't write a line if there was another person anywhere in the same house, or so he said at some point. I've tried to test it on myself, and my feeling is that your sense of being concentrated can deceive you. Writing in what seems to be a happy concentrated way, in a room in your own house with books and everything necessary to your life around you, produces something noticeably different, I think, from writing in some empty silent place far away from all that. Because however we concentrate, we remain aware at some level of everything around us. Fast asleep, we keep track of the time to the second. The person conversing at one end of a long table quite unconsciously uses the same unusual words, within a second or two, as the person conversing with somebody else at the other end—though they're amazed to learn they've done it. Also, different kinds of writing need different kinds of concentration. Goethe, picking up a transmission from the other side of his mind, from *beyond* his usual mind, needs different tuning than Enoch Powell when he writes a speech. Brain rhythms would show us what's going on, I expect. But for me, successful writing has usually been a case of having found good conditions for real, effortless concentration. When I was living in Boston, in my late twenties, I was so conscious of this that at one point I covered the windows with brown paper to blank out any view and wore earplugs—simply to isolate myself from distraction. That's how I worked for a year. When I came back to England, I think the best place I found in that first year or two was a tiny cubicle at the top of the stairs that was no bigger than a table really. But it was a wonderful place to write. I mean, I can see now, by what I wrote there, that it was a good place. At the time it just seemed like a convenient place.

INTERVIEWER

What tools do you require?

HUGHES

Just a pen.

INTERVIEWER

Just a pen? You write longhand?

HUGHES

I made an interesting discovery about myself when I first worked for a film company. I had to write brief summaries of novels and plays to give the directors some idea of their film potential — a page or so of prose about each book or play, and then my comment. That was where I began to write for the first time directly onto a typewriter. I was then about twenty-five. I realized instantly that when I composed directly onto the typewriter my sentences became three times as long, much longer. My subordinate clauses flowered and multiplied and ramified away down the length of the page, all much more eloquently than anything I would have written by hand. Recently I made another similar discovery. For about thirty years I've been on the judging panel of the W.H. Smith children's writing competition. Annually there are about sixty thousand entries. These are cut down to about eight hundred. Among these our panel finds seventy prizewinners. Usually the entries are a page, two pages, three pages. That's been the norm. Just a poem or a bit of prose, a little longer. But in the early 1980s we suddenly began to get seventy and eighty page works. These were usually space fiction, always very inventive and always extraordinarily fluent — a definite impression of a command of words and prose, but without exception strangely boring. It was almost impossible to read them through. After two or three years, as these became more nu-

NEW SUBSCRIBERS' DISCOUNT

SAVE $12 off the cover price and $6 off the regular subscription rates with this coupon.

THE PARIS REVIEW

Enclosed is my check for:

☐ $28 for 1 year (new subscriptions and gifts only)
☐ $34 for 1 year (4 issues)
☐ $1,000 for a lifetime subscription
(All payment must be in U.S. funds. Postal surcharge of $7 per 4 issues outside USA)

☐ Send me information on becoming a *Paris Review* Associate.

Bill this to my Visa/MasterCard:

_____
Card number   Exp. date

☐ New subscription   ☐ Renewal subscription
☐ New address

Name _____

Address _____

City _____ State _____ Zip code _____

Please send gift subscription to:

Name _____

Address _____

City _____ State _____ Zip code _____

Gift announcement signature _____

Please send me the following:

☐   The Paris Review T-Shirt   ($15.00)
    Color _____ Size _____ Quantity _____
☐   The following back issues: Nos. _____

    See listing at back of book for availability.

☐   The Paris Review Print Series catalogue ($1.00)

Name _____

Address _____

City _____ State _____ Zip code _____

☐ Enclosed is my check for $ _____
☐ Bill this to my Visa/MasterCard:

_____
Card number   Exp. date

Impress someone, and save.

Give *The Paris Review* for only $28 a year when you renew your subscription at the regular rate. You save $12 off the newsstand price!

No postage
stamp necessary
if mailed in the
United States

BUSINESS REPLY MAIL

FIRST CLASS   PERMIT NO. 3119   FLUSHING, N.Y.

POSTAGE WILL BE PAID BY ADDRESSEE

THE PARIS REVIEW
45-39 171 Place
FLUSHING NY   11358-9892

No postage
stamp necessary
if mailed in the
United States

BUSINESS REPLY MAIL

FIRST CLASS   PERMIT NO. 3119   FLUSHING, N.Y.

POSTAGE WILL BE PAID BY ADDRESSEE

THE PARIS REVIEW
45-39 171 Place
FLUSHING NY   11358-9892

merous, we realized that this was a new thing. So we inquired. It turned out that these were pieces that children had composed on word processors. What's happening is that as the actual tools for getting words onto the page become more flexible and externalized, the writer can get down almost every thought or every extension of thought. That ought to be an advantage. But in fact, in all these cases, it just extends everything slightly too much. Every sentence is too long. Everything is taken a bit too far, too attenuated. There's always a bit too much there, and it's too thin. Whereas when writing by hand you meet the terrible resistance of what happened your first year at it when you couldn't write at all . . . when you were making attempts, pretending to form letters. These ancient feelings are there, wanting to be expressed. When you sit with your pen, every year of your life is right there, wired into the communication between your brain and your writing hand. There is a natural characteristic resistance that produces a certain kind of result analogous to your actual handwriting. As you force your expression against that built-in resistance, things become automatically more compressed, more summary and, perhaps, psychologically denser. I suppose if you use a word processor and deliberately prune everything back, alert to the tendencies, it should be possible to get the best of both worlds.

Maybe what I'm saying applies only to those who have gone through the long conditioning of writing only with a pen or pencil up through their mid-twenties. For those who start early on a typewriter or, these days, on a computer screen, things must be different. The wiring must be different. In handwriting the brain is mediated by the drawing hand, in typewriting by the fingers hitting the keyboard, in dictation by the idea of a vocal style, in word processing by touching the keyboard and by the screen's feedback. The fact seems to be that each of these methods produces a different syntactic result from the same brain. Maybe the crucial element in handwriting is that the hand is simultaneously drawing. I know I'm very conscious of hidden imagery in handwriting—a subtext of a rudimentary picture language. Perhaps that tends to enforce more cooperation from the other side of the brain. And perhaps that extra load of right brain suggestions prompts a different succession of words and ideas. Perhaps that's what I am talking about.

INTERVIEWER

So word processing is a new discipline.

HUGHES

It's a new discipline that these particular children haven't learned. And which I think some novelists haven't learned. "Brevity is the soul of wit." It makes the imagination jump. I think I recognize among some modern novels the supersonic hand of the word processor uncurbed. When Henry James started dictating, his sentences became interminable, didn't they? And the physical world, as his brother William complained, suddenly disappeared from them. Henry hadn't realized. He was astonished.

INTERVIEWER

How long does it take to write a poem? Of course it depends on length and hibernation time, but still . . .

HUGHES

Well, in looking back over the whole lot, the best ones took just as long as it took to write them down; the not-so-satisfactory ones I'd tinker with sometimes for two or three years, but certainly for a few days, and I'd continue making changes over months. Some of them I'd still like to change.

INTERVIEWER

Are poems ever truly finished?

HUGHES

My experience with the things that arrive instantaneously is that I can't change them. They are finished. There is one particular poem, an often anthologized piece that just came —

"Hawk Roosting." I simply wrote it out, just as it appeared in front of me. There is a word in the middle that I'm not sure about. I always have this internal hiccup when I get to it because I had to make the choice between the singular and the plural form and neither of them is right.

INTERVIEWER

Has the answer occurred to you since?

HUGHES

No. I don't know that it could be solved. It's just one of those funny things. So that poem was abandoned insofar as I couldn't solve that problem. But otherwise it's a poem that I could no more think of changing than physically changing myself. Poems get to the point where they are stronger than you are. They come up from some other depth and they find a place on the page. You can never find that depth again, that same kind of authority and voice. I might *feel* I would like to change something about them, but they're still stronger than I am, and I cannot.

INTERVIEWER

Do you read or show your work to others while it is in progress?

HUGHES

I try not to. There's a Jewish proverb that Leonard Baskin's always quoting: Never show fools half-work. That "fools" is a bit hard, but I imagine most people who make things know what is meant.

INTERVIEWER

How has criticism of your work affected you or your poetry?

HUGHES

I think it's the shock of every writer's life when their first book is published. The shock of their lives. One has somehow to adjust from being anonymous, a figure in ambush, working from concealment, to being and working in full public view. It had an enormous effect on me. My impression was that I had suddenly walked into a wall of heavy hostile fire. That first year I wrote verses with three magical assonances to the line with the intention of abolishing certain critics! Now I read those reviews and they seem quite good. So it was writer's paranoia. The shock to a person who's never been named in public of being mentioned in newspapers can be absolutely traumatic. To everybody else it looks fairly harmless, even enviable. What I *can* see was that it enormously accelerated my determination to bring my whole operation into my own terms, to make my own form of writing and to abandon a lot of more casual paths that I might have followed. If I'd remained completely unknown, a writer not commented on, I think I might have gone off in all kinds of other directions. One can never be sure, of course.

INTERVIEWER
Wasn't there ever a desire to do something else?

HUGHES
Yes, always. Yes. I've sometimes wondered if it wouldn't be a good idea to write under a few pseudonyms. Keep several quite different lines of writing going. Like Fernando Pessoa, the Portuguese poet who tried four different poetic personalities. They all worked simultaneously. He simply lived with the four. What does Eliot say? "Dance, dance, / Like a dancing bear, / Cry like a parrot, chatter like an ape, / To find expression." It's certainly limiting to confine your writing to one public persona, because the moment you publish your own name you lose freedom. It's like being in a close-knit family. The moment you do anything new, the whole family jumps on it, comments, teases, advises against, does everything to make you self-conscious. There's a unanimous reaction to keep you as you were. You'd suppose any writer worth his salt could be bold and fearless and not give a damn. But in fact very

few can. We're at the mercy of the groups that shaped our early days. We're so helplessly social — like cells in an organ. Maybe that's why madness sometimes works — it knocks out the oversensitive connection. And maybe that's why exile is good. I wonder if the subjective impression of most writers is that whenever they take a new step, some big, unconscious reaction among readers tries to stop them . . . often a big conscious reaction among colleagues. Hardy stopped writing novels by just that. In his late years, while he was up in an apple tree, pruning it, he had a vision of the most magnificent novel — all the characters, many episodes, even some dialogue . . . the one ultimate novel that he absolutely had to write. What happened? By the time he came down out of the tree the whole vision had fled. And it never reappeared. Even Goethe, back then, made some remark about the impossibility of producing a natural oeuvre of fully ripened works when everything was instantly before the public and its hectic, printed reactions. Of course Goethe himself was a terrible stopper of other young writers. One of the strongest arguments that Shakespeare's plays were written by somebody unsuspected, maybe, was the uniquely *complete* development of that creative mind and its vision.

Also, there's a tendency to lay down laws for yourself about the kind of thing you want to do: an ideal of style, an exemplary probity of some kind, or maybe an ideal of thuggery, a release into disregard for all conventions and so on. Once they become your expected product, these are all traps. One way out of this might be to write a kind of provisional drama where you can explore all sorts of different provisional attitudes and voices. Remember the unresolved opposition of Trigorin and Treplev in Chekov's *The Seagull*? Chekov had a huge nostalgia for Treplev's weird vision. Somewhere he described the sort of work he longed to write — full of passionate, howling women, Greek tragedy dimension — and he bemoans the gentle doctor's attentiveness that imbues his actual writing. Now, if he'd been anonymous from the start, might he have explored the other things too? In poetry, living as a public persona in your writing is maybe even more crippling. Once you've contracted to write only the truth about yourself — as in some respected kinds of modern verse, or as in Shakespeare's sonnets — then you can too easily limit yourself to what you imagine are the truths of the ego that claims your conscious biography. Your own equivalent of what Shakespeare got into his plays is simply foregone. But being experimental isn't enough. The plunge has to be for real. The new thing has to be not you or has to seem so till it turns out to be the new you or the other you.

INTERVIEWER

You say that every writer should have a pseudonym for writing things different than their usual work. Have you ever used one?

HUGHES

Never — except once or twice at university. But I wish I had. I wish I'd established one or two out there. The danger, I suppose, of using pseudonyms is that it interferes with that desirable process — the unification of the personality. Goethe said that even the writing of plays, dividing the imagination up among different fictional personalities, damaged what he valued — the mind's wholeness. I wonder what he meant, exactly, since he also described his mode of thinking as imagined conversations with various people. Maybe the pseudonyms, like other personalities conjured up in a dramatic work, can be a preliminary stage of identifying and exploring new parts of yourself. Then the next stage would be to incorporate them in the unifying process. Accept responsibility for them. Maybe that's what Yeats meant by seeking his opposite. The great Sufi master Ibn el-Arabi described the essential method of spiritual advancement as an inner conversation with the personalities that seem to exist beyond what you regard as your own limits . . . getting those personalities to tell you what you did not know, or what you could not easily conceive of within your habitual limits. This is commonplace in some therapies, of course.

INTERVIEWER

What kind of working relationship have you had with editors of both poetry and prose?

HUGHES

On the whole I've been lucky with them. Extremely lucky. I was more than lucky to have T.S. Eliot as my first editor in England. Sylvia had typed up and sent off my manuscript to a 92nd Street Y First Poetry Book Competition—judged by Marianne Moore, Stephen Spender and Auden. First prize was publication by Harper Brothers. When it won, Sylvia sent Faber the typescript and a letter with that information in which, in American style, she referred to me as Ted. They replied that Faber did not publish first books by American authors. When she told them I was British, they took it. That's how I came to be Ted rather than something else.

Eliot's editorial hand on me could not have been lighter. In my second book of verse he suggested one verbal change, but I didn't follow it. I should have. He made some very useful suggestions in a book of verse for children that I wrote. I certainly followed those. My present children's editor at Faber, Janice Thompson, is brilliant in that she definitely gets me to write more things than I otherwise might and makes very acute judgments and suggestions about what I do produce. Editors in the U.S.—well, I've liked and got on with them all. But at that long distance I've never got to know any so well as I've known the Faber succession. Except for Fran McCullough at Harpers. Fran became a close friend while she was editing Sylvia's books and mine. She edited Sylvia's novel, *The Bell Jar*, and *Letters Home*. Later she edited Sylvia's *Journals*. Some explosive drama in all that. Only the beginning of bigger explosions. I hope we've remained friends in the fallout.

INTERVIEWER

Has it ever become impossible to write?

HUGHES

The nearest I've ever felt to a block was a sort of unfitness, in the athletic sense: the need for an all-out sustained effort of writing simply to get myself into shape before starting on what I imagined would be the real thing. One whole book arrived like that, not a very long book, but one which I felt I needed to galvanize my inertia, break through the huge sloth I was up against. On the spur I invented a little plot: nine birds come to the fallen Adam urging him to get up and be birdlike. I wrote the whole as a bagatelle, to sweat myself out of that inertia — and to conjure myself to be a bit more birdlike. Then, suddenly there it was, a sort of book. *Adam and the Sacred Nine*. I'd written a book just trying to get to the point where I might begin to write something that might go into a book. Still, did it break through to the real thing? That's the question, isn't it? A block is when we can't get through to the real thing. Many writers write a great deal, but very few write more than a very little of the real thing. So most writing must be displaced activity. When cockerels confront each other and daren't fight, they busily start pecking imaginary grains off to the side. That's displaced activity. Much of what we do at any level is a bit like that, I fancy. But hard to know which is which. On the other hand, the machinery has to be kept running. The big problem for those who write verse is keeping the machine running without simply exercising evasion of the real confrontation. If Ulanova, the ballerina, missed one day of practice, she couldn't get back to peak fitness without a week of hard work. Dickens said the same about his writing — if he missed a day he needed a week of hard slog to get back into the flow.

INTERVIEWER

Could I ask about your relationship with other poets? You knew Auden and Eliot.

HUGHES

I met Auden for more than a hello only twice. It was at a poetry festival, in 1966. Our conversation was very brief. He said, "What do you make of David Jones's *Anathemata*?" I replied, "A work of genius, a masterpiece." "Correct," he said.

That was it. The other occasion was after one of the 1966 International Poetry Festival evenings on the South Bank in London, when he was fuming against Neruda. I listened to his diatribe. We'd asked Neruda to read for twelve minutes, maybe fifteen. He'd read for over half an hour, longer—apparently from a piece of paper about four inches square. Auden always timed his readings to the minute. Neruda and Auden died almost on the same day; *The New Statesman* gave Neruda the front page and tucked Auden inside. I felt pained by that, though I have no doubt that Neruda is in a different class, a world class, as a poet. I sort of swallowed Auden whole some time in my early twenties—or tried to. He was so much part of the atmosphere. Some of his work I have always admired a lot. And I admire him—the Goethean side, the dazzle of natural brilliance in all his remarks. But I never felt any real poetic affinity with him. I suppose he is not a poet who taps the sort of things I am trying to tap in myself. Eliot was. I met Eliot only rarely and briefly. Once he and his wife Valerie invited Sylvia and myself to dinner. We were a bit overawed. Fortunately Stephen Spender, who was there, knew how to handle it. What do I recall? Many small humorous remarks. His very slow eating. The size of his hands—very large hands. Once I asked him if the *Landscapes*, those short beautiful little pieces, each so different from the others, were selections from a great many similar unpublished things. I thought they might be the sort of poem he whittled away at between the bigger works. No, he said. That's all there were. "They just came." It's a mystery. He wins the big races with such ease—but how did he keep in trim? How did he get into form? He seems to me one of the very great poets. One of the very few.

INTERVIEWER

What did you think of Ezra Pound? Did he give you pleasure?

HUGHES

He did, yes. Still does. But as a personality—he doesn't have the power to fascinate as a personality that, for instance,

Eliot does, or Yeats, perhaps because his internal evolution, or whatever it was, was so broken, so confused by a militance that took it over from the outside. Perhaps one recoils from what feels like a disintegration. But many pages of the verse seem to me wonderful, in all kinds of ways.

INTERVIEWER

You have been associated with Mark Strand and W.S. Merwin. How do you see their work as compared to yours?

HUGHES

I know Merwin's work pretty well. Mark Strand's less well, though I look at it very closely wherever I find it. I've been close to Bill Merwin in the past. I got to know him in the late fifties through Jack Sweeney who was then running the Lamont Poetry Library at Harvard. They had a house in London, and when Sylvia and I got back there in late 1959 they helped us a lot, in practical and other ways. Dido Merwin found us our flat, then half furnished it, then cooked things for Sylvia in the run up to our daughter being born. That was the high point of my friendship with Bill. He was an important writer for me at that time. It was a crucial moment in his poetry — very big transformations were going on in there; it was coming out of its chrysalis. And I suppose because we were so close, living only a couple of hundred yards apart, his inner changes were part of the osmotic flow of feelings between us. Very important for me. That's when I began to get out of my second collection of poems and into my third — which became the book entitled *Wodwo*. He helped me out of my chrysalis, too. Part way out. And he was pretty important for Sylvia a little later, when the *Ariel* poems began to arrive in early 1962. One of the hidden supply lines behind *Ariel* was the set of Neruda translations that Bill did for the BBC at that time. I still have her copy. It wasn't just Neruda that helped her. It was the way she saw how Bill used Neruda. That wasn't her only supply line, but it was one. I think Bill's traveled further on his road than any contemporary U.S. or British writer I can think of. Amazing resources and skills.

INTERVIEWER

What do you think of the label "confessional poetry" and the tendency for more and more poets to work in that mode?

HUGHES

Goethe called his work one big confession, didn't he? Looking at his work in the broadest sense, you could say the same of Shakespeare: a total self-examination and self-accusation, a total confession — very naked, I think, when you look into it. Maybe it's the same with any writing that has real poetic life. Maybe all poetry, insofar as it moves us and connects with us, is a revealing of something that the writer doesn't actually want to say, but desperately needs to communicate, to be delivered of. Perhaps it's the need to keep it hidden that makes it poetic — makes it poetry. The writer daren't actually put it into words, so it leaks out obliquely, smuggled through analogies. We think we're writing something to amuse, but we're actually saying something we desperately need to share. The real mystery is this strange need. Why can't we just hide it and shut up? Why do we have to blab? Why do human beings need to confess? Maybe, if you don't have that secret confession, you don't have a poem — don't even have a story. Don't have a writer. If most poetry doesn't seem to be in any sense confessional, it's because the strategy of concealment, of obliquity, can be so compulsive that it's almost entirely successful. The smuggling analogy is loaded with interesting cargo that seems to be there for its own sake — subject matter of general interest — but at the bottom of *Paradise Lost* and *Samson Agonistes*, for instance, Milton tells us what nearly got him executed. The novelty of some of Robert Lowell's most affecting pieces in *Life Studies*, some of Anne Sexton's poems and some of Sylvia's, was the way they tried to throw off that luggage, the deliberate way they stripped off the veiling analogies. Sylvia went furthest in the sense that her secret was most dangerous to her. She desperately needed to reveal it. You can't overestimate her compulsion to write like that. She had to write those things — even against her most vital interests. She died before she knew what *The Bell*

Jar and the *Ariel* poems were going to do to her life, but she
had to get them out. She had to tell everybody . . . like those
Native American groups who periodically told everything that
was wrong and painful in their lives in the presence of the
whole tribe. It was no good doing it in secret; it had to be
done in front of everybody else. Maybe that's why poets go
to such lengths to get their poems published. It's no good
whispering them to a priest or a confessional. And it's not for
fame, because they go on doing it after they've learned what
fame amounts to. No, until the revelation's actually published, the poet feels no release. In all that, Sylvia was an
extreme case, I think.

INTERVIEWER
Could you talk a bit more about Sylvia?

HUGHES
Sylvia and I met because she was curious about my group
of friends at university and I was curious about her. I was
working in London but I used to go back up to Cambridge
at weekends. Half a dozen or so of us made a poetic gang.
Our main cooperative activity was drinking in the Anchor
and our main common interest, apart from fellow feeling and
mutual attraction, was Irish, Scottish and Welsh traditional
songs—folk songs and broadsheet ballads. We sang a lot. Recorded folk song was rare in those days. Our poetic interests
were more mutually understood than talked about. But we
did print a broadsheet of literary comment. In one issue, one
of our group, our Welshman, Dan Huws, demolished a poem
that Sylvia had published, "Caryatids." He later became a
close friend of hers, wrote a beautiful elegy when she died.
That attack attracted her attention. Also, she had met one of
our group, Lucas Myers, an American, who was an especially
close friend of mine. Luke was very dark and skinny. He could
be incredibly wild. Just what you hoped for from Tennessee.
His poems were startling to us—Hart Crane, Wallace Stevens
vocabulary, zany. He interested Sylvia. In her journals she

records the occasional dream in which Luke appears unmistakably. When we published a magazine full of our own poems, the only issue of *St. Botolph's*, and launched it at a big dance party, Sylvia came to see what the rest of us looked like. Up to that point I'd never set eyes on her. I'd heard plenty about her from an English girlfriend who shared supervisions with her. There she suddenly was, raving Luke's verses at Luke and my verses at me.

Once I got to know her and read her poems, I saw straight off that she was a genius of some kind. Quite suddenly we were completely committed to each other and to each other's writing. The year before, I had started writing again, after the years of the devastation of university. I'd just written what have become some of my more anthologized pieces—"The Thought Fox," the Jaguar poems, "Wind." I see now that when we met, my writing, like hers, left its old path and started to circle and search. To me, of course, she was not only herself: she was America and American literature in person. I don't know what I was to her. Apart from the more monumental classics—Tolstoy, Dostoyevsky and so on—my background reading was utterly different from hers. But our minds soon became two parts of one operation. We dreamed a lot of shared or complementary dreams. Our telepathy was intrusive. I don't know whether our verse exchanged much, if we influenced one another that way—not in the early days. Maybe others see that differently. Our methods were not the same. Hers was to collect a heap of vivid objects and good words and make a pattern; the pattern would be projected from somewhere deep inside, from her very distinctly evolved myth. It appears distinctly evolved to a reader now—despite having been totally unconscious to her then. My method was to find a thread end and draw the rest out of a hidden tangle. Her method was more painterly, mine more narrative, perhaps. Throughout our time together we looked at each other's verses at every stage—up to the *Ariel* poems of October 1962, which was when we separated.

INTERVIEWER

Do you know how Sylvia used her journals? Were they diaries, or notebooks for her poetry and fiction?

HUGHES

Well, I think Janet Malcolm in the *New Yorker* made a fair point about the journals: a lot of what's in them is practice . . . shaping up for some possible novel, little chapters for novels. She was constantly sketching something that happened and working it into something she thought might fit into a novel. She thought of her journals as working notes for some ultimate novel, although, in fact, I don't think any of it ever went into *The Bell Jar*. She changed certain things to make them *work*, to make some kind of symbolic statement of a feeling. She wasn't writing an account of this or that event; she was trying to get to some other kind of ancient, i.e., childhood, material. Some of her short stories take the technique a stage further. Wanting to express that ancient feeling.

INTERVIEWER

What happened to Plath's last novel that was never published?

HUGHES

Well, what I was aware of was a fragment of a novel, about seventy pages. Her mother said she saw a whole novel, but I never knew about it. What I was aware of was sixty, seventy pages which disappeared. And to tell you the truth, I always assumed her mother took them all, on one of her visits.

INTERVIEWER

Would you talk about burning Plath's journals?

HUGHES

What I actually destroyed was one journal which covered maybe two or three months, the last months. And it was just sad. I just didn't want her children to see it, no. Particularly her last days.

INTERVIEWER

What about *Ariel*? Did you reorder the poems there?

HUGHES

Well, nobody in the U.S. wanted to publish the collection as she left it. The one publisher over there who was interested wanted to cut it to twenty poems. The fear seemed to be that the whole lot might provoke some sort of backlash—some revulsion. And at the time, you know, few magazine editors would publish the *Ariel* poems, few liked them. The qualities weren't so obvious in those days. So right from the start there was a question over just how the book was to be presented. I wanted the book that would display the whole range and variety. I remember writing to the man who suggested cutting it to twenty—a longish intemperate letter, as I recall—and saying I felt that was simply impossible. I was torn between cutting some things out and putting some more things in. I was keen to get some of the last poems in. But the real problem was, as I've said, that the U.S. publishers I approached did not want Sylvia's collection as it stood. Faber in England were happy to publish the book in any form. Finally, it was a compromise—I cut some things out and I put others in. As a result I have been mightily accused of disordering her intentions and even suppressing part of her work. But those charges have evolved twenty, thirty years after the event. They are based on simple ignorance of how it all happened. Within six years of that first publication all her late poems were published in collections—all that she'd put in her own *Ariel*, and those she'd kept out. It was her growing frame, of course, that made it possible to publish them. And years ago, for anybody who was curious, I published the contents and order of her own typescript—so if anybody wants to see what her *Ariel* was it's quite easy. On the other hand, how final was her order? She was forever shuffling the poems in her typescripts—looking for different connections, better sequences. She knew there were always new possibilities, all fluid.

Could you say a bit more about how your own poems origi-
nate and how you begin writing?

Well, I have a sort of notion. Just the tail end of an idea,
usually just the thread of an idea. If I can feel behind that a
sort of waiting momentum, a sense of some charge there to tap,
then I just plunge in. What usually happens then — inevitably I
would say — is that I go off in some wholly different direction.
The thread end of an idea burns away, and I'm pulled in —
on the momentum of whatever was there waiting. Then that
feeling opens up other energies, all the possibilities in my
head, I suppose. That's the pleasure, never quite knowing
what's there, being surprised. Once I get onto something I
usually finish it. In a way it goes on finishing itself while I
attend to its needs. It might be days, months. Later, often
enough, I see exactly what it needs to be, and I finish it in
moments, usually by getting rid of things.

What do birds mean for you? The figures of the hawk and
the crow — so astonishing. Are you tired to death of explaining
them?

I don't know how to explain them. There are certain things
that are just impressive, aren't there? One stone can be impressive, and the stones around it aren't. It's the same with animals.
Some, for some reason, are strangely impressive. They just
get into you in a strange way. Certain birds obviously have
this extra quality which fascinates your attention. Obviously
hawks have always been that for me, as for a great many others,
not only impressive in themselves but also in that they've
accumulated an enormous literature making them even more
impressive. And crows too. Crows are the central bird in many
mythologies. The crow is at every extreme, lives on every piece
of land on earth, the most intelligent bird.

INTERVIEWER
Your poem "The Thought Fox" is thought to be your ars poetica. Do you agree with that?

HUGHES
There is a sense in which every poem that comes off is a description or a dramatization of its own creation. Within the poem, I sometimes think, is all the evidence you need for explaining how the poem came to be and why it is as it is. Then again, every poem that works is like a metaphor of the whole mind writing, the solution of all the oppositions and imbalances going on at that time. When the mind finds the balance of all those things and projects it, that's a poem. It's a kind of hologram of the mental condition at that moment, which then immediately changes and moves on to some other sort of balance and rearrangement. What counts is that it be a symbol of that momentary wholeness. That's how I see it.

INTERVIEWER
Why do you choose to speak through animals so often?

HUGHES
I suppose, because they were there at the beginning. Like parents. Since I spent my first seventeen or eighteen years constantly thinking about them more or less, they became a language — a symbolic language which is also the language of my whole life. It was not something I began to learn about at university or something that happened to me when I was thirty, but part of the machinery of my mind from the beginning. They are a way of connecting all my deepest feelings together. So, when I look for, or get hold of a feeling of that kind, it tends to bring up the image of an animal or animals simply because that's the deepest, earliest language that my imagination learned. Or one of the deepest, earliest languages. People were there too.

INTERVIEWER
What would you say is the function of poetry as opposed to the function of prose?

HUGHES
In the seventies I got to know one or two healers. The one
I knew best believed that since everybody has access to the
energies of the autoimmune system, some individuals develop
a surplus. His own history was one of needing more than most:
forty years of ankylosing spondylitis. In the end, when he was
past sixty, a medium told him that no one could heal him,
but that he could heal himself if he would start to heal others.
So he started healing and within six months was virtually
cured. Watching and listening to him, the idea occurred to
me that art was perhaps this: the psychological component of
the autoimmune system. It works on the artist as a healing.
But it works on others too, as a medicine. Hence our great,
insatiable thirst for it. However it comes out—whether a design in a carpet, a painting on a wall, the shaping of a door-
way—we recognize that medicinal element because of the instant healing effect, and we call it art. It consoles and heals
something in us. That's why that aspect of things is so important, and why what we want to preserve in civilizations
and societies is their art: because it's a living medicine that
we can still use. It still works. We feel it working. Prose,
narratives, etc., can carry this healing. Poetry does it more
intensely. Music, maybe, most intensely of all.

INTERVIEWER
On another matter entirely, do you think the literary com-
munities in England and America differ from each other?

HUGHES
Yes, profoundly. The world and the whole grounding of
experience for American writers is so utterly different from
that of English writers. The hinterlands of American writing
are so much more varied, and the scope of their hinterlands
is so infinitely vast. Many more natural and social worlds are
available to American writers. For every generation of Americans there's more material that is utterly new and strange. I
think the problem for American writers is to keep up with

their material, whereas the problem for English writers is to find new material — material that isn't already in some real sense secondhand, used-up, dog-eared, pre-digested. You see this in a very simple way in the contrast between the American and English writing about field sports — shooting and fishing. The range, richness, variety, quantity, quality of the American sports writing is stupefying. There are some fine writers on these subjects in the U.K., but one has the impression that they are simply updating, modernizing material that was used up generations ago, and a very limited range of material it is.

INTERVIEWER

What do you think of writing workshops and MFA programs?

HUGHES

Sometimes they work wonders. When the Arvon Writing Foundation — what would be called a creative writing college in the U.S. — was started here in England in 1969, I was asked to join the founders. I had taught creative writing classes at the University of Massachusetts, and it had been rather a wonderful experience. I learned an awful lot from the students themselves. I saw how those classes worked, how the students educated each other in writing skills, how one talented student can somehow transform the talents of a whole class. But on the whole I felt that the idea was impractical for England. I thought I knew too well the bigoted antagonism that most of our older writers felt about transatlantic ideas of creative writing. I'd heard it expressed too often. So I thought the idea could not work here simply because the writers would not cooperate. But the founders of Arvon, two poets, went ahead and invited me to give a reading of my verses to the first course. The students were a group of fourteen year olds from a local school. Within that one week they had produced work that astonished me. Within five days, in fact. They were in an incredible state of creative excitement. Here in England the idea worked in a way that I had never seen in the U.S. So Arvon developed. Younger writers, and most of the older writers as it turned out, tutored the courses with an almost natural skill and very often with amazing results. The experience persuaded me that a creative writing course of the Arvon's kind has more impact here, perhaps because the English personality and character tend to be comparatively fixed and set, rigid, so that any change comes with a bang. You get revelations of talent in people who had never dreamed they could write a word. Amazing conversions.

INTERVIEWER
Would you like to have had such a program available to you when you started out?

HUGHES
I've often wondered. I'm not sure if I would have gone. What I wanted to do was work it all out in my own terms and at my own pace. I didn't want to be influenced, or at least I wanted to choose my influences for myself. Between the age when I began to write seriously and the time I left the university at the age of twenty-four, I read very little in poetry, novels and drama apart from the great authors — the authors I considered to be great. Within that literature I was a hundred-great-books reader. My first real encounter with the possibilities of contemporary poetry came only in 1954 or 1955, when a Penguin anthology of American poetry came out. I'd become aware of some names of course — Frost, Wallace Stevens, even Theodore Roethke, Hart Crane. That anthology came out just as I was ready to look further. So I completely bypassed contemporary English poetry, apart from Auden and Dylan Thomas, and came fresh to the American. Everything in that book seemed exciting to me — exciting and familiar. Wilbur, Bill Merwin, Elizabeth Bishop, Lowell. But most of all John Crowe Ransom. For two or three years Ransom became a craze of mine, and he still was when I met Sylvia. I managed to enthuse her to the point that he seriously affected

her style for a period. But many things in that anthology hit
me, pieces like Karl Shapiro's "Auto Wreck." When I met
Sylvia I also met her library, and the whole wave hit me. I
began to devour everything American. But my point is that
up to then, my exciting new discoveries in poetry had been
things like the first act of *Two Noble Kinsmen*, (not usually
included in Shakespeare's Complete Works), or Lady Gregory's
translation of the Arran song: "It was late last night the dog
was speaking of you." What I felt I wanted to do didn't seem
to exist. I was conscious mainly of a kind of musical energy.
My notion was to make real and solid what would contain
it — something to do with the way I read poems to myself.

INTERVIEWER

And you eventually burst out of that.

HUGHES

The earliest piece of mine that I kept was a lyric titled "Song"
that came to me as such things should in your nineteenth
year — literally a voice in the air at about 3:00 A.M. when I
was on night duty just after I'd started national service. Between that and the next piece that I saved, the poem I titled
"The Thought Fox," lay six years of total confusion. Six years!
That's when I read myself to bits, as Nietzsche said students
do. Also, I ran smack into the first part of the English lit tripos
at Cambridge. I got out of that and into anthropology none
too soon. I was writing all the time, but in confusion. I mopped
up everything that was going on inside me with Beethoven's
music. Throughout that time, he was my therapy. After university I lived in London, did various jobs — but I was removed
from friends and from constant Beethoven, and for the first
time in years I thought about nothing but the poem I was
trying to write. Then one night up came "The Thought Fox"
and, soon after, the other pieces I mentioned. But I had less
a sense of bursting out, I think, more a sense of tuning in to
my own transmission. Tuning out the influences, the static

and interference. I didn't get there by explosives. My whole understanding of it was that I could get it only by concentration.

In the late twentieth century is there a tradition of British poetry that is different from other English-speaking nations?

HUGHES
Well, when I began to write, I certainly felt there to be. The tradition had its gods, the great sacred national figures of the past. Some of them not so great. But they policed the behavior of young poets, and they policed the tastes of readers — most of all the tastes of readers. Yes, in the 1950s it was still a strong orthodoxy. Eliot and Pound had challenged it, but they hadn't fractured it. I'm not even sure if they modified it much. Mainly you were aware that this tradition was distinctly not-continental and distinctly not-American. It had hypersensitive detectors for any trace of contamination from those two sources. In general, I suppose, it was defensive. We were made very aware of it in the early fifties by Robert Graves. He gave a series of lectures at Cambridge which purged the tradition of its heretics — bad Wordsworth and so on — and of its alien stowaways: Eliot and Pound. Graves had a strange kind of authority through the late fifties — the man of tradition, the learned champion of the British tradition. I fancied he had an effect even on Auden, who certainly admired him a lot. But then came the sixties. In the U.K. the shock of the sixties is usually tied to the Beatles. But as far as poetry was concerned, their influence was marginal, I think. The poetry shock that hit the U.K. in the sixties started before the Beatles. Sylvia responded to the first ripples of it. In a sense, *Ariel* is a response to those first signs, and she never heard the Beatles. What happened were two big simultaneous events in the world of poetry — the first was the sudden waking up of the world from the ice age of the war. Countries that had

been separated by blockades or crushed under the communist ice suddenly seemed to wake up. In poetry, they rushed to embrace one another, first on that amazing boom of translation, then in the International Poetry Festivals that got going mid-decade. Maybe the Pasternak explosion in the late fifties was the beginning. But in general, Bill Merwin had translated a huge amount of various authors. We had Robert Bly's first volumes of his *Sixties* magazine. We collected the first translations of Zbigniew Herbert and Holub — unearthed by Alvarez in, I think, 1962. I'm not sure when the Penguin translations began, but their first Lorca edition had appeared in 1960. The boom began early and then simply grew right through the decade.

The other momentous event came from the U.S. — the shockwave not so much of pop music but of the lifestyle of the Beat poets, with Allen Ginsberg as high priest. That shockwave, which swept America at the end of the fifties, hit England in the beginning of the sixties. The Beatles were its English amplifiers, in one sense, but the actual thing at the time was the lifestyle. You saw all your friends transformed in a slow flash. And with the lifestyle came the poetry, the transcendentalism, the Beat publications. Those two big waves — one of international poetry and the other, the California revolution, blend into one. What was really very strange was the way the fans of the new pop music and folk music craze all took to buying poetry — especially translated modern poetry. Penguin stepped up their output of new titles; every publisher seemed to be commissioning new translations of foreign poets. Those fans bought huge numbers of the books. They were packed in at the first of the Art Council's big International Poetry Festivals in 1966, which I helped organize. Our program was based on an issue of Daniel Weissbort's new magazine, *Modern Poetry in Translation*, which I think was the first such magazine in Britain. It was an amazing occasion. Almost every big figure I invited accepted and came. And by chance, on the day of the festival London happened to be full of poets from all over the place. We invited quite a few and

they joined in. Any young poet in the U.K. aware of that must
have been hit pretty hard. The variety of different poetries that
were not only suddenly available, but in high fashion, was
staggering. The mad atmosphere of those early International Festivals
only lasted a year or two. Probably that one in 1966 and the
earlier, more spontaneous one in 1965 were the great ones.
But the rest of it reeled on into the early seventies until finally
the translation boom began to flag. Still, the best of the books
haven't gone away. And that awakening of all the countries
to one another's poetry hasn't gone to sleep. Poets like Holub
have become almost honorary British poets. In many ways,
none of that has closed down. Has it modified British tradition? Well, it must have modified it one way: at least all young
British poets now know that the British tradition is not the
only one among the traditions of the globe. Everything is now
completely open, every approach, with infinite possibilities.
Obviously the British tradition still exists as a staple of certain
historically hard-earned qualities if anybody is still there who
knows how to inherit them. Raleigh's qualities haven't become
irrelevant. When I read Primo Levi's verse I'm reminded of
Raleigh. But for young British poets, it's no longer the only
tradition, no longer a tradition closed in on itself and defensive.

INTERVIEWER
You've just come back from Macedonia — a poetry festival
that was obviously very important. What was the understanding of British poetry there?

HUGHES
I had a curious experience on the airplane coming back. I
boarded in Skopje and noticed this young woman on the opposite side of the aisle, oh, about thirty-five. I saw her look at
me and I thought because the whole festival in Struga had
been so publicized and televised throughout Macedonia — that

maybe she felt she had seen me, maybe even recognized me, since they gave me the Laurel Wreath of Gold this year, and there'd been a certain amount of camera concentration. But neither of us said anything. Then there she was again on the next leg of the flight, in the seat in front of me, and she asked if I was who I was. She had seen me on TV. Finally she said, "I was very surprised that they gave the prize to British poetry." Naturally I asked her why. And she replied, "Well, I thought British poetry was dead." It turned out she was a doctor in Dubai. I had with me this rather magnificent Macedonian-made volume of my poems translated into Macedonian. So I handed her the book and said, "Here's an opportunity to examine the patient." When she returned it to me half an hour later she was very gracious. Ten minutes after that I saw she was reading the latest *Times Literary Supplement*!

INTERVIEWER

It's like the British poet is dead every few years, isn't it?

HUGHES

What struck me was that it came out so pat. A sort of obvious truism, as if everybody over the continental landmass simply knew it. And in the *TLS* she had her finger on the pulse.

INTERVIEWER

Is poetry as vital to people now as it was thirty years ago? Aren't sales of poetry going up?

HUGHES

Well, it's a fact — not much observed maybe except by the judges of children's writing competitions — that the teaching of how to write poetry is now producing extraordinary results. Mainly at the lower ages. This might not be so new in the U.S., but in the U.K. it's a phenomenon of the last fifteen years, especially of the last ten. The twenty-five-year influence of the Arvon Foundation can't be ignored. You only have to

ask around among young published poets and look at the
prizewinners of the various competitions. And Arvon has
spawned a host of other places doing a similar job. All this
must be helping sales in the U.K. It's a new kind of reading
and writing public that simply didn't exist in Britain before
the early seventies. And it's definitely not confined to the
universities.

But I expect the real reasons must be deeper. Poetry sales
are supposed to rise during a war, aren't they, when people
are forced to become aware of what really matters. You could
invent an explanation, I'm sure. Maybe something to do with
the way we all live on two levels — a top level where we scramble
to respond moment by moment to the bombardment of impressions, demands, opportunities. And a bottom level where
our last-ditch human values live — the long-term feelings like
instinct, the bedrock facts of our character. Usually, we can
live happily on the top level and forget the bottom level. But,
all it takes to dump the population on the top level to the
lowest pits of the bottom level, with all their values and all
their ideas totally changed, is a war. I would suggest that
poetry is one of the voices of the bottom level.

The poetry translation boom of the sixties was inseparable,
I think, from the Vietnam War. That war felt like the Cold
War finally bursting into flames — the beginning of war with
the combined communist regimes. And the translated modern
poetry boom was inseparable from that catastrophe. It per-
vaded everything. Two societies, the U.S. and the U.K., that
were notably stuck on the top level were trying to divine the
bottom-level reality being lived out in South East Asia. But
in general everyone under the communist regimes was on the
bottom level. You remember all those attempts to actualize
it, to live it secondhand? To be part of it somehow?

Pasternak was the first big voice to be heard from under
the Russian ice. But then came Yevtushenko and Voznesensky
on their reading tours through the West. Their popularity,
their glamour, was amazing. I remember C.P. Snow introducing Yevtushenko onstage at the South Bank by characterizing

him as "what we really mean by a celebrity." Behind that,
Mandelshtam, Akhmatova, Mayakovsky and the rest were suddenly the greatest names; translations began to pour out.
There was a huge thirst. And I remember the big shock —
another of the big literary shocks in my life — of discovering
the poetry of Russia's victims, in Herbert, Holub, Popa and
so on, and along with that the poetry of Amichai, Celan . . .
So you could say the great craving of the U.S. and the U.K.
on the top level to anticipate and experience that reality on
the bottom level did take in one way the form of a craze for
translated poetry, an almost undiscriminating appetite for any
news whatsoever through that hotline. The market for those
books was colossal.

Now what's going on in the Balkans is making that bottom
level resonate again, as well as the African famines, the thirty-
odd horrible little wars crackling away, and behind all that a
new sense of impending global disaster, an obscure mix of
environmental and political breakdowns, runaway popula-
tions and the economic threat of the Far East. Anyway, a sense
of big trouble coming, with all the evidence of the first phases
jamming the TV screens. Here in the U.K. we're still only an
audience on the top level watching the calamities taking place
on the bottom level. But we're a twenty-four-hour-a-day top-
level audience, supersaturated with impressions of life on the
bottom level. The war in former Yugoslavia has raised the
curtain on it all. So, given that model of the two levels, the
appetite for poetry should be rising again, a little. Or slowly.

INTERVIEWER

Finally, what does this progression mean in terms of form?
What are your thoughts on free as opposed to formal verse?

HUGHES

In the way you've put the question "formal" suggests regular
metrics, regular stanzas and, usually, rhyme. But it also suggests some absolute form that doesn't have those more evident

features; it suggests any form governed by a strong, inflexible inner law that the writer finds himself having to obey, that he can't just play around with, as he can play around with, say, the wording of a letter. That kind of deeper, hidden form, though it doesn't show regular metrical or stanzaic patterning or end rhyme, can't in any way be called "free." Take any passage of "The Waste Land," or maybe a better example is Eliot's poem "Marina." Every word in those poems is as formally fixed, as locked into flexible inner laws, as words can be. The music of those words, the musical inevitability of the pitch, the pacing, the combination of inflections—all that is in some way absolute, unalterable, the ultimate perfect containment of unusually powerful poetic forces. You could say the same of many other examples: Smart's "Jubilate Agno," any passages in Shakespeare's blank verse, Shakespeare's prose. To my mind, the best of the kind of verse usually called free always aspires towards that kind of formal inevitability—a fixed, unalterable, musical and yet hidden dramatic shape. One difference between this kind of verse and regular, metrical, rhymed stanzas, is the problem it sets the reader at first reading. Regular formal features give the reader immediate bearings, the A-B-C directions for reading or performing the piece being nursery simple: the poem has a familiar, friendly look from that very first encounter. But when these are missing—no regular meter, no stanza shape, no obvious rhyme—the reader has to grope, searching for that less obvious, deeper set of musical dramatic laws. That takes time, more than one or two readings. And it takes poetic imagination—or some talent for rhythmical, expressive speech. But if those laws are actually there, as they are in the Eliot, the Smart and the Shakespeare, sooner or later they assert their inevitability in the reader's mind, and the reader begins to recognize the presence of some absolute, inner form. Of course, if those laws aren't there, they can never assert themselves. The piece never gets a grip on the reader. It might be interesting and even exciting to read at first encounter, but then it will slowly fall to bits. The reader will begin to recognize the absence of any law that makes it go one way rather than another . . . the absence of any deeper pattern of hidden forces. So the thing ceases to be read.

In the long run, the same fate — to be rejected and forgotten — overtakes most formally shaped verse too, no matter how strict its meter or how accurate and dexterous its rhymes. Good metrical rhymed verse, if it's to grip the imagination and stay readable, has to have, as well as those external formal features, the same dynamo of hidden musical dramatic laws as the apparently free verse.

Having said that, I think you are then left with the pro and contra arguments for using or not using those features of regular meter, stanza, rhyme. The main argument, to my mind, for *not* using them is to gain access to the huge variety of musical patterns that they shut out. Imagine if Shakespeare had stuck to sonnets and long rhymed poems and had never got onto the explorations of his blank verse and those wonderful musical flights of dialogue or onto his prose. Imagine what might have come out of the eighteenth century in England if the regime of the couplet hadn't been so absolute. How could Whitman ever have happened if he'd stuck to his crabby rhymes? That seems to me a strong argument. But the main argument for using meter, rhyme, stanza also seems strong. It's not just that rhymes and the requirement of meter actually stimulate invention — which they obviously do, at certain levels — but it's the strange satisfaction of making that square treasure chest and packing it. Or making that locket with its jewel or its portrait. Or making that periscope box of precisely arranged lenses. There's a mystery to it, I'm quite sure. Maybe a mathematical satisfaction. Take the ballad stanza, which is basically just an old English couplet. The best of those quatrains have a kind of primal force, not just musical finality but an inner force, a weight of paid-for experience that most people can recognize. Yet when you break the meter, lose or disarray the rhymes, everything's gone. Then there's Primo Levi's remark. He found that in the death camps, where it became very important to dig poems out of the memory, the poems of regular meter and rhyme proved more loyal, and I'm not sure he didn't say that they were more consoling. You don't forget his remark.

—Drue Heinz

Etchings

Tony Fitzpatrick

The Last Vegas Bird

The Watch Man's Bird

The Little Man's Bird

The Griot's Bird

The Shipwrecked Sailor's Bird

The Sad Diva's Fire Bird

The Host

Marcia Guthridge

I've never understood about fishing and buffalo stomachs.
I admit it freely. I am no cannibal. But there are connections
between me and the world. I'm not a cog. I'm a bolt. People
who know me find me reasonable — neither gluttonous nor
profligate. It is only my wife who thinks I devour without
permission and eschew what I should eat.

Only yesterday, for example, just back from vacation, I was
driving across the city, the water glittering in the lake on
one side of me, skyscraping apartment buildings — clean steel
Mies — glittering on the other side, Bach's "Air on the G
String" on the radio. I soared. The road was newly paved and
the high places were long, the dips so smooth and quick the
nose of my little car never turned down, just fell for a second
vertically and rose again, me with it. Two birds pumped up-
ward in the distance and then a perfectly proportioned curve
in the road — a classical Grecian curve — turned me to see an
airplane, barely moving, opposite the birds but on the same
slant, heading down for the airport I had just left. The plane
disappeared behind a building; and when I saw it again, a

trick of the sun, I guess, had it sinking straight down now,
no slant, falling lazily like a parachute, like me and my little
car when the beautiful road dipped. I knew my place.

• • •

Even the shells are bleached white here on my seashore.
The Gulf of Mexico is so light a gray that the sun above it
can blur it nearly to white. Directly across the same Gulf, on
the edge of Florida where we went one spring on vacation
because he likes color and baseball, the water is altogether
different: blue. There are lots of palm trees and sea oats among
clumps of long-bladed humid green grass, sea grapes with flat
round red leaves, mossy pine trees and a sky hectic with birds,
such birds: blue herons and egrets with necks as slim and
wavy as the sea-oat stalks and shockingly yellow beaks, greedy
mud-colored pelicans flap-elbowing each other off the crowded
fishing piers. The sun is red and sweet, unreal. The shells are
striped and glossy. I found one that looked like the hide of
a green zebra with one perfect straight orange line up the
middle, as if painted on with a fine Japanese brush.

So after we went to Florida that one spring because he
wanted to, after I'd spent the whole week comparing where
we were to where I'd rather be—the shore of my childhood
summers, the resort of my adult dreams—he said he'd see this
beach of beaches. "Let's go to Texas. We'll take a few days
off at the end of August. I want to see this place." He said
it on the plane going home from Florida. Immediately I
blanched innerly, like one of my Texas shells, like a brittle
white sand dollar with a secret rattling in its closed chambers.

But I said it was a nice idea (indeed it was), and I said to
myself that sensing danger would help me to avoid it. I knew
he wouldn't like Port Aransas. I knew to him it would seem
primitive and brutal. I knew to me it would seem primitive
and brutal now, except it was inside me in the way places are
inside creatures like creatures are inside places, like mountains
are inside mountain goats, like mollusks are inside shells. I
knew he was not my brother or my father, or even my cousin

(he was my husband), and I knew that would be a problem. Blood bonds to places, and everything there is is layered and surrounded.

I thought I was ready. He would be my guest. But I did not foresee the argument about murdering fish. How could anyone foresee such a thing?

We flew into Corpus Christi and drove the short distance to the tip of Padre Island in a rented Buick. Already this was wrong. When I was a child, my family strapped plastic buckets and rubber floats and beer coolers atop the car and drove down from Central Texas, where we lived. We crossed from the mainland on the car ferry, so the water snuck right up under us, car and all, first thing. Every year we took the same vacation, my uncle's family too; all eleven of us stayed in one cabin. One pair of grown-ups slept in the bedroom and the other pair in the sitting room, which was the same as the kitchen. Until my little sister and my youngest cousin grew up a little, they slept in the sitting room too, on a pallet made of beach towels on the sandy floor. The older kids got to sleep on the screened porch, on salt-smelling mattresses that felt as if they were stuffed with ancient oyster shells. We tossed and twitched on our crunchy beds gingerly, because of our sunburns. We giggled softly late into the night, and listened to the roar of trucks on the main island road a hundred yards away, and sometimes, as the trucks glided onto the Corpus Christi highway, we imagined we heard the Gulf waves whispering among the tall wheels.

Every morning we packed the two cars full of food and Coca-Cola and beer, and drove to the beach about a mile away. Sometimes the cars were so full of stuff we older kids were allowed to ride sitting on the doors, our legs inside and the rest of us out. You drive—still do—your car right up to the water, and then you could sit on top of it, stare at the Gulf and pretend to be a pirate or a renowned fisherperson scouting schools. The car glinted in the sun and heated up like a roasting pan with you on it. We made sand animals. We buried each other: we'd dig a deep hole and put somebody in it, then smooth a mound of sand around his shoulders till

it was a perfect dune with a head on it, and finally the buried
kid's muscles went crampy, and he'd burst from the white
earth like a white-hot rock from a volcano. We floated for
hours at a time in the steamy salt water, to boil for a while
instead of roast. The grown-ups fished in the surf.

We recognized the end of the day by how red our skin was,
not by the color or position of the sun, which stayed high and
strong till dusk, when it changed momentarily from white to
yellow and popped suddenly into the water while no one was
watching. When we were red enough we packed the cars and
drove back to our cabin. My mother and aunt cleaned vegeta-
bles; my father and uncle cleaned fish. It was the children's
job to take the laundry to the laundromat without dragging
the towels through the sticker burrs in the pale lawn, and to
fetch eggs or fruit or pickle relish from the Island Food Store
which smelled of hot wood and bread. One afternoon we
resolved to help with supper by trapping crabs. It took us
hours to catch a dozen from the pier, none bigger than my
youngest cousin's tiny fist, with legs like hairs, fleshless. By
the time we got them back to the cabin they were dead in
our dry creel. My father and uncle came home from fishing
and found the bodies where we dumped them in the grass
burrs by the back door. They made us boil them and (though
my mother fought them on this—she said they'd already
started to smell off) eat them. There was no more than a
teaspoonful of meat in each crab. We scraped smidgens from
crevices in the enameled labyrinths of inner shell, sucked the
juice from spider legs, and then my uncle re-boiled the shards
and strained the liquid for broth. My father thought it was
necessary to eat what you kill. "It's not magic," I heard him
say forcefully to someone later in the house, while I lay with
the other children on the screened porch thinking of sleep.
"It's common consideration. It's keeping things right between
us and the fish."

The condo my husband had booked for us this time had
a view of the Gulf and a Weber grill. When I saw the modern
kitchen with its butcher-block island, I remembered how my

mother and aunt laughed as they moved between the sink and the little table in our kitchen–sitting room, working with shoulders touching. I told him about that, and when he looked at me as if there must be more to the story, I added: "My mother didn't laugh when she cooked supper at home."

Immediately I went hunting the thermostat, turned off the air-conditioning and began tugging at the window over the carport. "Don't you think we'll be hot without air-conditioning?" he asked. "It must be a hundred and ten out there." "This is urgent. There's got to be a crowbar here somewhere," I said. "I need a window open. I need a window open now." The windows were all painted shut. I pulled barbecue tools out of kitchen drawers until I found a hammer and a sturdy spatula. On my way back to the bedroom I saw his face. It looked all flattened out, pulled tight by the ears, so I smiled affectionately. "We're lucky to have the Gulf so close, you know." I didn't want him to be afraid.

I went to work furiously on the window. From well behind me, he peered toward outside. "There are cars right up on the beach," he called out, plainly astonished. "Would you look at that? People are driving their cars right up to the water!" Wood cracked, the sash zinged, and the window rolled open. I stepped back, sweating. Dead white paint chips littered the sill.

"I know. That's what you do here."

"Don't kids get run over?"

"Every once in a while. Not very often, I don't think."

We spent four days going to the beach. The wind was high the whole week. He sat on a towel decorated with the Coca-Cola logo and weighted on the corners by two Top-Siders, a Pat Conroy novel and a bottle of SPF 30 sunscreen. He squinted at me through eyelashes studded with sand. He didn't wear sunglasses because he didn't want to tan like a raccoon. "Why are there so few birds here?" he asked. "No pelicans or herons like in Florida."

"There are gulls," I said, pointing to a homely line of them gazing with us at the water and staggering in the hot wind.

"Maybe for the same reason there are so few people," he

answered himself. It was a Friday morning, and only a pickup and a sun-silvered Camaro were beached near us, pulled up to the high tide mark in line with the gulls.

I made peanut-butter sandwiches with jalapeño peppers on flour tortillas every noon, and carried mine down from the condo to eat them sitting in the breakers. Bits of tar swirled in the water around me. When one hit me it stuck like a leech. Sand blew into my mouth with every bite. Grit silted among my teeth after I swallowed. He usually stayed in the kitchen to eat his lunch, and then took a nap. He never wanted to go back to the beach after that because he'd already cleaned himself up once. It took quite a while to scrub, with mayonnaise, the tar from our skin. He wondered if it would ever come off his new trunks.

Evenings, we walked on the fishing pier to see what people were catching. We dodged flying hooks cast inexpertly by children off the windy rock jetty a mile or so down from the pier. "Sometimes you can catch crabs around here," I informed him.

Tuesday night we brought some shrimp back from Aransas Pass. I told him we might find a good restaurant over there on the mainland, but what I really wanted to do was ride the ferry. So we did, and we saw one restaurant that looked all right to him—a steak house built with stones on the bottom, logs on top and a concrete Indian tepee on the roof like a chimney. We got as far as the crowded parking lot (it was the crowd that soothed and attracted him), and he stopped the rental car halfway nosed into a space. He left his hands on the wheel and turned to me. His eyes moved from my feet up to my neck. "You know," he began, still not looking at my face. "I don't want to embarrass you."

I can't say I wasn't surprised. The betrayal was too soon and too overt. "Yes?" was all I said.

"Well, it just occurred to me—I just noticed what you're wearing."

"I never knew you to pay much attention to my clothes." I had on a polyester muumuu I had bought at the Island Food Store and rubber flip-flop thong sandals.

"I never saw you looking like this before. You don't wear this outfit at home, do you?"

"No."

"Anyway, I don't think we ought to go in this place. These people look pretty dressed up." There was a group of women getting out of a car near ours. They had on high heels and carried patent-leather purses.

"Okay, forget it then." I didn't care about eating at a crowded steak house with a tepee on top anyway. I wanted to get back on the ferry. "Let's go back."

A couple of miles before the ferry landing, we stopped at an open-backed van by the side of the road and bought some shrimp in a plastic bag. "We'll take them home and boil them," I said. "You won't believe how fresh they'll taste." The fat woman who sold us the shrimp had three fat children playing in the front seat of the van, no front teeth and flip-flops the same color as mine.

On the ferry I got out of the car, as usual, to feel the wind and look for porpoises as we chugged across the gassy little strip of water from the mainland. I considered the shrimp. I was fascinated by them, and had taken the plastic bag out with me to the ferry's front rail. They were dead, of course, but still perfect: their feelers and legs unbroken, black eye-beads, pale pink stripes. Their last meals were still visible through their fragile shells in their alimentary veins.

"I'd like to eat them with their skins still on," I said to him after we'd boiled them. "Eyes and all." They were pinker, done being cooked but each one still intact. They drained in a colander. Two of them embraced a limp half-lemon, their legs twined about it on either side. They were like mythological figures balancing a symbolic orb over an antique door. Steam rose from the colander: the absolute last of their pale pink spirits.

I relented and did not eat the eyes and shells; but I refused to let him de-vein my portion. Happily, I ate what the shrimp had eaten. I tried not to chew too many times, as if they were holy things, and so I could imagine them coming to life and swimming in my gut, eating what I ate, pink parasites in a gracious host.

It got hotter and hotter. We lay in bed one night at the end of the week listening to the hungry gulls calling for help. Pools of sweat rose in the hollows between my breasts and ribs when I lay on my back. I felt him sighing beside me, awake.

After a time, he got up. He flopped once, disentangled his long feet from the top sheet and popped out of the bed. He fumbled through a drawer and found his blousy seersucker trousers. He hopped on one leg around the room, fighting for his balance as he put them on. "I'm going for a walk, but I don't have much hope of cooling off. Even the goddamn wind is hot."

Now I sighed, answering his sleepless breathing, "Watch out for the snakes as you're crossing the dunes. They come out onto the paths at night."

He changed his mind, refolded his trousers carefully into the drawer and returned to the sticky bed. Finally, I felt the springs soften and I could tell he was asleep. As I drifted off myself I remembered, too late, that we could have turned on the air conditioner.

When there was only one more day left, I decided we should go out on one of the party boats to fish. I had thought of it a few other times, earlier, but we hadn't gotten to it. I don't think he much cared what we did, and I had been happy floating in the waves, baking in the sand and eating peanut-butter and jalapeño sandwiches. Now, I thought, it was time to go fishing.

And what caused the trouble was not the fishing, nor even my putting it off until it was so late. It was my real self, which had been flexing inside of me for the whole trip, and which burst out, wide awake, well grown and ready to kick ass the minute I stepped onto that boat.

Every married person has a real self, I guess (as well as people who live with their mothers and with roommates), which over the years of being only in common places is slowly bludgeoned unconscious by a gathering of small blows with very blunt instruments: dishrags, bedsheets, dandelion roots, now and then a snow shovel. The real self hides like a small fish in a grotto, coils to save itself like a snake in the dunes and sleeps. Around it, cell by cell, grows another more pliant personage to live in the common places: it knows how to avoid unpleasantness, Mexican food, excessive sun, ecstasy. Still the real self wakes sometimes at night to moon-bask on the cool dune paths and to star in dreams of rebellion and courage, or to fish in the Gulf for its darkly swimming buried kin.

It was a rough trip out that day. It always was, as I remember from when my father and uncle used to take me and the other kids out on these big boats designed for groups of inexperienced fishermen. One side of the boat is designated for being seasick and the other for fishing. I have never been among the seasick. In fact, the happiest I have ever been, I think, is when standing with my hips fitted snug into the point of the bow riding up a swell and crashing down, shrieking, salt water soaking me, stinging my sunburn. I did it this day too, now adult and undignified, having ignored the warnings of the old sailor who captained the boat. Still I shriek and sing; again I am the happiest I can be.

As soon as we stopped, the men around us made a shiny pop-top reef around the boat and let out their lines. I baited my double hook with a ribbon fish and wiped my hands on my orange terry-cloth shorts, which I had bought years ago for my father. He had died a few days before his birthday. I had kept them in a box and had finally decided to wear them myself.

"These guys are drinking beer?" he said. "Jesus, it's 8:30 in the morning." He looked queasy. He hadn't enjoyed the ride out. "But it is hot."

The steel deck rail was becoming uncomfortable to the touch. He leaned over the side, then came back upright but swaying. "This water looks like it's about to boil. I think I'll buy a soda. You want something?"

"Beer." He headed for the cabin. I fished. "Maybe you should get yourself some crackers to settle your stomach," I called after him.

He was wrong: this water was not about to boil. It was still, bubbleless, foamless, as secret as frozen soil in winter. We had left the clattering gulls behind with the shore. I saw one lone shrimper at the very edge of sight, its nets hoisted up, head past us and home somewhere. I trusted the leathery old sailor who had brought us here. Indeed, he even had an electronic fish-finder up on the bridge, if the sign by the dock was true. There were fish below us. But I firmly felt, staring at my slack line, they were asleep at the faraway mud-misted bottom of the Gulf, as soundly asleep as jonquil bulbs in Yankee January.

It was a half-day trip. We were supposed to be ashore again by noon. By eleven, the captain had moved us twice and all that had been caught was one dark-fleshed jack (my father called them liverfish), two puny kingfish off the stern, and a large pitted gray rock by someone's grandson who had been fishing near me and who, in the process of reeling in his rock, managed to tangle my line hopelessly with his. For a rushing moment, I'd thought we'd awakened the fish and we both had bites; but instead, when the rock was decked I had to squat and cramp my fingers unthreading our lines from it. Many people lost bait. Something down there was nibbling in its dreams.

As I re-baited my hook we moved again. In the new place I lowered my line with a benediction; in answer, ten minutes later, ten minutes before we would have turned for shore, there was a flicker of fish fifteen yards from the bow where I stood. It gamboled near the surface, twisting like a puppy, its energy mixing and shining with the sun. "There's my fish," I whispered.

"That's no kingfish! It's a tarpon," yelled the captain from above me on the bridge.

My line zinged taut. With the calm of the prescient, I raised my pole to set the hook, and in an instant that hook was on its way to Florida. "Let her run awhile," the captain told me. He was right behind me now. "Reel in," he ordered everybody else. "This little lady's got a fish on here, big one. Never expected a tarpon today. Don't see them all that much." He sounded as if he doubted whether I deserved such a fish.

"Now you start inching her in," he advised me. My arms ached already just from holding onto the pole while the fish ran. When the fish rested I braced the end of the pole against my stomach and turned and turned the reel. When it jerked and swam sideways the captain pushed me along with it. Up and down either side of the boat I sashayed and sidestepped to fool the fish into thinking it was pulling me; then, when the captain gave the word, I pulled it. My arms went numb early on. "You want me to take over?" he asked.

I shook my head. "My fish," I gasped. The dearth of breath in my lungs gave this the sound of a question.

It was a fish fight from one of my father and uncle's tales. I had caught a fish or two as a kid, dragged it myself off a boat like this to the scale by the fish-cleaning house, hugging it on the way like a dead child. We used to catch small sharks and kingfish, jack, once a big tuna I didn't like the taste of. They fought, but not like this fish, my fish.

Suddenly the line went slack. I thought my fish was lost. But it was only breathing under the boat, trying to trick me. I waited.

The numbness spread to my legs. By the time the fish started running again I had braced myself against the railing in a V shape, the grip of the pole poking my midsection out into a point, my heels on the deck and my toes smashed up against the side of the boat, my arms stretched to the utmost to keep from losing the tackle. I reeled and waited, holding tight. Finally, I could feel where the fish was: less deep and very close. It lolled, enervated by the warm surface water. I reeled some more, and unbraced my legs enough to lean and peep over at the water. My fish flashed at me a silver greeting from an eighth of a mile underwater.

"I saw it," I sighed.

"Damn straight," the captain whispered in my ear. "You want this fish?" I nodded and shrugged to catch some sweat from my chin. "Then reel." I felt blisters rising on my hands with each heartbeat. I knew how the fish felt. I too had surrendered in warm salt water, unable to swim for the lapping of waves in my mouth. I knew how the hook hurt as it pulled, how it jabbed as I gnawed it; so when my fish began its last run and the pole slipped in my chafed and sweaty hands, I considered going with it over the side, letting my fish catch me.

I re-gripped. And when the fish was done running I reeled with the end of my strength. I bore down like a mother for the last push in a birthing, and up came the fish with a splash like a gunshot. It flipped, looping the line round its tail in the air. It was miraculously silver-blue-and-green, the same colors as the winking hot gulf. Blood covered its face. The captain and I were both soaked by its explosion out of the water. He climbed to a perch on the deck rail, ready with his gaffing hook, and kept coaching: "*Up*. Keep the tip up!"

The fish out of water was too heavy for me. I let it drop back down. It was gone again. But I sat on the end of my pole as if it were a seesaw and pried it up again. The bones in my crotch ached, but the fish was caught. The captain and one of his teenaged assistants gaffed it through its middle and levered it onto the boat.

"That is a nice fish," the teenager dryly opined. We were all flattened against the side of the boat watching it die. Decked, it flopped and faded from blue-green to gray. Its gills pulsed hugely and irregularly. I could not see its eye for the blood from around the hook. I could hardly breathe. Some of us on deck hopped and slid around to avoid the thrashing fishtail. The grandson who had caught the rock climbed with me onto the railing and stared enviously at me as I watched my fish. The teenaged assistant reversed his gaffer and slammed the fish in the head a few times with the handle. Soon after that it stopped caroming about the deck. It lifted itself twice from the slimy pinkened boards, its middle rising first, then up-ended the curve in the air and thudded down. Finally it died with its gill chamber wide open. Each filament was discrete: you could have counted them, hung like harpstrings. If you were small enough and careful you could have walked among them in the spaces where the breath had been, like a Chinese weaver in an ancient silk factory with the worms next door.

"I can recommend a taxidermist in Fulton," the captain said to me. His teenager had started the boat and was turning us around. Someone had dragged my fish to the cooler astern, where it lay ignominiously among mackerel. For a moment I didn't understand the word.

"Taxidermist. Oh, I don't want a trophy," I said. "I'm going to eat it."

"Oh no ma'am," advised the captain, politely laughing. "Most people around here don't like to eat tarpon." The men around me tittered.

"Why not?"

"It's no eatin' fish. My way of thinking, fish like this, you mount it."

"I'll eat it."

He searched for another way to explain, forcefully: "It ain't good eatin'."

"You expect me to hang it on the wall?"

"Hell yes. That is one good-looking fish. Skull's in pretty good shape." All the men on deck began talking and gesturing about trophies. They didn't know anything about eating tarpon. They were just siding with the old sailor. "Here, we'll see what your old man thinks about it." He had come up behind me, and saluted with his beer can. It was close enough to lunch for him to have one now, and I guess he had gotten used to feeling on the border of sick. He still looked yellow.

"Did you see?" I asked him.

"Of course I saw. I was right here the whole time. Look how wet I am." He jiggled his knees so I could hear his shorts sloshing. "That is a big fish. You should be proud."

"I am proud. I caught it. I'm going to eat it."

"I think we should have it mounted."

"This fish is too important to stuff," I said. The captain wheeled and waved a hand at my face as if I were a fool and words were useless. I hated to lose his approval, but my real self was now in control. He headed for the ladder to the bridge.

My husband reasoned: "It's because the fish is so important

that I think it should be mounted. We'll find someone in Corpus Christi and have them send it to us when it's done. We'll leave early tomorrow for the plane and drop it off."

"No."

"Well, we don't have time to eat it, even if we wanted to. We're going home tomorrow." He was becoming annoyed. I could see the tightness in his throat as the words passed through. "You should have gone fishing earlier in the week, okay?"

"I don't care. I'll find some dry ice and take it on the plane in coolers. I'll have it cleaned and cut up."

"They won't let you on an airplane with dry ice. My daddy's a pilot," offered the boy who had caught a rock.

"How many coolers do you think we'll need for a forty-pound fish? Or more?" he yelled, waving his arms and spilling his beer.

"I'll give some away."

"Nobody wants to eat this kind of fish. You heard him. He says it's not good."

"It is good. I'll figure it all out."

I had to eat what I caught. Or, at least, what I caught had to be eaten. If there were someone to help me eat it, I could share. I didn't have to eat it all myself, but it couldn't be wasted. I had been taught this as a child. It was part of my family's science. My father's people claimed kinship with the Plains Indians, a tenuous connection, which my mother maintained was no more than fancy dress for an ancestor's sexual indiscretion; still my father loved to talk about buffalo hunting—eating the meat, making spoons from horns, clothing from skins and toys from bladders—wasting nothing. It was important that if you killed something you kept its life going by taking the whole of the dead into yourself. I don't know that he ever said it to me just that way, but I know it to be true.

• • •

I've never seen anyone act so crazy and be so convinced she's right. If I pulled the car over by this curb and stopped a

hundred people at random and told them the whole story, I
bet they'd all side with me. She said her father made her eat
dead crabs. She said I had no soul. She said there was nothing
real left of me. She said she was descended from Native Americans who used all of the buffalo. She made no sense.

I came home on the flight we had tickets for. Christ, I had
to be back at work—and she stayed so she could find enough
dry ice and coolers to pack up her stinking fish. Maybe they
won't let her on any plane. Maybe she'll have to eat the whole
thing there, frying it up in chunks on a hot plate in that
lousy beach house. Maybe she'll stay down there forever eating
tarpons. She's gone completely nuts. She'll swallow the eyes
and crunch up the tail, eat the liver and turn into a fish. Isn't
that what the Indians did? I tried to calm her, smooth her
down. She was bristly. "Let's not make this into life and
death," I said.

"What the hell else do you think it is?" she screamed back
at me, spitting. The back seat of the rental car was piled high
with slimy, bloody plastic bags containing bits of fish. She'd
wrestled the thing by herself down the dock and had it
chopped up at a fish house. She was covered with blood and
the car smelled awful. (Oh, my own little car calms me, now
I'm home. It smells so good, and it fits so well around me.)
"My fish is bleeding, bleaching into me. It is exactly just life
and death," she raved.

"You're scaring me," I said. Her left forearm was clean of
fish blood. I touched the salty skin there. I remember we
passed one of those big spiraling plastic slides that dump kids
into pools of water and I thought how the kids on that one,
shadeless in this wild place, must be getting their butts burnt
off, and I remember thinking I was glad we were going home.

At first she wheedled me. Her voice was low and monoto-
nous, humming. She suggested we take the fish back to that
hot little condo and stay another week (a week or so is what
she said—"or so": how long?). We'd jam the refrigerator full
of fish and start eating. "We'll eat the fish together. You'll
help me eat it."

I pictured that cheap Formica table in the kitchen dripping

with slippery fish, the butcher-block island twinkling with scales. I saw barrels of tartar sauce, mountains of lemons, fried filets, ceviche, tarpon chowder in a washtub, minced-fish-and-onion cakes the size of basketballs. I saw the little Weber grill smoking up the carport full-time for a week "or so," scarring slabs of fish with charcoal stripes, and I saw her sweating and grinning through the smoke. I glimpsed the edge of lunacy myself. I thought of fish fritters for breakfast, and my stomach quivered. "I don't really care that much for fish, you know."

That was all I said, and then she cut loose and sang her anger at me. She chanted like a TV evangelist or a witch doctor in a Tarzan movie. Her face was bright orange and shining — sunburnt I guess, but it occurred to me that she'd caught fire from sitting in this deadly sun all week and was about to combust spontaneously, right there on the bloody car seat. Her features looked blurred, as if they were starting to melt like the plastic on the baking water slide. To touch her now would burn me. Her hair was mashed flat on the top of her head from this ugly fishing cap she'd been wearing, and it jutted out in stiff salty tufts around her ears.

She said I had no connections with things. She went on and on about the sea and the fish and the plains and the buffalo and life and death and her childhood. She said even the Christian culture knows how to redeem violence: through sacrament. She would take communion, eat her fish. If she didn't, nothing made sense. I don't remember half the things she said. She said Indians ate what they loved. She said it was a kind of cannibalism, so I should understand it: I had swallowed her.

Two Poems by Kevin Cantwell

Advent Day at Mumford Quarry Nursery

Gray flagstone steps, mean staggered discard graves
on which engravers botched a line or date,
or split the granite's flaw; a stream-cut groove's
water slows; headstones prop an iron grate
through which the azure pool drains inhuman
cold; but green of mistletoe and holly
wreaths sell briskly, sold by the home for men,
who seem unmindful of the pitched, hilly
walks; speechless, they seem yet unamazed
as they fetch poinsettia by the armfuls,
or mulch, for those who look beyond the fall
come to solstice dark and these fallow days.
Alms or extravagance of crème de menthe —
we write it off to get us by lean months.

Adam and Eve

   And now they have already begun to go,
in Albrecht Dürer's piece, a little soft
   around the waist; she has, at least; and slow
to leave, they must, as sand begins to sift
   inexorably through its narrow waist of glass.
Her flesh grown thick we take to be a son.
   Those awful woods, untouched by ray of sun,
go still; hence this study and his early gloss
   of melancholia; hence her touching smile,
which never fades completely, nor the leaves,
   which stay, and free their hands for the small
tasks at which they've grown so clumsy, and loaves
   which sour by that cause, that which so divides,
   yet which of pleasure is not so devoid.

Two Poems by George Bradley

New Age Night at the Nuyorican

Like I get this phone call from Shirley MacLaine,
it's the middle of the night, right,
she's all confused about time,
and she's like how in this previous existence
I was maybe a nomenclator for a forum,
only I was crucified
for incompetence,
which was totally really bogus,
so then I became a logothete in Constantinople,
and I got to wear one of those hats
that look kind of like bandaged volley balls,
but I was way unorthodox,
so they put my eyes out,
you know on purpose,
which was way unempowering,
so then I became a soteriologist
in this library in this monastery in Switzerland,
but there was a problem, sheepskin makes my nose stress,
I was probably already vegetarian only I didn't know,
and even today I can't eat Swiss cheese,
the holes give me gas,
so anyway I like ran away,
and I got caught and burned on this like stake,
like fondue,
so then I became a cynarchtomachist
in this Renaissance,
it's the stake thing all over again, right,
only it was completely humanocentric,
so instead I became Victorian, an opsimath,
but it just got old,
and all along there were lots of wars,

and I was in them all probably to the max,
and so eventually I moved to New York City,
and then I became a poet
and forgot all the words and hung up.

Tobias, or
The Idea Whose Time Had Come

Less bright it was slighter
than your recollection
miniature in fact
the hands upon its breast
withered thin as claws
to see those thread-like lips
it needed all your strength
to think that they pronounced
hosannas once or ever knew
the trumpet's embouchure

so you sat down to mourn
what became a corpse of light
eased it out of samite robes
helped it from its fillet
of crowning artifice
beheld it unembellished
naked or any aura
an echo in the eyes
as aspect of the self
sloughed off like scaley skin

a splendor faded
as if you had believed
dream logic
and now been undeceived
as if a spirit sent to guide

abandoned you instead
parable gone wrong
apocryphal account
tale of a wandered child
but with one little twist

that though you heeded
the strange instructions
found the flashing river
and labored to extract
bright creatures from its side
yet when you strayed
and the effulgence came
to lead you home   O bliss
you knew in grasping
reaching for that hand   its gaze

held something other than
the adoration in your own
contained some composite
of pity and amusement
wit and wistfulness
accustomed as the angel was
to what the light was like
and knowing soon
it would release you
an orphan of the sun

Molly Bendall

The Book of Sharp Silhouettes

Gothic flowers bedded themselves
in the edges of this night, the night
when a bullet pierced her rib precisely,
even musically, and another, her throat,
and threads of blood gathered on her blouse
into the brocade of a costume,
and she was thrown back

into a perfect arch, a balletic
plunge, her chin tilting up, until
she saw the window behind her and
in its corner the half-lit clouds
and old moon. She'd forgotten
him already—her betrayed
betrayer. He didn't know where

her gaze had traveled but jeweled eyes
had sparkled on her arms and his own
body as he noted the sequins
so purposefully arranged and sewn.
And she fell to that needle of moon
out into the woods behind her house,
where her sister took her, pulled

her away into the low-tones of dusk
to look again at the screech owl's
sculpted nest, an earth-colored pitcher,
full and comfortable at its distance,
set against the signatures of
peaks and spires—they imagined once
it held Chinese tea for them.

And this time the owl was there too,
a canopy to their conversation about
leaving the stifling humidity of home,
about the poison of diamond-shaped leaves,
about the 7 P.M. freight train
that thundered miles away through the brown
petals of the canyon. Her hair

and her sister's poured down like the dark
tea of summer to meet the uneasy ferns and
torn leaves that complemented the mink wings
of the owl—its strange, aristocratic
hovering. And how the wings pursued
and interrogated, then folded
into the crackling burnt paper

of the hills behind them.
Was this lemon-eyed spy
a changeling or an interloper,
or a distraction in her own portrait
of night? It was as if the mesh of trees
had chosen her and knelt over her,
and evening's cloaked arms came

to her face, then the edges of its sleeves
into her open mouth—ruthless sleeves,
like those of a queen from a story ballet
with heavy, widowy cloth.
And the sleeves reached into
her throat, past her heart,
into her voice, a voice her sister heard,

the sound that fell deeply, almost easily
until their stage was brimming
and lush, lush with the fragrance
of birds and tea that rises
on the fitful conscience of this blackened page.

Fred Dings

The Evening After

I

"Death is also the *thief* of beauty," he says,
as a slow disquietude replaces morning's calm.
The pink light fades from ashen clouds,
and an icy luminosity begins to wax
above the highlands of eternity.
The willow, weeping all evening over rocks
beside the pond, darkens to an arch hunched
above a wafer of sacramental light,
a fallen moon too faint to give much sight.
There were minds which might have ripened into suns
had not the body failed, the nursing vine
sallowed and withered before the fruit was ripe.
We are flowers of light in a field of darkness,
brief in our pulse of generations. We open
and close, wax and wane, open and close.

II

Death of the body is not the only death.
Our seasons of loss prepare us for the end,
the gardens withered in droughts of circumstance,
the taut and cold receding lips of love,
the glance that lowers and turns away forever,
the fires of hope snuffed by the winds of change
on the ledges above, the dim glitter of stars
in the pond's eye like distant citadels
we'll never know but we had once lived by.
Death of the body is not the only death.
A winter mind that never turns to spring
has had too much of suffering. Its crystal eyes
no longer see the colors of our lives.

An empty house collapses under snow
in whiteness cleansed of feeling long ago.

III

In the pointed night, where *are* the stars of death?
Is it sacrilege or only emulation
to want to be a god? A brazen boy
flings against the Goliaths of circumstance,
his sling, a frayed genetic rope he weaves
to the furthest nebulae at the end of thought,
a human tree whose height might reach eternity.
The fire-feathered bird among its branches
sings a human song on the edge of space.
It beckons through the rocks of time and place.
It sings of fire and ice, but not of death.
It sings of change and dreams, but not of death.
An ancient king who lingers on his throne
hears its song and dreams of wanderings,
of odysseys among the distant stars.

Sue Kwock Kim

Women Singing in the Deep Sea
after an eighteenth-century Korean painting

They are far from shore.
Foam-glittering, they rise from the waves
    in a pure fountain
of flesh. Nothing lifts them

    upward; nothing lies beneath them
but salt-blaze, dulse, the ocean's acid
    scud and boil. The waters
are not human. Yet the women soar

    through the brine as if giddy
with birth, mouths open, bursting from the deep
    into the sweet world. As if they were
singing themselves to life. How else

    could they swim this far?
There are no ships, no ragged hulls,
    no trace of travel: only the women
themselves, playing in the blood-dark waters—

    they are their own vessels.
Their lips pulse with light. What world
    do they dream of making, as they sing
the sea to sleep, calming its hiss and coil—

    as foaming scalps recede
from scoured reefs, and hordes of the unborn
    swarm upward, racing
to be, to breach the waters of the infinite

and shed their silence
like an unbearable skin. . . . Light pours
from the women's throats like cries.
As their voices lift them higher, spume slips

from their bodies in molten gold,
folds baring shoulder and breast. One woman
swims above the surf, floating in the air.
Another glides among liquid furrows,

harvesting sea-roses, coral, gold leaf.
A third rises in slower strokes. Dripping
with silver water, she spreads her hair
over the lap of the first. They could be

in love; but caught in the clear amber
of their present, they will always have to dream
of the next moment. Their bodies are frozen.
And to shiver on someone's thigh, hair forever

spilling in a wet cascade, glittering
like black wheat: who wouldn't be bewildered
by possibility? The future lies
beyond reaping. To wake here, dazzled

by choirs of flesh, light, water,
the women ripening in each other's arms —
yes, this could be paradise.
The singing is everywhere. Their lips are open.

But they are silent. You are the one
who is singing, your voice cries out to give
breath to their dreaming, to bear
the fruit of change, which they must always desire.

Two Poems by Scott Hightower

For Maffeo Barberini

Sacrifice of Abraham, 1603; Uffizi.

There is no longer just the knife, a bundle
    of sticks, and a pot with fire.
    Other things have made their appearance.
A young stranger appeals to Abraham; has
    already stayed his hand,
    the right one with the glinting knife.
The boy no longer needs fear Abraham's
    ecstatic precision. (Though
    the patriarch turns away, his thumb
still presses sharply into Isaac's hollow cheek.)

    No registry note relays
    to us any of Barberini's
insight into the nature of Caravaggio's
    imagination.
    We can only guess. Had he
the chance, his paymaster might have
    recorded three consecutive
    payments for Andy Warhol's straddling
(six-shooter drawn) *Elvis*, emerging like a
    giant, a single handed
    renaissance out of one of the New York School's
abject grids. The figures here, Hibbard coyly notes,
    "are linked more intimately
    than in some of his earlier paintings."

Here, we have Caravaggio parrying
    in the game of signs; Cardinal
    Barberini paradoxically

imploding in his fashionable generation's
           violent and destructive
      systems of interpretation. Traps
within a trap. "There is no longer just the knife,
      a bundle of sticks." No, to
original sin. No, to final
salvation. No, to . . . innocence. Three payments
      for a metaphor. "A pot
      with fire." Three payments for
Caravaggio's interpretation
      of a myth; one we
      recognize to be both as real
and as fanatic as a dark massing of birds.

A World Without Art

Today I had a postcard from a friend
traveling the other coast — how pleasant
the modest arabesque, the unsolicited
thought and script, the self-expense.

At first, I thought (upside down) it was
a basic sky-blue Idaho. Turns out to be
San Francisco and the sky wedging down
between the Palace of Fine Arts and a corner
of one of the figure-graced garden boxes
atop its colonnade; 1915.

Over its Corinthian-capped (from this
angle, calliope-like) columns, from one
of the round portico's broken plinths,
a statue beckons.

Four draped muses emerged to the coordinates
from a swirling curtain of acanthus leaves.

Atop the flanking colonnade are empty boxes.
All their corners are attended by a grieving woman
whose shoulders extend akimbo. These,
with her upper arms, slope out to rest
on the top of the empty skyward planter.
Her hands fold back into her lowered face.
The card implies that she is only one of many:

"The weeping women that grace the Palace
of Fine Arts's colonnade were conceived,
according to their sculptor, to express
the melancholy of life without art."

I will tack it up on my condiment shelf in my kitchen
with the bannered, neatly rowed cornfields of Iowa,
Michelangelo's "Bearded Slave," and Siena's Palio.

Stephen Dunn

Missing

> *Frank was missing something,*
> *and women would do anything*
> *to find out what it was.*
> —James Salter

He disappeared, often, even as he was speaking,
though he could finish those sentences
from which he had disengaged himself,
finish them well. And when I spoke
he was interested just enough to make me
want to continue speaking. Strange,
that I was flattered by this; it seemed
he was giving me all of half of himself,
the best he could do.
                    In bed, after lovemaking,
which was always good, I knew he'd learned
his post-coital manners — caring, tender —
and was performing them. I was sure
he was planning his next day, his secret
heart checking its secret watch.
I'd known other men like this, of course,
but he was so poor at concealing these faults,
and would admit to them if asked,
they seemed part of his presence, part of
the way he was always *there* for me,
if you know what I mean.
                    I felt, in time,
I could locate, perhaps give life to,
his missing half. I felt love could do this.
And I felt even an odd love for his vacancies,
the way, I suppose, most of us will kiss

a terrible scar to prove we can live with it.
He had a good job. Men admired him
because he brought the entire half of himself
to work every day, brought it with intelligence
and charm. It was enough for them.
And all my women friends adored him,
said how lucky I was.
                              But I must admit
it isn't easy to love a man like him.
There's so little asked of you; after a while
you forget you're using half of yourself,
and then something reminds you
and an enormous sense of deprivation follows,
then anger—a quiet fury, I'd call it.
Which is why, finally, I left.
But I've never stopped wondering about him.
And I'm past my anger. If he walked in
right now, I think I'd put my arms around him
and breathe him in, ask him how he was.

Two Poems by Barbara Hamby

Nose

I am trying on an especially evil-looking pair of shoes
when the shopgirl points to the middle of her face and says,

"This is called what?" For a moment I draw a blank as I search
My mind for the Italian word for snoot, schnozzola, beak

but when "il naso" finally surfaces, I realize
that she is Italian and probably knows the Italian word

for nose, so what she wants is the English,
which is relatively easy for me, so I say, "Nose."

"Nose," she replies, smiling. "You have a beautiful nose."
I am looking at the shoes on my feet. I have dangerous feet,

especially in these particular shoes, but my nose
is rather white-bread, too much like my skinflint
    grandmother's

for me to ever be entirely ecstatic about it,
and this girl's is spectacular, an aquiline viaduct

spanning the interval from her eyes to her delicious lips.
A friend once told me, "My sister paid $2,000

for a nose like yours, a perfect shiksa nose,
but it ending up looking like Bob Hope's."

Suddenly, I feel as if I have no nose, like Gogol's Kovelev
riding around St. Petersburg looking for his proboscis.

What is a nose? Obviously not simply a smeller, sniffer,
or a mere searcher-out of olfactory sensation,

but something more — an aesthetic appendage to the facial
construction, a slope from the brow to the philtrum,

with symmetrical phalanges. Aren't I precise, who knows
     precisely
nothing about having an unsatisfactory nose, or ever thinking

about it for one second? Perhaps my offending part
is somewhere else, or am I as hapless as Gogol's hero —

with too little nose for my purposes, like Miss Ruby Diamond,
the richest woman in my hometown, who lost her nose to
     cancer,

and had two counterfeit noses, one lifelike and the other
a simple plastic flap to hide the scar of ninety years.

A nose is a nose is a nose is a nose,
Gertrude Stein did not say and why would she

as it is obviously untrue? Though each nose is an island
in the sea of the face, sticking out in a more or less

inadequate fashion. Like Cyrano, I marshal my couplets,
ragtag though they be, to celebrate all noses unloved

and those lost to disease or, like Kovelev's, inadvertently
misplaced, and the nose of the shopgirl on the Via Roma in
     Firenze,

her eyes red from either smoking pot or heartbreak
and the many other indignities gathered like humps on our
     backs,

which we touch for luck, as if floods, bombings, murders
could only happen to others, who are beautiful and pure.

Delirium

Just before I fainted in the restaurant that evening,
    I was telling you a story about a madman
    I saw earlier in the day
as I walked home from my ballet class
    just off the Piazza Santa Maria del Carmine.
After crossing the bridge of Santa Trìnita,
    looking in at the Ghirlandaio frescoes
    of the Sassetti family,
then wondering how many women there were
    who were young and rich enough
to wear the see-through lace cowboy shirts
    in the Gianni Versace windows
    on the Via Tornabuoni,
at the intersection of the Via de Calzaioli
    and the Via del Corso,
I walked into the hullabaloo being drummed up
    by a bearded man who was stalking back and forth,
    screaming something in Italian, of course,
    and waving his arms in the air.
But when he turned he would reach down with one hand,
    clamp his crotch,
    and then pull his body around
as though his hips were a bad dog
    and his genitals a leash he was yanking.
After each turn he'd continue stalking and flailing,
    until time to turn again.
So I am trying to explain this and our pizza comes,
    and I saw off a bite, but it is too hot,
so what do I do but swallow it, and it's too hot,
    and I think, it's too hot,
and my voice decelerates as if it is a recording
    on a slowly melting tape and the scene

in the restaurant begins to recede:
in the far distance I see the bearded man ranting
    on the street,
then, nearer but retreating quickly, you
    and the long corridor of the restaurant,
then it's as if I am falling into a cavity behind me,
    one that is always there, though I've learned to ignore it,
but I'm falling now, first through a riot of red rooms,
    then gold, green, blue and darker
    until I finally drift into the black room
    where my mind can rest.
I wake up in the kitchen, lying on a wooden bench,
    with you and the waiter staring at me.
"I'm fine," I say, though it's as if I am pulling
    my mind up from a deep well.
The waiter brings me a bowl of soup,
    which I don't want, but it doesn't matter because
the lights go out and a man at the next table says,
    "*Primo quella signora ed ora la luce*,"
which means, first that woman and now the light,
    and it's so dark that I can't see myself or you,
and I feel as if I'm turning and a mad voice
    rises from my stomach
and cries where are we anyway, and who, and what, and why?

Jane Flanders

Ma Goose: The Interrogation

Who killed Cock Robin?
Where is the boy who looks after the sheep?
What's in the cupboard?
Have you any wool?

Where is the boy who looks after the sheep?
Where have you been?
Have you any wool?
How many hairs to make a wig?

Where have you been?
How many miles to Babylon?
How many hairs to make a wig?
Wasn't that a dainty dish to set before the king?

How many miles to Babylon?
How many were going to St. Ives?
Wasn't that a dainty dish to set before the king?
Whose dog art thou?

How many were going to St. Ives?
How does your garden grow?
Whose dog art thou?
Are the children in their beds?

How does your garden grow?
What's in the cupboard?
Are the children in their beds?
Who killed Cock Robin?

Three Poems from Desire *by Frank Bidart*

Love Incarnate

Dante, *Vita Nuova*

To all those driven berserk or humanized by love
this is offered, for I need help
deciphering my dream.
When we love our lord is LOVE.

When I recall that at the fourth hour
of the night, watched by shining stars,
LOVE at last became incarnate,
the memory is horror.

In his hands smiling LOVE held my burning
heart, and in his arms, the body whose greeting
pierces my soul, now wrapped in bloodred, sleeping.

He made him wake. He ordered him to eat
my heart. He ate my burning heart. He ate it
submissively, as if afraid, as LOVE wept.

Overheard Through the Walls
of the Invisible City

. . . telling those who swarm around him his desire
is that an appendage from each of them
fill, invade each of his orifices, —

repeating, chanting,
Oh yeah   Oh yeah   Oh yeah   Oh yeah   Oh yeah

until, as if in darkness he craved the sun, at last he reached
consummation.

—Until telling those who swarm around him begins again

(we are the wheel to which we are bound).

Lady Bird

Neither an invalid aunt who had been asked to care for a
                                                    sister's
little girl, to fill the dead sister's place, nor the child herself

did, could: not in my Daddy's eyes—nor
should they;

                    so when we followed that golden couple into the
                                                    White House

    I was aware that people look at
the living, and wish for the dead.

Mishima in 1958
Donald Keene

Yukio Mishima was born Kimitake Hiraoka on January 14, 1925 in uptown Tokyo. His father was the deputy director of the Bureau of Fisheries in the Agriculture Ministry; his mother, from a family of educators and Confucian scholars, was herself well-versed in literature. The family lived in a well-to-do neighborhood, in a rented two-floor house with a houseboy and six maids, an unusual extravagance. But for the first twelve years Mishima lived downstairs with his grandmother in her sickroom, leaving the room only with her permission.

His first fiction pieces, which he wrote at the age of twelve as a student at the Peers School, attracted the attention of the editor of Bungei-Bunka (Art and Culture) *who invited him to write a story for that magazine. It was the first piece published under his new pen name, Yukio Mishima.*

Despite his literary accomplishments, Mishima's father discouraged his writing: in a 1941 letter to his son he wrote, "I hear that some high-and-mighty writers speak of you as a genius, or precocious, or some kind of deviate, or just unpleasant. I think it is high time you took stock of yourself." Four years later, at the end of 1944, Mishima enrolled at the Impe-

rial University as a student of German law. Classes were almost immediately interrupted by the war, and he received his draft notice in February, 1945; he did not serve in the army, but instead was assigned to work in an airplane factory. He eventually graduated in November of 1947.

His first literary success came in 1949 with the publication of Confessions of a Mask (Kamen no kokuhaku). *By the time Donald Keene interviewed him for* The Paris Review *in 1958, Mishima's literary talents had been widely recognized in Japan with the publication of* Thirst for Love (Ai no kawaki), Forbidden Colors I (Kinjiki), Forbidden Colors II (Higyo), The Sound of Waves (Shiosai), The Temple of Golden Pavilion (Kinkakuji). *So too was his reputation beginning to expand into the international arena: a year earlier he had traveled to New York to promote the English translation of his* Five Modern Nō Plays (Kindai Nogakushu). *But Keene never completed the interview he began. The essay that follows has been put together from his recollections of their original meeting.*

Mishima's non-literary accomplishments also contributed to his expanding celebrity. In 1955 he began a bodybuilding regimen that became an obsession for him and eventually led him to the study of karate and the samurai arts of kendo and Bushido.

In later years Mishima denounced the western influence in Japan. He became interested in ultra-nationalist efforts to defend traditional Japanese culture from outside influence. Soon his name was increasingly associated with the military in Japan. In 1967 he participated in the Army Self-Defense Force's basic-training camp. The following year he decided to create his own civilian army, the Shield Society, which was often construed as a right-wing militaristic organization but was intended, according to Mishima, to promote Japan's return to the ethical traditions of the samurai.

Despite his increasing attention to the affairs of the Shield Society (in addition to training the cadets, he also designed their uniforms and wrote a march song for the society), Mishima's literary pursuits were not interrupted. He continued what had become a nightly routine, writing through the hours be-

tween midnight and dawn. In 1969, the first two volumes of his final work, The Sea of Fertility, *were published; the same year he also wrote a ballet and two three-act plays. When the cadets threatened to interrupt his writing schedule with frequent nighttime visits, he rented the lower floor of a coffee shop, the* Salon de Claire, *where they could meet with him for two hours every Wednesday. Indeed, Mishima maintained a distinct separation between his two worlds: the members of the Shield Society were unfamiliar with his novels and plays, and Mishima thought literary youth unsuited to the military.*

On November 3, 1969 Mishima arranged a dress parade to celebrate the first anniversary of the Shield Society. He invited one hundred guests, both foreigners and Japanese; those who did not attend he never spoke to again. Near the time of this anniversary he also began to plot his own suicide. He recruited three cadets to assist him: Masakatsu Morita, Masayoshi Koga, and Masahiro Ogawa. As the anniversary approached he began severing connections. He backed away from new literary projects and resigned from the Board of Directors of the Japan Symposium on Culture.

Then, on November 25, 1970, after submitting the final pages of the last volume of The Sea of Fertility *to his publishers, he and his Shield Society cadets entered the ASDF headquarters where they had an appointment with the commander, Lieutenant General Kanetoshi Mashida. When Mashida ushered them into his office, he was promptly taken hostage while members of the ASDF were gathered (at Mishima's demand) in the plaza outside. From the balcony of the commander's office, Mishima delivered a ten-minute speech on his political theories to a jeering audience. At the end of his speech he returned to the commander's chambers, sat on the floor and committed hara-kiri, the ritual suicide of the samurai: he plunged his dagger into his abdomen and drew it across his body, making an incision seventeen centimeters long—representing a tremendous degree of control over physical reflex; he was then beheaded by the cadets.*

Mishima was dressed in his Shield Society uniform for his final "leave-taking" as he had requested in a letter written in

*the days before his death. In another letter he had asked that
"since I die not as a literary man but entirely as a military
man, I would like the character for sword — bu — to be included
in my Buddhist name. The character for pen — bun — need not
appear."*

—B.H.

Shortly before leaving New York for Japan in the spring of
1958 I was asked by George Plimpton to interview Yukio
Mishima. Interviews with writers were a regular feature of *The
Paris Review*, and I gladly accepted the request, in part because
(like others who have devoted themselves to literatures not
widely known in this country) I am something of a propagan-
dist, and I was therefore delighted that a Japanese would be
included among the celebrated writers who had already been
interviewed.

Mishima readily agreed to the interview. Because his house
was then being renovated — as I recall, air conditioning was
being installed — he suggested that we hold the interview instead in the recently opened Nikkatsu Hotel. The lobby was
not only unusually spacious for Tokyo, but the air-conditioning was thrillingly frigid.

I confess I do not recall how Mishima looked on that occasion. Judging from the photographs of Mishima printed on
the dust jackets of his first books published in America, at
that time — before he took up weight lifting — he had wavy
hair, and an open, uncomplicated face marked by an engaging
smile; but my recollections tend to be of the later Mishima,
when his face had become a samurai mask with cropped hair
and a prevailingly resolute expression. Of course, even in his
samurai period he laughed, but it was a roar of a laugh; a
mutual friend once told me that Mishima's eyes never laughed.
Mishima had taken up "bodybuilding" by the time of the
interview, but (as I recall) he had yet to transform his face.

I had not conducted an interview with anyone (except for
Japanese prisoners during the war years) since junior high
school days, and I had totally forgotten how it was done.
I had not even prepared any questions, but asked Mishima
whatever came into my head, in no particular order. I wrote

down his answers in a script which I now have great difficulty in deciphering. Most unfortunately, I failed to write down my own questions. All that remains, therefore, are Mishima's answers, written with cryptic brevity in a mixture of Japanese and English. If I had written out my impressions of the interview the same night I probably could have recalled my questions, but I procrastinated, apparently dissatisfied with the interview. In the end, I decided that my record of the interview was too fragmentary and too disconnected to be published in *The Paris Review*. I suppose I could have asked Mishima to submit to another interview, but no doubt I was embarrassed by the failure of my first attempt.

On looking over my notes, some forty years later, it seemed to me that perhaps readers today might be interested even in these incomplete answers. Mishima may well have been annoyed by the amateurishness of my questioning, but his answers were frank and unevasive.

Here is my first note: "I have been writing ever since I can remember. I was raised by a grandmother who was ill most of the time. I was kept by her side in her room. Reading was my only amusement. I was never allowed to play outside the house. My grandmother thought this was dangerous, that I might make bad friends. I read all kinds of stories—*Arabian Nights*, *Children's Literature of the World*. I even wrote my own children's stories."

Needless to say, these were not Mishima's own words. The interview was conducted in Japanese, but in order to write as quickly as possible, I sometimes translated his words into English, and I eliminated all but essential words.

The next reply suggests that I pursued the question of his early writings: "I first published in the school magazine when I was twelve."

The earliest work included in Mishima's *Complete Works*, published after his death, is the article "Memories of Elementary School," which appeared in the literary magazine of the Peers School in 1937, when Mishima was twelve. This multivolume set of Mishima's works is extraordinarily complete, including everything he ever wrote, even childhood compositions and the captions to photographs.

His next answer was more interesting: "The style of my early works was modeled on Tanizaki's. He was the first writer I ever read, especially 'A Blind Man's Tale,' 'A Portrait of Shunkin,' 'Tattoo' and *Naomi*. I didn't read *Some Prefer Nettles* until later on."

Mishima's admiration for the works of Tanizaki Jun'ichirō, though not as often expressed as his admiration for Kawabata Yasunari, remained with him from adolescence. It is hard for me to imagine any child reading with pleasure "A Blind Man's Tale," a difficult work, but I am reassured by Mishima's next response, which is recorded merely as "*Robinson Crusoe. Treasure Island*." These sound like more plausible books for a boy of twelve or thirteen to be reading; but another reply, recorded somewhat later in the interview, indicates that Mishima about the same age saw a performance of Oscar Wilde's *Salome* and was so impressed that he went to a bookshop to examine a copy of the text with the famous illustrations by Aubrey Beardsley. He said, "From there I went on to Tanizaki, who was said to be the Japanese Wilde." Perhaps that was, in fact, the order of events, but my notes are too fragmentary to be sure. The next entry states: "I read cruel stories and vulgar children's stories."

A taste for "cruel stories" lingered with Mishima to the end. Next to the last time I saw Mishima, in 1970, at the hotel in Shimoda where he spent the month of August with his family, he showed me what he had been reading. One book had particularly grotesque illustrations in the style of the 1920s. It was an account of a man who made textiles out of human blood. Mishima said, "I won't give you this book." He often gave me books if I showed any special interest in them, but this was evidently one book with which he would not part. He told me at this time that nothing in contemporary Japanese literature interested him, and that was why he turned to such "cruel" books.

Mishima's next reply was, "I was not taken to Kabuki until I was thirteen. I was allowed to see foreign movies, as well as

French and German operettas, but my grandmother feared
that Kabuki would have a bad effect on me. When I finally
got to see Kabuki I was in fact tremendously shocked and
excited. I read a lot of Kabuki and puppet plays towards the
end of my junior high school days. My grandmother and
mother were both interested in Kabuki, but my other grandmother preferred Nō. *Miwa* was the first Nō I ever saw. I saw
Kakitsubata when I was fifteen and began to read the texts
of Nō afterwards."

The importance of the theater to Mishima is apparent from
his life and writings. He once told me that the only Japanese
thing he missed in New York was Kabuki. We went together
to Kabuki often, sometimes seeing the plays from a glassed-in
booth at the back of the Kabuki Theatre, sometimes sitting
in the most expensive seats. We also attended Bunraku (the
puppet theater) together, but Mishima did not really enjoy
the puppets themselves. He preferred the Tokyo variation —
a puppet theatre without puppets, narrated by a chanter who
sat with his samisen accompanist in the middle of the vast
Kabuki Theatre stage.

Mention of Mishima's "other grandmother" came as a surprise when I reread my notes. I do not recall any other instance
of his alluding to his maternal grandmother. I had wondered
about his interest in Nō for other reasons. In 1966, when we
visited the Miwa Shrine together, as part of his field work for
the novel *Runaway Horses*, he told the chief priest of the
shrine that *Miwa* was the first Nō play he ever saw. It was also
the first, or possibly the second Nō play I ever saw, a strange
coincidence considering that I have not seen it since and it is
seldom performed. I went to see Nō with Mishima about once
a month. He had a subscription ticket and sat in the front
row of the audience. I do not doubt that he was genuinely
interested in Nō, but it did not mean as much to him as
Kabuki. He never wanted to see more than a single Nō in an
evening and would generally ask me which of the two plays
to be presented I preferred to see. Sometimes he dozed off
during the performance, which did not embarrass him in the
least.

I can recall Mishima speaking with special enthusiasm about one play, *Okina*, a ritual work without a recognizable plot that is performed only on special occasions. He told me that he did not feel that the New Year had really begun until he heard the meaningless but somehow auspicious lines declaimed in the play, *tō tō tarari tararira*. Mishima also liked the character Munemori in *Yuya*, because he suggested a Renaissance tyrant, interested only in his own pleasures. I remember, too, that he expressed great admiration when I identified a passage from *Matsukaze* — not much of an achievement, considering it is the most famous of all Nō plays. But although Mishima's emotional commitment to Nō was relatively limited, his intellectual appreciation was intuitively right, as his *Five Modern Nō Plays* demonstrate.

The next comment in my notes seems to be Mishima's response to a question from me about whether or not he ever read foreign books in the original languages: "I am poor in languages. I read only translations. Occasionally I have read a novel in English, for example, James Baldwin's *Giovanni's Room* and Gore Vidal's *The City and the Pillar*."

I wonder if it was merely modesty that induced Mishima to say that he was poor at languages. Perhaps he was comparing himself to professional translators. German was his first foreign language, and he retained an affection for it, as we can tell from his scribblings on the manuscript of *The Thieves*, the only one of his working notebooks ever published, or from the German subtitle he gave to his popular *Sound of the Waves*. Not long ago, during the course of a lecture I gave on Mishima at the University of Trier, I remarked that I had no idea how good Mishima's German was. After the lecture an elderly gentleman in the audience raised his hand and informed me that he was Mishima's German teacher at the Peers School, and that Mishima was by far the most accomplished in the class.

Most Japanese learn their English from textbooks of grammar, and even if incapable of uttering a single intelligible sentence know all the rules governing the use of "will" and "shall" or "would" and "should," but Mishima's English was acquired conversationally, and even when rules of grammar were broken, he was entirely intelligible. Unlike most Japanese, he showed no hesitation about speaking or writing English, and when he spoke it was usually in a loud voice, not the hesitant tones of someone who fears he will not be understood. He had the habit of picking up whatever words were in vogue and using them incessantly. When he was in New York in 1957 the adjective "monumental" occurred in nearly every sentence, though I cannot recall ever having said it myself. Mishima enjoyed not only speaking English but writing it, even to people who could easily read Japanese, like my late colleague Ivan Morris. It is noteworthy, too, that although he had learned English conversationally, he was able to read the two novels he mentioned.

These novels — Vidal's and Baldwin's — represented an interesting choice of reading matter. Neither novel had been translated into Japanese; Mishima was obliged to read them in English. But he seems to have chosen them neither because they were masterpieces nor because he was specially interested in the author. As far as I know, he never met Gore Vidal. I was present on the one occasion when Mishima met Baldwin at a publication party for *Five Modern Nō Plays* at the Gotham Bookmart. I could tell that Mishima was repelled by Baldwin's face, and he made a visible effort before he could shake his hand. Clearly there was some other reason for choosing these particular books. Both openly treat homosexuality, and this was a subject in which Mishima was particularly interested.

The next section of my interview dealt with Mishima's early novel *Confessions of a Mask*. Did I proceed to questions about this novel because of a connection I detected between it and the two American novels? Or was I merely tracing the chronology of his literary career from the beginnings? There is no way I can determine this now, but Mishima's answer to my first question was startling: "The whole of *Confessions of a Mask* was based on personal experiences. Everything originated in what I had actually felt, though I twisted or exaggerated my feelings. I even used materials from school compositions in the book. The section on Ryōtarō was originally written when I was thirteen, and the one on St. Sebastian when I was sixteen."

Mishima at times denied emphatically that *Confessions of a Mask* was autobiographical, but here was clear testimony that he had described, in literary form, of course, actual experiences. I can still remember that I was startled to hear him say these unambiguous words at a time when Japanese critics tended to refer to *Confessions of a Mask* as a "parody" or drew allegorical meanings from the account of the narrator's sexual preferences. Mishima underlined the factual truth with his next remarks, concerning Sonoko, the young woman whom the narrator of *Confessions of a Mask* loves but does not desire: "Sonoko was described as a Christian because she really was one. It was the only thing about her I disliked — or, to be more exact, which didn't suit me. Sonoko read *Confessions of a Mask*. She said that it made her very happy, and that everything was exactly as she remembered it. I was amazed by her attitude."

Years later, in fact shortly before his death in 1970, Mishima told me that the model for Ōmi in *Confessions of a Mask* had recently come to his door. Mishima, from a perch on the balcony of his house, was able to get a good look at the man without being observed. Unlike the dashing Ōmi, with whom the narrator is in love, the man looked down-and-out and wore wooden clogs instead of shoes. Mishima decided not to meet him. Other incidents in *Confessions of a Mask* can be verified by references in his autobiographical essays and similar works, but this was the only time, as far as I know, that he so openly mentioned his relations with Sonoko.

The next note reads: "I feel I first became a novelist with *Thirst for Love*."

Reading this statement more than thirty years after the interview, I was astonished because I had always supposed that this was *my* discovery. On several occasions, in the course of discussing Mishima's writings, I had made the same statement, always believing that I was the first to discover the special importance of *Thirst for Love*. Only on rereading my notes did I realize that Mishima himself had told me this. *Thirst for Love* (1950) was the work in which he definitively separated himself from the confessional novel. His next comment was: "I was strongly influenced by François Mauriac at the time. I was very fond of his writings, but that is no longer the case. He is just too clever. *Thérèse Desqueyroux* is *too* well written."

The interview at this point seems to have gone back to an earlier period in Mishima's career. He briefly described the situation prevailing in the Japanese literary world during the postwar period, when some celebrated writers like Tanizaki, who had maintained silence during the war, began to appear in the magazines again, and when some younger writers were enabled by the defeat to publish works they had kept hidden from the censors. Mishima was still unknown. He commented, "Even the publication of *Confessions of a Mask* brought me no sensational fame. It did not sell many copies. I thought while I was writing it that everybody would hate it, that it was very daring, and that perhaps only a hundred copies would sell. As a matter of fact, 10,000 copies were sold. This was not bad, but it was not a best-seller. It brought me a kind of fame for my technique and style, not because of the content of the book. The book was said by some reviewers to constitute a new analysis of human character, but it caused no shock. Most people thought *Confessions of a Mask* was a novel about impotence, rather than homosexuality. Not until I published *Forbidden Colors* did anyone bring up the question of homosexuality. It was probably because in Japan there had been no such novel since the seventeenth century, when Saikaku wrote about homosexuality among the samurai. But there were plenty of stories of impotence brought about by war wounds or by lack of food. Hemingway's *The Sun Also Rises* is a novel about an impotent hero, after all. People at the time spoke about "spiritual impotence" as if it were the malady of the generation.

"When I wrote *Confessions of a Mask* a complete translation of Proust into Japanese had not yet been made. I had never read Saikaku. Cocteau influenced me, especially the character Dargelos in *Les enfants terribles*. I had read Gide's *Corydon* and *Si le grain ne meurt*, but they did not influence me. In fact, I disliked Gide, though he was very popular in Japan, especially as a thinker. I am even now not very fond of Proust, perhaps because of the translation. I like Cocteau — he reminds me of haiku. Raymond Radiguet, whom I first read at sixteen, became an obsession for six or seven years. I was insanely fond of his works.

"After publishing *Forbidden Colors* there was a lot of gossip about my private life, but no one said a word after *Confessions of a Mask*. I am glad that an American translation of *Confessions of a Mask* will appear. I am particularly glad that this will be my third book in English translation."

Confessions of a Mask, translated by Meredith Weatherby, was in fact the first novel of Mishima's to be translated into English, but Harold Strauss at Knopf, the editor who did more than anyone else in the New York publishing world to promote interest in modern Japanese novels, rejected the book, saying that it would "brand" Mishima as a homosexual in the eyes of the American reading public. It certainly had not branded him in the eyes of Japanese readers, and even today most Japanese interpret the novel as a description of immature, rather than homosexual love. In America, where the writings of Proust, Gide and others had made readers familiar with the persona of the author as homosexual, and where the lives of such writers as Tennessee Williams and Truman Capote attracted attention for this reason, it was nevertheless felt undesirable to associate Mishima with this body of writing. Mishima evidently agreed. *Confessions of a Mask* appeared after *The Sound of Waves* and *Five Modern Nō Plays*.

The Sound of Waves was popular with American readers and created the kind of interest in Mishima that the publisher hoped for, but Mishima commented during the interview: "I have never written with Western readers in mind and will not do so in the future. I have no idea why my books are popular in the West."

Only at the end of his career, shortly before his dramatic suicide, would Mishima change his mind and actively seek to win success with foreign readers. For some years he had been desperately eager to win the Nobel Prize as the supreme recognition of literary merit. He became convinced at some point that the way to win the prize was to have as many of his books translated as possible. I had previously agreed to translate *Thirst for Love*, but only on the condition that there would be no deadline. Mishima at first agreed, but later became impatient and asked me to yield my rights to make the translation. I immediately agreed. The translation that appeared, as it happens, was not good, and I doubt that it helped Mishima's chances with the Nobel Prize Committee, but his need for foreign recognition became increasingly urgent. He had come to feel disgust with Japanese critics, especially because of their failure to review his final tetralogy, *The Sea of Fertility*. Some critics disqualified themselves, on the grounds that they did not know enough about Buddhism, treated at length in *The Temple of Dawn*, the third volume of the series; but it is more likely that Mishima's right-wing activities made them fear to praise his books lest they lay themselves open to the charge of being fascists. Mishima, contemptuous of their cowardice, decided that the reactions of foreign reviewers would be the real test of the worth of his books. His last letters, sent to Ivan Morris and myself, asked that we do what we could to ensure the publication of the translations of the final two volumes of the tetralogy. He had somehow obtained the impression that American editors were unwilling to publish the works of dead foreign authors. Even if this had been true, it was strange that a man, about to commit a "suicide of remonstrance" in the traditional manner of the samurai of the past, was concerned with his popularity among foreign readers.

But to return to *The Sound of Waves*. Mishima explained to me why he had written this novel: "I had always written about the underside of human relationships, and wanted for a change to write about the surface. I felt this was necessary because I had begun to doubt the appropriateness of always depicting hidden motivations. I had come to realize that it was not true that the surface must be a lie. I wondered if confession, the characteristic of literature written from the underside, was not the result of Christian influence. I tried to write *The Sound of Waves* from the front."

The inspiration for *The Sound of Waves* was originally provided by Mishima's visit to Greece in 1952. The sunlight and the simplicity of the life he observed aroused a revulsion against the way of life of the Japanese intellectual and particularly against the haggard look they typically wore as the badge of their suffering. He never recovered from this revulsion. Mishima obviously enjoyed the company of some intellectuals, but it probably gave him greater pleasure to associate with members of the Self-Defense Force or, later, his own Shield Society than with other writers. He also enjoyed the company of non-Japanese, though he satirized them mercilessly in some of his books. His manner was not that of some Japanese who turn to foreigners for wisdom and guidance, but the opposite: he seems to have found Western people appealingly childish and uncomplicated in contrast to the deviousness of the Japanese intellectuals. Of course, the perception of Europeans and Americans as appealingly childish owed much to Mishima's inability to speak English (or German) well enough to engage in intellectual discourse with Western equivalents of the Japanese intelligentsia.

All the same, Mishima constantly turned to the West for inspiration after his first discovery of the sunlit simplicity of Greece. He recreated in his *Sound of the Waves* the old Greek romance *Daphnis and Chloë*, substituting for the shepherd and shepherdess of the original more plausible Japanese protagonists, a fisher boy and a fisher girl. He did not expect that this novel would be a great success, considering it to be mainly an exercise in stylistics, imparting new life to a very old story by means of local color, and persuading readers that something like pastoral beauty existed in Japan.

Mishima termed both *Forbidden Colors* (1951) and *The Temple of the Golden Pavilion* (1956) philosophical novels. *Forbidden Colors* was influenced in its manner, though not in its content, by the works of Thomas Mann, whom Mishima at the time considered to be the greatest living writer. He did not say much else in the interview about *Forbidden Colors*, but my notes contain some hints as to what impelled him to write *The Temple of the Golden Pavilion*, perhaps his finest work, in which he related the circumstances that led a priest to burn down a celebrated Kyoto temple. The notes, rather incoherently, say: "Already existing beauty. That alone is alive, exists, and will never die. The 'I' of the novel is cut off from that world. He can't become beautiful and he can't create anything because there is before him a perfectly beautiful object. Being cut off from beauty, he must destroy the obstacle in his path before he can become free. He tries to live. We must all try to live, though we are imprisoned in art. Probably I will write no more works about beauty."

We seem to have moved on then to a more general discussion of literature, though the notes are again unclear: "I gained liberation through literature, though I never sought it. Proust is spiritual, but I am physiological. Literature enabled me to free myself from many complexes and from tension. I became interested in all aspects of human life and I shed my adherence to self. In this I think I am unlike most Western writers. I have come to think that I am *not* dissimilar to other people, though when I wrote *Confessions of a Mask* I thought I was. Goethe thought he was better than other people, not different from them. The same was true of Mori Ōgai.

"I have almost never found anything in Western literature that seemed alien to me. Even within Japanese society, of course, I like only certain people, and at times it is harder to understand the behavior of members of my own family than those depicted in the works of Western literature. But the methods of description followed by some Western novelists seem unnecessarily detailed to Japanese readers, who are accustomed to make the intuitive leap necessary to understand a haiku. Zola always felt it necessary to explain that a desk has four legs, that a room has four walls."

I remember asking Mishima if he thought that the emotions of the characters in a Dostoevsky novel were not too violent for the Japanese to comprehend. I asked this question because a Japanese friend had told me that a Japanese, faced with the mental torture experienced by characters in the novels of

Dostoevsky, would rather kill himself or go mad. Mishima answered, "The extremes of passion in Dostoevsky are not much worse than those in a Bunraku (puppet) play." But, he added, the Japanese are like the Spaniards in the quickness with which they boil over with passion. Suicide or murder tends to be decided on in an instant, rather than after a long process of cogitation.

Our conversation shifted from his novels to other kinds of literature that he had written: "For a time I thought I would become a poet. I was mistaken. Just as a woman supposes she is beautiful and only gradually comes to know what her face really looks like, I wanted to be a poet because poets — at least in their portraits — were so much handsomer than novelists. Poets looked like Byron, Shelley or Keats, but novelists were all bearded old men. I wrote poetry between the ages of fourteen and seventeen, sometimes in free verse, sometimes in the normal Japanese meters."

Mishima wrote little poetry in his maturity. Apart from the stylized dramatic poetry in which he cast his version for the puppet theater of Racine's *Phèdre*, there were only sporadic examples, such as the song he composed for the Shield Society or the valedictory poem to the world written shortly before he killed himself. But I recall that one year, soon after I had returned to Japan, he asked me to a restaurant where he had me examine his translations of some poems by James Merrill, whom he had met in New York. I was surprised that Mishima, despite his disclaimers about his knowledge of English, was able to interpret accurately modern poetry, and I thought that the translations were in themselves poetry. Sometimes, too, his prose came so close to poetry that is was difficult to distinguish between the two. This was true especially of the dialogue in his plays, where the language is usually not that of everyday speech (which Mishima, of course, could write easily and accurately) but of poetic intensity.

Mishima was attracted to the classical Japanese theater because, even when the plot of a play could have been treated realistically, it managed always to maintain a stylization of language that at times approached the highest reaches of Japanese poetry. He said during the interview, "The theater has been the strongest influence on me. I doubt anyone could form an attachment to Japanese literature merely by reading the classics. The appeal must be more sensual."

While at the Peers School, Mishima had been influenced by his teachers of classical Japanese literature. He was better acquainted with this literature than any other writer of his generation and returned to it again and again in his own works. But, at least when we had our interview, he was less interested in the traditionally admired works of classical poetry and prose than in works written for the theater, and some of the scenes in his novels were created in a deliberately theatrical manner.

Mishima, unlike many who read or see classical plays, seems to have been uninterested in discovering characters in the old masterpieces who resembled himself or his acquaintances. He preferred more abstractly conceived characters, who speak in a poetic language that often contrasted with their station in life. He felt that a dramatist's fidelity to his time limited the interest of his themes. This may be why he was not especially interested in the most famous Japanese dramatist, Monzaemon Chikamatsu (1653–1725). When my volume of translations of the plays of Chikamatsu appeared in 1960, Mishima quite seriously proposed that these translations should be translated into modern Japanese, so that the texts might acquire greater stylization in passing through the medium of a foreign language. On the other hand, he sharply criticized the attempts of the management of the National Theater to make Kabuki popular with the young by modernizing the language. He enjoyed the texts because of their language, even when the plots were absurd or grossly inflated, and he hoped that later generations of Japanese would come to know the same pleasure rather than have the texts fed to them in simplified, banal modern language.

The next reply by Mishima indicates that I asked him if he had ever thought of becoming an actor. Mishima's reply was: "I thought I would like to become an imaginary person, but never an actor!"

The answer was typical of his humor, but I wonder if it was true. In later years he seemed to enjoy appearing on the stage, where on occasion he sang French *chansons* dressed in a sailor suit, or appeared as a Roman guard in the final performance of his translation of Racine's *Britannicus*. He also appeared in the films, once as a gangster, another time as an army officer who commits hara-kiri, and in a third film as a fire-eating swordsman of the nineteenth century. He also took bit parts on occasion, especially in plays he had written. I recall him telling me that once, while he was sitting in a bar somewhere, he was approached by a stranger who spoke mysteriously of a deal in which they were both involved. Little by little Mishima realized that the stranger had confused him, because of the part he played in a gangster film, with a real *yakuza* of his acquaintance. The story sounds too ingenious to be true, but even if Mishima invented it, it suggests his pleasure in assuming other identities.

Mishima had a special fondness for *yakuza* films, de-

UPI/Bettmann

Mishima before his suicide in Tokyo in 1970.

lighting in their bad taste and overall stupidity. They certainly did not afford anything resembling the aesthetic pleasure of Nō or Kabuki, but he not only attended such films regularly but occasionally insisted that I accompany him. I did not share his enthusiasm, but that may be because I was unable to forget my professorial dignity.

Mishima remarked during the interview that he thought of the novel as his wife and the theater as his mistress. He said the same thing on later occasions. He believed that he so easily took to writing plays because of the conversational gifts he had inherited from his family. Unlike some Japanese families, whose remarks at table are restricted to monosyllables, his family kept up a flow of witty conversations, and he eagerly took part. This enabled him in later years to write theatrical dialogue with great speed, about five times as fast as writing a novel. I asked Mishima specifically about *Five Modern Nō Plays*, which had been published in my translation the previous year. He answered, "I had considered the possibilities available to me for writing poetic drama. I first tried writing some Kabuki plays because I wanted to create something in the manner of the old texts, but I never felt there was a future in writing new Kabuki plays in the old language, however nostalgic it made me. It was no more than a whim. I had to look up the old words in a dictionary, but these words had come naturally to the dramatists of the past.

"I came to realize also that Nō, unlike Kabuki, is not fixed to any one period. It is complete and perfect in absolute terms. It occurred to me that I could take the themes of Nō and use them in modern plays of my own. In the case of Kabuki plays, the themes and the expression are one and they cannot be separated from their time. Nō is an abstract art, but Kabuki is quite concrete. Everything is overtly expressed in Kabuki."

As I reread these remarks of Mishima I felt a twinge of guilt. For years I had been telling students precisely what Mishima told me about the differences involved in making modern plays out of Nō and Kabuki, forgetting that I had heard this from him, and supposing I had made a fresh discovery.

Mishima went on to discuss *shingeki*, the modern theater, created in the twentieth century after European prototypes: "I believe that *shingeki* will become more refined and will enjoy a development peculiar to Japan, a drama of dialogue. I doubt that modern Japanese drama will come any closer to European drama. In the case of the novel, there is not much chance of a distinctively Japanese form to develop if only because the novel has no form, but I think that a Japanese form will evolve in the modern theater. Perhaps there will be a revival of Nō or of Kabuki, though there is no sign of it as yet. The *shingeki* actors still imitate the West too much, and as a result Western people find Japanese modern drama uninteresting. But perhaps in a hundred or two hundred years they will decide that our *shingeki* is unique. I hope that some day there will be plays of Ibsen, Racine or Chekhov that can be seen only in Japan. At present the Japanese perform slavish imitations of the Moscow Art Theater when staging Chekhov, and of British companies when staging Shakespeare. But one day there will be a *Hamlet* or a *Macbeth* that can be seen only in Japan, though I don't know what form it will take."

This is where the notes for the interview conclude. Perhaps Mishima had another appointment or he may have become tired of answering my questions. As I have mentioned, I never made any conscious use of the remarks he made during the interview, though some of his words evidently sank so deeply into my mind that I thought they were my own.

I remained Mishima's friend until the day of his death on November 25, 1970. While I was in Japan (generally, the three months of the Columbia summer vacation) I saw him frequently, and we corresponded when I was in New York. He was an excellent correspondent, but during the last few months before his spectacular suicide his letters became irregular, and their tone suggested an increasingly bleak outlook on the world. I naturally did not suspect the cause was the emotional turmoil he experienced as the day for his self-appointed death approached, the day he was to deliver to the publisher the final episode of his four-volume novel.

On the night of his death (it occurred about midnight by New York time) I had gone with a Japanese friend to see *Oh Calcutta!*. Soon after I got back home the telephone rang. It was a Japanese newspaperman in Washington who informed me briefly of what Mishima had done that day and asked my impressions. He apparently did not know I was a close friend of Mishima's, and had telephoned simply because I was a professor of Japanese literature. I was too shocked to say anything intelligible, but the telephone rang all through that night from newspaper and magazine people in Japan, and by dawn I was speaking rather glibly. I have since then written on several occasions about what I felt that night, or when I saw the newspaper photograph of Mishima's head, or when I read his letter (which reached me three days later) opening, "When your read this I will be dead." I have given numerous lectures about Mishima and, in response to questions from members of the audience, offered explanations of his spectacular death. I confess I do not really believe my own explanations. Did he really kill himself because he couldn't bear the thought of becoming old? Or was it because, having written far more than most authors in a full lifetime, he felt he had written enough? Or was he so infatuated with samurai ideals (like the ideals of the suicide-bent kamikaze pilots) that in the end he had to experience disembowelment? I still keep searching for clues. Perhaps a vital one, yet undetected by me, lies hidden in that interview of forty years ago.

Rachel Hadas

Peculiar Sanctity

> *. . . the tradition which affirmed the peculiar sanc-*
> *tity of the sick, the weak, and the dying . . . per-*
> *haps came to an end for literature with the death*
> *of Milly Theale.*
>
> —Lionel Trilling, "Mansfield Park"

Except it didn't. It went underground
as some diseases have been known to do,
returning with a vengeance in our time.
To note the renaissance of elegy
as the defining genre of our day
is not to claim for form
merely the reflex of a pendulum
stupidly swinging. There are differences.
First of all, a fierce self-righteousness
beats its drum through our diffused distress.
Secondly, people take enormous pride
in giving utterance to grief and loss.
It is as if we shoved huge stones aside
to make room for our little threnodies.
Silence is shameful, more than shameful, death.
Is speech not life, then, animal instinct,
survival's automatic pilot, breath?
No; it requires courage. Thirdly, though
for silence and for speech the penalty
our plague exacts is utterly the same,
we are supposed to rage, seethe, overflow
with fury; brandish, not just grief, but blame,
level reproaches at the government.
How could so many be allowed to die?
Fourthly, it is not correct to say
"I'm dying of"; one says "I'm living with,"
thus adding to the gallantry of myth.

In mortal sickness, courage is no lie.
With or without peculiar sanctity,
people have always managed as they could.
And once the sick one takes the downward road
to that broad region shrouded in twilight,
similarities with those before
become more marked than differences of mode.
The figures look the same: tall Tenderness
bends by the bed to offer a caress.
And everyone who passes or who stays
must grapple with the place's doubleness:
the tremulous wish to live at any price
versus the drawn-out longing for release.
When what the scourge can do is done at last,
the bystanders all having done their best;
when everyone's acknowledged this to be
something not curable by elegy
(silence is death, and so is poetry),
they rise, go out, and seek the light of day
for a little while. They turn away,
yes, but only for a breathing space
from the old, new, peculiar sanctity,
before returning to their grisly task.

Max Winter

Sixteen Visions of the Immaculate Conception

1.
She thrust upwards and screamed.
Her cat woke, leapt off the windowsill,
and broke a vase containing dried Latvian flowers.
Many nights she had lain this way.

2.
She seemed to hunt
for a bar of soap.
Something slipped between her doubled legs;
she sighed and was quiet
until the end of the hour.

3.
A small blue Volkswagen rolled down the hill.
When its window opened, the dents in its hood
vanished.
She climbed inside slowly and reluctantly.

4.
Who has removed this young woman's dress?
Why are her arms thus akimbo?
What is the name of this hill?
Where are her feet?
When did this occurrence occur?

5.
She unlatched and opened the door
cautiously. She was frightened by the brightness
of the day.

6.
It had been weeks
since she had felt
his hands
on her back.

7.
When the waves came to wake her feet
her eyes rolled
and she could write her name in the shells
no more.

8.
She opened the card,
expecting nothing.
She received a sprig of holly which,
when she sniffed it,
took the breath from her body.

9.
Underwear thrown on antenna,
she found nothing in her purse
but a weary penny and a cracker.
The cupboard was empty,
the refrigerator dim.
A broom fell in the closet.

10.
She was trying to find Omaha
on a small map of the United States.
A needle poked up through New Mexico.

11.
She was carried over autumn,
thrown through forests,
bred with angels.

12.
She let him have it,
whoever he was.

13.
It tapped her gently on the forehead and ears.
She breathed expectant breaths in the yard
as the night became longer and longer.

14.
Oh baby,
come on baby,
the night time
is the right time
to be with the one
you love,
he said.
She did not answer
because he was not in the room.

15.
She lost her place.
She napped.
She started the book, yes, again.

16.
Someone had taken her blankets
and opened the window wide.
It was Christmas Eve.
She had been dizzy of late.

Phillip Sterling

Duplicate Scenes of the Earthly Paradise

(Eighteenth-century fireplace insert,
Musée de la Vie wallonne)

For the sake of argument pretend
we don't know who they are, this couple,
one on either side of a cast-iron tree
entwined with reptilian repose, dog-

faced, drooling. Obviously, the two are
not the same. On the right,
she confronts us, unashamed,
her not-quite-smile withheld to a smirk

in her pose, as if her model had meant
to shoulder innocence, all the while her flush
belying the artist's bed and not his brush.
The other's standing sidewise, from waist

down, more serious,
and yet his nub's a subtle
giveaway to the black gravity of his gaze,
a black apple in each hand.

Duplicate, but not identical,
molded in smokeless sheen
for some elaborate Walloon firepit:
on the right the tree takes hold of him,

enflames him, offshoots fired from his loins;
on the left the miscasting encircles her,
as though she bathes in rottled leaves
and fruit, molten earth, fecundity. Only

the serpent in both is the same, distracted
by the fragrance of apples in her hair
and heedless of the other side of the tree
wound in snakeskin.

Joan Murray

Augustine Speaks

No, I'm not the Austrian—you're confusing me
with Dora—the one who deserted Freud
before he had his chance to perfect her.
She would have been his chef d'oeuvre:
the proof of all his theories. But she refused
to accept his preformed version of her truth,
and up off the couch she went,
robbing him of the glorious ending
after he'd written her whole story.
All the journals were waiting.
It's no wonder he never
forgave her.

For me it was different. Whatever others say,
I thank God—and Charcot—for every minute of
those years I spent with him at Salpetrière.
Though I called him *maître,* we were more like
partners in a pas de deux: I was so attuned to
his cues, I could snap in and out of catatonia, howl
like a dog, or touch myself—here and here—and
reenact the rape that he said "continued to
obsess" me. What he created went beyond
science. Or even art. It was more like
religion. He turned humiliation to
ecstasy.

I performed it daily for the artists and writers.
For gentlemen with wealth or titles. Or undeniable
connections. And the new politicians who came
each year after the arrondissement elections.
And then I listened to their breathing, deepening

and quickening, till I hardly needed Charcot's
subtle promptings. I was painted and photographed.
I became literature and theater. My bodice grew looser.
And Charcot (who sometimes fantasized that he
was Jesus Christ, or even Napoleon) grew in
stature each time my rapture
swept the crowd.

At the height, he had five thousand patients. Most
were women. Many were foreigners. There were
several Americans. And he blamed me
for the burdens my success had placed on him.
He was suffering from profound professional
stress until he took it in his head to *cure* me.
Years before, he had achieved a minor reputation
for performing cervical cauterizations as
a cure for emotional instabilities.
(I never asked him what they did
with men — I think they sent them
off to school.)

But the rest of Salpetrière still favored hysterectomies.
And Charcot was prodded by their jealously to
get me up on the table and take my insides out of me —
as if the devil were in there, calling out the motions
of our dance. He might have let me go if I had asked him.
But seeing him so deranged by their pressure, I arranged
a quick departure: I didn't say good-bye or even
thank him. And I regret that now. I don't expect
he'll find me after so many years. Yet still I listen
for the sounds of wheels coming down the road.
And I wonder if it's him, if I'll let him
take me back.

Two Poems by David Breskin

Poem for a Businessman (Me)

Sympathy, to begin with, is a problem.
The hotels are okay and there's free soap
to smuggle home. Lunches are not lavish
but good food mothers want their sons to eat.
There's pay. And hours. Vacations follow
seasons like soldiers in obedient
retreat. Plus the silent love of men
waiting for their bags at whirring airport
carousels. Someone says that stewardi
are hardly what they used to be. What is?
Sex is sex and politics, and speed has killed
the shoeshine boys. Eat fast or be eaten.

Being on hold is what hurts. Life stops
and static fills: fiber-optic calls
so still my empty neurons firing echo.
For this fiscal my thinking is bearish
the man says. Projections get fired
like rockets or people. A real bear, I think,
would empty that office pretty quick, but
loading docks full of debt is fear enough.
First-in, first-out: FIFO. Last-in, first-out:
LIFO. Inventories stand in place like slaves
until they're laid, casually, by demand.
While I hold the line, spreadsheets wink at me.

Between the gates of night, domestic flights
from wives and kids I never had run counter
to the clock and land at lots of rental cars.
When I hit the lights, the windshield wipers
mock me. The parking brake unlocks the trunk.

A map displays my ignorance. Buying
everything in sight would solve some problems.
Jail would be a new one. Under rumbles
of descending jets the car-lot sentry
dances inside headphones. He checks my contract,
makes his mark and, smiling, hands it back.
The bottom line can't be read but shows my name.

Bugs

When humans watch the sky for holes, then kiss
all plants goodbye and suck down freeze-dried food
our ancient, desperate souls with pens ablaze
write debt-for-nature swaps like let's do lunch.

If gams are schools of whales but also legs
then maybe Moby's caught, her fishnet hose
so torn by drift net's yen for cash she bleeds
above the thigh, the moon blood red with coins.

If five of six animals are insect
and most of those are beetle, who are we
to save the world from orgies of the small?
One good bomb and they own the place, and cheap.

Wax and silk and pigment and honey: bugs
work so hard for us it's odd they sting
instead of strike. Butterflies near factories
turn black to hide from predators. Success.

Across the wobbly fist of earth, blue whales
are whispering to elephants: let's dance,
make love, burn swords of ivory and baleen,
stay up late, drink like there's no tomorrow.

Two Poems by Robert Hahn

Summer and Winter at the Mount

1975 and 1985

1.
Lost souls in Chekhov watch the fireflies emerge
from the woods, haltingly, and mope: "One day we'll know
the reason we have lived and why we have worked
and soon winter will come to cover us with snow"—

in our case, we prayed for summer, for the accomplishment
of its round tones. When it came, we scavenged the green
world for alternate selves, frantic as aesthetes
from the fin de siècle on a querulous tour of the continent.

The Tempest saved us. One midsummer night,
a spritely poly-accented troupe arrived
at Edith Wharton's "Mount": white, Palladian,
but her own design, down to the last brocaded

bolster, complete, and abandoned when her husband's mind
shattered. In the shuttered windows, lights
came on. Below the sloping lawn, released
spirits poised to spring from the webbed trees.

Now our lives could begin! At the porch railing,
whole in a flick of hissing light, a young sailor
leaned to wrestle an invisible wheel. Voices
blinked from the pines. Present, restored, we rejoiced

to find ourselves marooned in their company, lost,
where being there together could be enough at last.

2.
Today, ten years later, more or less
the same, we've returned. It's winter in Lenox, Mass.

We circle her flaking house, rehearsing our bleak
themes (the life or the work, marriage or betrayal).
The brilliant crust breaks beneath our feet.
Distraught calligraphy! Snow lies in draped

folds on the paired stairways falling like the arms
of Undine, alas, dropped to her sides in petulant
exasperation. Poor thing, she's exhausted. Her charmed
innocence is all in the mind of her husband, the poet

manqué. What's to be done? A crow veers
overhead, a scratch of sound across the scene.
No company. What's here but our wish to be here
completely, compose the music for a new season,

to weave a new life for Edith Wharton and the slanting
ghost in the dark hallway, the mad husband?

3.
Let their voices emerge altered in a dimming light
where sonorous imagined spouses at last grow wise

together. We pray that their spirits may be beguiled
as they were the summer Edith's guest, arriving
with his great valise of overlaid intonations,
was the singular Henry James. *Ènchanté!*

What more could she have wished—a marriage of minds
in supple talk, all afternoon in her patterned
gardens, their white petals trembling *en point*,
distinct. Shadows disentangle from the pines

and lengthen over the lawn, which becomes an obedient
wave rolling to the porch where the lamps are lit,
where he opens the book he has brought to read, and reads
aloud, *Leaves of Grass*, its looping anapestic

flow a counter-spell to their own interiors,
landings where her confessions are staged, and corridors
crossed with odd moted lights, suggestions
he greets as *mon bon*. But tonight their labors are set

aside as he leans to his book and she leans back
in the high-backed brocaded chair, as he croons
the phrases sonorous and strange. Her rings catch
in the lamplight. How hard her mind is tonight! How soon

winter will come again with work and snow
and trooping hallucinations of death the distinguished
thing. How clearly he sees it, his work finished,
in the glow of her assembled lamps flowing

to fuse with the dusky pines and the cedars dim,
the tallying chant, our presence conjured, our winter

4.
eluded again. It's an August night. From the verge
of our back yard, the plucked voices emerge

in halting rhythm, like fireflies the dazed, lonely
Ruskin saw in Tuscany, and labored to describe
in a last unfinished work: "How they shone,
moving through the black leaves like fine-broken starlight!"

Olmsted's Fens Corrected by Shircliff

Aroused by the way it sounded, *fens* —
compact, dense, with secrets one could reveal
in a slow disclosure, a kindling, of *glade, glen,*
a flare of darker green, unhearable sounds
of water fingering through spongy soil —

you brought the word back in your steamer trunk,
a lens: one could see that the raw, prosaic banks
of Muddy River, if disguised, would emerge
more beguiling, sinuous, mazier than they were
in nature, if cloaked in nature, secrets sunk

within secrets. When you thrust the river underground,
insinuated in hidden pipes, your lagoons
unwound and languished in green, random spaces,
off-balance and shadowed, like the beckoning recesses
so alluring, in stone, to your neighbor Richardson,

of the barrel-chest, the vaulted bellow, your swinish
guest and dark familiar. You lived on coffee.
He dyed the air with dripping joints of beef,
chewed up blueprints and spilled out designs
for warehouses, trains, jails, wasting the night

while you dozed and schemed, another way to loop
two woodland paths, a pair of wooded rivers,
loosely together as if by chance, seduced
to a darker wrestle, in loam, in shadow, lovers
vanishing to reappear draped in more elusive

words, altered by their secrets. But soon
you slept for good in sandstone, and your rotund friend
did too. This is where Arthur Shircliff comes in.
The fens, he concluded, alarmed, were far too unruly.
He sealed the underground pipes. The pools

where weeds had spun in dark swirls
like hair in sleep were reduced to a stream
beneath a wrought-iron footbridge, lacy, petite. . . .
The leftover river he dumped in the Charles.
A new broom. A new expanse, pristine,

platonic, unrolled from Isabella Gardner's palace,
clean as a parade ground, a tabula rasa.
Gravel walks radiated out from the core
of its compass. Tulips braced in the formal
declamatory gardens. This was no place

for a willful shadow, carelessly flung, a blur
of green, dark as the red Medoc, black
where Richardson sits by his torch, where he turns
in his vast chair, and hails you. None of that.
Of what is hidden, veiled, withheld, not a word.

Two Poems by Jody Gladding

Eclipse

Now. And now, a tiny foot, like
a shooting star, draws an arc
inside my belly.

But if my belly were the whole
sky, would I wake at night to rise like this,
cumbersome as the moon?

And would the moon reveal so
much to me — the heavy globe she is
behind the bright disc, expanding, contracting?

New Moon

To do this, said the moon, you must
give up everything.

Everything, she said, and I watched
the light drain from her
like milk.

I watched the light trail
down her legs, her cheeks,
fall out in clumps as she brushed it.

I could barely see her now,
a watery curd in the evening sky.
You must even give up the night,

she said, and that plan of yours
to rock by the window.
Give, she said.

I lifted my gown. Just give,
she said. Shadows pooled under me.
I lay naked on my side.

More, she said. My neck was damp
now, and crooked like a spout.
This hurts, I said.

Give it up, said the moon, and I curled
around the hunger.

Joseph Harrison

Not Playing Possum

I'd seen him scuttling under a parked car
In the oil-stained side street near the auto shop,
Or peering from beneath the juniper bush
That guarded our old weather-peeled bow porch.
Weirdly primeval, and adaptable
To mutations in ever more unnatural orders,
Partly because they will eat almost anything,
His kind is famous for a curious ruse
They undertake in paralytic terror:
If cornered, they play at being carrion
And pray that what's discovered them won't eat them,
A ploy not wholly unlike human tricks,
Like pretending one isn't present while the phone
Rings and rings with the call you refuse to answer,
Or quietly ignoring an ugly scene
Out of discretion or plain cowardice,
Or claiming a meaning is merely literal.
Even the most absurd of these games works
Only because it mimics a moment of truth,
Absence or absent-mindedness or poems
Anchored by an unavoidable fact,
And when, one brutal week in mid-July,
The city baked in triple-digit heat
Till its cement was blasting like a furnace,
Drying the last greasy puddles that passed
For water among the staggering animals,
The juniper bush emitted a sickening reek,
A fetid message that soon crossed the street,
It meant, no matter what the old phrase said,
This possum wasn't playing. He was dead.

The Oven Bird by Robert Frost: a story

Daniel Stern

for Frank Kermode

It was the long bad time after the long good time.

Stocks a puzzle, real estate stalled, the bond market iffy, Wall Street firms down to half their size. Two of his former associates under indictment: Sorkin and Menninger, Menninger probably guilty. To Lee Binstock, good times had always come like sunshine on a holiday weekend; a feeling of surprise but of pleasure deserved. Now, out of work for the first time in twenty years, bad times came with the unpleasant surprise of being caught and punished in spite of feeling innocent. And, of course, there was the matter of Binstock's mouth.

Always, he'd been able to make his own extracurricular comfort: the clarinet's woody breath of independence—his horn of romance. He had partners in crime. Callahan, advertising copy, ruddy, volatile on the violin, with his quiet academic wife, second fiddle in more ways than one; Menninger, mutual funds, intense, humorless on viola; Sorkin, smooth but folksy, arbitrage, controlling the pulse on cello. No "civilian," as they called those who could only listen, could know what a Sunday afternoon spent summoning the Brahms quintet could do—a single-minded song to ransom the frustrations of buying too much and selling too little, to pardon the mistakes of the week, the wrong choices of a lifetime.

You can see why, once it was clear that he could not make a clean, steady sound on the clarinet anymore, might never again, Binstock was thrown into despair. He had actually—at rock bottom one night—called a suicide hot line advertised in the *Village Voice*. The woman on the phone had answered: "Suicide hot line—please hold." And then clicked him off onto recorded music for waiting. By the time seven minutes had gone by, the idea of being put on hold to wait for a suicide counselor seemed so absurd that his mood began to clear. Also, the music they played was a Marcello oboe concerto, sublimely lyric even on the phone, and he made plans to buy the recording as soon as he could get to Tower Records—which he supposed was the same as saying he'd decided to live and had not been really serious about dying.

Nevertheless, the misery returned the next day, apparently to stay. Binstock supposed he should be grateful that he never had to play for a living. But it didn't help when Eugenia suggested he try to switch over to the piano since after the bloody fight the clarinet seem to be finished for him.

"It's nothing *you* did, Lee," she said. "Don't forget that. Those guys in the car—*they* did something to you."

"I could have kept my mouth shut," Binstock said. "I might not have a job but at least I'd still have a mouth."

She kissed him quickly on that cue. His lips were askew since the surgery—hence the difficulty in forming a proper embouchure and getting a clean sound out of the clarinet—but he could still taste a kiss. It tasted cool and sweet—a hint of some cherry-like lipstick flavor.

"Where the hell do you think you're going?"

"Move your ass. I've got the light."

"And I've got the right of way."

"Hey, we got a walking lawyer here. Right of way . . ."

"I just meant that you're such a good musician you shouldn't waste it. It's always been more than a hobby to you. You were never just a businessman."

"Disgusting word."

"Which? Musician? Businessman—?"

"*Hobby*. What a word to use about music."

"I knew you'd say that."

"We've been married too long. You know everything I'm going to say—"

"Married talk is like music. Just because you know how a Mozart sonata goes doesn't mean it's not going to surprise you every now and then."

"Don't be clever and charming. I'm in pain."

"Mouth pain or life pain."

"Same thing."

"Think about trying the piano. We'll always keep body and soul together. But you have to care for your soul. L.A. didn't help with that either."

When the market had collapsed, when the open possibilities of the last few years all seemed to turn into dead ends, Binstock had taken them to California. Eugenia, New York to her bones as only an out-of-towner can be—Connecticut born—objected to the choice of L.A. But Binstock was in need of hope and hid behind a joke, somebody's remark that Hollywood was the only place in the world where you could die from encouragement. That was the one commodity he needed, he told her, after most of the other commodities in his world had failed him. They escaped to the Beverly Hills branch of Dean Witter, in search of hope, of encouragement.

Eugenia could do her work on either coast. She ran a newsletter for educators from home . . . wrote, edited, mailed— the works. "I'm pre-Industrial Revolution," went her running joke. "The last cottage industry." This made for laughter at parties but said nothing about younger ambitions, about newspaper jobs not landed, about magazines not created. The newsletter won journalism awards. It provided a modest income and it could be moved with the luggage. They waited a few weeks because the gynecologist thought Eugenia might be pregnant, but it was another false alarm.

In Los Angeles they economized: one car for the two of them. On weekends, Eugenia out playing women's doubles, Binstock took a small, aristocratic pleasure in noting how cars slowed down for you when you walked across Santa Monica Boulevard, a rare West Coast bird, a pedestrian. Even so Los Angeles gave little comfort, less encouragement. They were back in New York in seven months.

"If you're such a tough guy get out of the car."

"Just move, buster. I get out of this car you're going to be damned sorry . . ."

Then the comedy of errors on upper Broadway, a car pressing him to move as he crossed Eighty-sixth Street, an angry Binstock deciding to move at his own pace, even not to move at all — then the fistfight, the only such encounter in Binstock's adult years, crunched bone, spitting, choking on blood filling his mouth with the taste of pennies, Binstock dizzy on his knees, the police siren singing in his ears.

"Son of a bitch didn't even stick around. Broke my mouth and beat it."

That was what he'd tried to say, but it didn't come out clear enough for the cops or Eugenia to understand. He said it to her, carefully, after the operation.

"Blame it on L.A.," Eugenia said. "The cars there slow down when they're a mile away from a pedestrian. You got used to that. You forgot how they drive in New York."

Binstock murmured, stiff-mouthed, "I was born a pedestrian. When this bastard started to push me with his damn BMW I just got pissed off. I was too tired of being pushed."

"Because he was pushing you — or because it was a BMW?" They'd sold their's the year after the big slowdown when they sold the house in East Hampton. They were city mice again; reacquainted with the IRT, the crosstown bus.

Back from the hospital, too weak to look for the next job, he looked over the mail one day, sitting on the bed, only to find a disturbing letter from Sorkin in the mail. It was a rambling note full of regrets, *I guess I did wrong things but, in some strange way, not bad things. I don't know . . . I should have known better . . . don't care about myself . . . ashamed to face Ruthie and David — I read a poem the other day, "The Oven Bird" by Carl Sandburg. You should read it — we should all read it . . ."*

These days, post-operation, Binstock was exhausted by midday, and it was 2:00 PM. He fell asleep lying on top of the covers, right where he was. The instant his eyes were closed he thought — the letter from Sorkin sounded like a suicide note. He'd never seen one but the notion troubled him. He would call as soon as he woke up to see how the poor bastard was doing. But it was the phone call from Sorkin's son, David, that woke him an hour later.

The funeral service was mercifully brief though Riverside Memorial Chapel was crowded. The rabbi made no mention of suicide, speaking only, a little tactlessly Binstock thought, of temptations and sin. Binstock did not linger. The letter in his pocket was on fire — and the only way to put it out was to find out what Sorkin had meant about the Sandburg poem. You couldn't put off acting on instructions from the grave. Look what had happened to Hamlet. The trouble was, Binstock had a pretty decent library but Sandburg was not a writer he'd ever cared enough about to keep. So the poem would have to be searched out.

Before he could find a bookstore he actually passed a public library. There was something about a public library in the middle of the afternoon that mingled convalescence with the flavor of childhood. The library was half empty, but he remembered the libraries of the past exactly that way. The computer showed all of Sandburg, but there was nothing called "The Oven Bird."

Binstock found it hard to believe that Sorkin, hard-nosed, sharp-edged Sorkin, had actually read poetry. The one person in their group who busied herself with poetry readings downtown, maybe even wrote a few poems, had fallen out of touch

as soon as the going got rough: Jennie Maslow. It was worth
a shot, a quarter from a phone booth on the corner.

"Lee, I'm over here."

The bar in the Carlyle was blindingly dark after the cold
autumn sunlight, and Binstock blinked and blinked until he
saw her. He said: "I can't believe I called you out of the blue
and there you were."

It's hard to know who was more nervous, Binstock or this
slender, almost anorexic-looking young woman — younger
than he remembered.

"It just means I'm one of those people at home during the
day. But calling about a poem! Who's going to believe that?"

When he told her about Sorkin's letter she believed it. "The
tough ones melt down the quickest. I read the obit this morning, but I couldn't get myself to go."

The drinks came, a Coke for him and the real thing, something with tequila, for Jennie. "Not settled anywhere yet?"
he asked.

"Ah, well," she said. "I had a good long ride. I put some
cash away and I'm back to school. Are you still having those
wonderful chamber music evenings of yours? The Mozart
Quintet . . ."

It was the time to tell her about the fight and the operation
and to show her his mouth a little more closely. He was grateful
now that the bars in the afternoon were dark.

She braved it out. "I haven't been this close to your mouth
in years. Kind of nice."

Jennie had happened just before he'd met Eugenia, and
Binstock had been the one to break it off. That's why he'd
been too embarrassed to just ask her for information about
a poem on the phone, why he'd suggested a drink when it
was much too early for a drink and much too late for Jennie.
When it was clear he was not picking up on her auld lang
syne she said, "I'm sorry those bastards hurt you and I'm sorry
about the clarinet. I know how much you loved playing. I
found out in high school that I loved poetry — but I can't write
worth a damn. At least you can play."

"Could," he said. "You probably know this poem Sorkin wanted me to read."

She giggled, a nervous tic more than laughter. "The answer from the grave?"

"Or a warning."

"Sorkin was wrong. 'The Oven Bird' isn't Sandburg. Can you imagine your cold-blooded partner turning away from his computer running the price of gold in Tokyo and reading a poem to try to understand his life? He even got the poet wrong. My God! I mean, I'm sorry about what happened but Jesus — Sorkin, of all people."

"No soul?"

"Whatever passes for that these days — yeah, that's what I meant. But it's not Sandburg." She laughed. "The bird is way beyond old Carl Sandburg — Chicago, Hog Butcher to the world, et cetera. You know, Frost is really a dark poet — and God knows 'The Oven Bird' is one of the darker ones."

"Let's hear it." Binstock sipped his Coke carefully. He was using his mouth very carefully these days.

"Oh, I don't know it by heart." She raised her glass. A few seconds wait and she said, "I live around the corner on Eighty-fourth Street."

"I know," Binstock said.

"Come on back and I'll dig it out."

She read quite beautifully, a low husky voice without sentimental cadences, just right for this strange little item. He sipped a vodka — it was now late enough for a drink — and listened. Jennie said it was a sonnet, surprising him. Binstock didn't think people wrote sonnets after Shakespeare. It began:

There is a singer everyone has heard,
Loud, a mid-summer and a mid-wood bird.

It was not difficult, just hard to focus on — what the hell could Sorkin have had in mind? Then, with the last two lines, it was painful, it was clear.

The question that he frames in all but words
Is what to make of a diminished thing.

Jenny put the book down. "Poor bastard," she said.

"I liked him," Binstock said. "But I never quite trusted him. What kind of a man goes into arbitrage? After playing the viola in high school. Buying and selling money. Weird."

"You sound like Ezra Pound."

"What do you mean?"

"It doesn't matter," Jenny said. "Look at these lines — this was his mood when he — " She read:

The bird would cease and be as other birds
But that he knows in singing not to sing.
The question that he frames in all but words . . .

Binstock murmured the last line: 'Is what to make of a diminished thing.' Jesus, you know I could have done without this. Some favor from old Sorkin."

Jenny started to stand but instead leaned over him, the book in her hand. "I remember when I first read it. It makes your insides jump. Each time. It's always a shock. The question is *when* you read it. At what point. Sometimes you find those lines when you're ready for them. Other times they jump at you — a sad surprise."

"I guess Sorkin was looking for answers — and he found this."

"Found another question."

She traced his wounded mouth with a temporary caress. The kiss surprised them both. Not knowing what to do when their mouths separated she dropped the book into his hands. "Here," she said. "Take it. You can return it when you're done."

Binstock was torn — borrowed books had to be returned — usually in person. Her finger touched the scar above his lip.

"Is this where — ?"

Binstock stood up. What he didn't want was a mercy fuck. Nor anything from Jenny, not her book, not anything. Anyway, now the poem was his as much as hers — a dubious acquisition.

Back at his apartment, Eugenia was still out. The books on the shelves were waiting. But by this time Binstock was in a fuming rage. What was this shit about a poem that Sorkin was trying to pull on him? Was he implying that the two of them had been in the same boat, the same bag, the same scam, choose any crummy metaphor you want, he thought, running his fingers along the spines of books. He'd been such an idiot that between Sorkin and Menninger, he'd always assumed that maybe it was Menninger who deserved the indictment — had done something tricky, just beyond the law in some gray area of right and wrong.

Menninger had such a smooth style, while Sorkin was all sincerity. Mister Straight in his collection of tattersall vests, the country boy come to Wall Street who just got lucky, then luckier, then, very quickly, out of luck — finished. Was this poem by another country boy written in some code Binstock was supposed to break, a code that would reveal the truth of what had happened to all of them and all the others who'd been laid low after riding so high?

The problem was, Binstock didn't feel he belonged with the others. He'd been like the child at the grown-ups' party, only half understanding what they were talking about when their lunch deals got cryptic, mysterious. Maybe a broker who played the serious musician on weekends was not to be trusted with secrets full of dirt and danger. In which case his clarinet may have saved his ass. Who knows what he *would* have done given the opportunity. In any case, *he* wasn't knocking himself off. For Christ's sake, he wasn't forty yet — why should he read a fucking poem about diminished things?

Binstock pulled the book out so violently that a batch of neighboring books tumbled to the floor. Then, without understanding what he was doing, he grabbed the blue-covered

Frost book and tried to tear it in half. He'd never imagined what it might feel like to try to rip up a hardcover book, but he was sure it would be easy. It wasn't. The top part detached from the spine, pages ripped and dangling, but the whole thing stopped around halfway. His right hand hurt, and he felt like an idiot. He stood there, wondering how he would explain this scene if Eugenia walked in at that moment.

The ragged Frost was on the floor next to his foot as he kneeled, trying to pick up the books in time, but of course Eugenia arrived in the middle of it all.

"What's going on?"

"I don't know," Binstock said.

She zeroed in on the ripped-up Frost before he had a chance to hide it.

"My God, what is this?" She picked it up. It dangled from her hand, a wounded bird, survivor of some terrible accident.

"I'm sorry."

"It's not even yours. It belonged to Richard."

"I didn't think of that."

"Maybe you did. Are you still weird about him?"

Richard was Eugenia's first husband, an architect, first divorced, now dead in a plane crash three years ago.

"I was never weird about Richard."

"You acted like a crazy person whenever I mentioned him."

"Maybe you did that a little too often."

"Oh, for God's sake, Lee."

"Anyway, this is about Sorkin, my ex-partner, not your ex-husband."

She pushed her coat off her shoulders and let it fall among the books.

"I forgot about him mentioning some poem. Is this it? I thought it was Sandburg."

"It was Frost. Sorkin didn't know anything about poetry. Neither do I. But I don't go around writing letters scaring people and then dying; not just dying—killing myself."

"Did that scare you?"

"Well, it freaked me."

She carried the torn and flapping book into the living room. Binstock did not follow her. He knelt among the books and started replacing them on the shelves. Then he hung up Eugenia's coat. When he was finished he went into the living room. He lay down on the couch and picked up yesterday's *Wall Street Journal*, half-scanning it, half-hiding behind it.

She was quite a long time. He heard her exhale, a long slow breath.

Binstock has been hoping she would get to the lines in question and just read them in some cool and detached grown-up Eugenia way. Instead she seems taken out of herself.

"Diminished thing, — " she breathes. "How did he know?"

Binstock puts down the paper. Eugenia is leaning back, her finger marking the last two lines of the poem. He asks her what she means — know what? She tells him she'd always counted herself as reasonably happy, lucky, but if you think about diminished things, how could she not count up all the times, the lessening, the shrinking, the losing . . . "My God," she murmurs?

"What do you mean, exactly?" he asks, all innocence. "Be specific."

"It's not just now — early middle or whatever I'm in. It's every time. When I was fourteen I thought I would never again feel the heights of the year before when these two seniors, Larry and Bart competed for me — and I ignored them both and wrote an essay on independence for a school contest that got published in the *Atlantic Monthly*, special teenagers' section. And do you remember, when you first met me, how I played tennis with a natural backhand motion out of Balanchine. Now, I have to think carefully, Get the racket back, bend your knees . . . diminished things . . . " She gently folds the torn book closed.

It was a strange moment. She'd taken the whole question from him and made it her own, had gone from surprised anger to introspection so quickly. All it took was a few lines of a poem. At the same time, she took the idea of diminishment so lightly—just a minor joke played on us all . . . took the Oven Bird's song down to questions of a fourteen year old's essay . . . of a tennis backhand.

"Let's eat out tonight," he said.

"I have veal defrosting."

Eugenia had been cooking home every night for months, avoiding the hefty restaurant checks of the good old days.

"If I'm tearing up books you can melt some veal."

She left the Frost on the couch, looking like the survivor of some natural disaster, helpless, open to the Oven Bird's page.

They picked an Italian place which was on a special discount card: 20% off everything: tax and tip included. Binstock ordered a double vodka Gibson, surprising both of them.

"A double?" Eugenia used her eyebrows.

"Not to worry. Twenty percent off."

They both knew she hadn't meant the money but she let it pass.

"Did Richard really like poetry a lot?"

"Are we back to Richard?"

Eugenia ordered a glass of the house red while Binstock worked a little too swiftly on his double vodka. It was not Elio's, it was not Primola, it was certainly not 21, though the tables had white tablecloths, not checkered cloth or paper— they weren't down to that yet. But there was little likelihood of running into anybody they knew. They were between lives. Old friends still ate and summered in places they would not now be able to afford. New friends are not made so easily after thirty-five. Once, at two in the morning, Eugenia had wakened and murmured to him something about depending too much on each other. Binstock had said, "Who's to say what's too much?" and turned back to sleep.

"Actually," she said, "Richard was more visual. He liked some poetry but nothing too complicated. And God knows he wasn't the kind who would try to find some truth about himself from a poem. Have we now maybe had enough about Richard and have you maybe had enough Vodka?"

His hand had been in the air to catch the waiter's eye while she was talking. But by this time the waiter was there and he was ordering another double Gibson; Eugenia was carefully reading her way through the pastas. When he'd gotten irritated enough at her silent menu-reading act, Binstock tossed back about half of his second drink in one gulp. A dramatic toss, the way he'd seen actors do it in the movies.

But the drama backfired. The vodka went down the wrong way and he couldn't bring up a breath. Eugenia heard the awful wheeze and screech of his trying to breathe and she stood up.

"Lee, are you all right?"

Binstock couldn't answer, just kept trying to pull air up, desperately hoping that the block would give. He felt an instant away from being able to breathe again and at the same time an instant away from dying. He was terrified. It went on longer than he could have believed. He didn't think you could do without air for that long. People at the next table stared. The waiter appeared.

"Are you all right, sir?"

Eugenia came up from behind and grabbed him, pulling him up from his chair. She put her arms around his chest in some amateur's version of the rescue techniques they'd seen demonstrated on television. Then she squeezed hard. Binstock didn't want her to do that. He screeched even worse but felt a bit of air get through. Then, suddenly it was over. He could get a half breath in, then finally a sort of regular flow of air began.

All he could say was, "I'm sorry, I'm sorry . . . "

Binstock had never drunk so much so quickly and Eugenia had to put him to bed. But the alcohol made him edgy, alert even as it wore off. When Eugenia went to the kitchen to make coffee he sneaked into the bathroom and took a Valium—sneaked it because they both knew you didn't mix Valium and liquor. But when she came back with the coffee he told her; she just laughed and poured the coffee. "It's been that kind of day," she said. "Tearing up books, vodka, Valium, almost choking to death. Not necessarily in that order."

Sipping, sitting up, he said, "Maybe I was still competing with Sorkin."

"I don't think choking to death is highly recommended for suicide. Too painful, too unsure."

"It felt pretty close to dying — it feels that way when you can't breathe for so long."

"We keep talking about taking a course in CPR."

He put the empty cup down on the tray and lay back. "I feel like Lazarus back from the dead."

"How does it feel?"

"Strange. More peaceful than I've been for days, maybe weeks or months."

Eugenia picked up the tray to take it back to the kitchen. Binstock saw that her hands were trembling. He let her go without saying anything; he felt tranquil — too quick for the Valium — as if he'd come out on the other side of something. She came back to see him off to sleep and he was too sleepy now to notice if her hands were still shaky.

"Are you all right, Lee?"

"Yes. I'll get another job, a good one. Not to worry."

"You scared me to death when you couldn't breathe."

"Almost."

"Well, almost to death."

"I felt pretty close myself. No air, God . . . "

Eugenia tightened the sheets, smoothed the blankets with quick nervous movements and sat down on the bed.

"Will you be able to sleep?"

He was almost asleep already, he told her and, after all, he still had a mouth — to smile with, to kiss with, to eat with. Maybe a little more cautiously than before. Had he told her, he asked, with the odd solemnity of receding drunkenness, that he'd spent his childhood waiting in asthma clinics with his mother, that he'd desperately wanted to play the cello but they'd given him the clarinet instead because the doctor thought it would be good for his poor, constricted, twitchy lungs?"

"No." she said. "Did it work?"

"Yes. It worked, a lot of things work until they don't any-more." Eugenia folded blankets around him and said, "It's just an idea to you—a poem—but I've seen Oven Birds. They're a kind of warbler. We had lots of them at the farm in Haddam before my grandfather sold it. A brown back with white across the breast. It has a funny cry—it goes: Teacherteacherteacher-teacherTEACHER getting louder and louder—then it stops."

"Country girl," he murmured. "If it's a teacher we can ask it what all this means, what's happened to us."

"Maybe it doesn't know, maybe it's only calling for *its* teacher. And besides, it's a bird that doesn't answer ques-tions—only asks—and only asks one question, according to the poem . . . 'What to make of—' "

"Yes."

He murmured, "I wonder, did Sorkin's suicide note do this to us, tonight, or was it Mister Frost's bird?" He began to drift off even though he wanted to stay and be of some comfort to her as she had been to him, but he was too far gone. The risk of danger from mixing vodka and Valium was apparently avoided but not the drowsiness.

Drifting into sleep Binstock thinks about his mother, stand-ing in line at the clinic, holding the card with the visits checked off—her calm manner hiding the nervous chain-smoker, the courageous woman afraid of everything, supervising his pre-scribed home exercises: breathe in deeply, breathe out even more deeply, empty your lungs—push. His mother who'd always made do with so little, asked even less, but had been granted at least the largesse of height—a statuesque, lofty carriage. And Binstock remembers how even that had dimin-ished at the last, and she cast a short, sickly shadow on the way out.

Binstock wakes in a sudden state of joy. It is almost morning going by the light seeping in at the corners of the shutters. His mouth is dry and his head hurts but he has the answer. With the foolish clarity of dreams it presents itself as a sub-limely simple solution: sell the clarinet. He knows it is irra-tional, that it solves nothing, but somehow removing the physical presence of the clarinet as a reminder of loss, of what could no longer be performed at least not decently, feels like a freedom. Once it is out of the house Binstock can start again — find new opportunities, new consolations. He wonders how much you could get for a used Buffet B-flat clarinet in good condition. Quietly, Binstock steps out of bed, past his sleeping wife, out of the bedroom.

He unhooks the case and holds up the instrument. The silver keys glimmer in a strobe of light as he turns it in his hands, the black wood gleaming the only way wood knows how to gleam when competing with silver, but lovely in its own dark ways. If he kept it, it would not be like other clarinets, would never again sing the Brahms or the Mozart . . .

He hears the echo of the lines and goes into the living room where the ripped Frost book is still lying on the couch. He finds:

> *The bird would cease and be as other birds*
> *But that he knows in singing not to sing.*

His eyes roam the page looking for other lines that had pissed him off in yesterday's state of rage — confusing him but not consoling. It is different this morning. In the kitchen, holding the book, Binstock pours himself a glass of orange juice, comes back to the couch and reads the fourteen lines. Then he gets a white-lined pad from his desk, takes out the Montblanc fountain pen Eugenia had bought him when they'd first made him a vice-president at Merrill Lynch. He begins to copy out the sonnet. It is comforting to roll out the words; he understands why people in mourning go back to school so often.

Binstock thinks — this is not such a big deal. It's as if he'd spent his life reading and understanding poems.

> *There is a singer everyone has heard,*
> *Loud, a mid-summer and a mid-wood bird,*
> *Who makes the solid tree trunks sound again.*

A pause to reread. Mid-summer is what counts here, he
thinks. For this miserable bird mid-summer is already too late,
the peak is over. God! What a pain.

He says that leaves are old and that for flowers
Mid-summer is to spring as one to ten.

Mid-summer is practically the end of everything compared
to spring. And old leaves—a mysterious phrase: how old can
leaves be? Every year they must age about the same before
they fall . . .

He says the early petal-fall is past
When pear and cherry bloom went down in showers
On sunny days a moment overcast;

Everything good seems to be past—which rhymes with overcast . . . downer after downer . . .

And comes that other fall we name the fall.
He says the highway dust is over all.

The rabbi at the funeral chapel had made the obligatory
remarks concerning dust. It is no longer a problem to connect
poor Sorkin at the end of his rope with these lines. Binstock
writes slowly, with care:

The bird would cease and be as other birds
But that he knows in singing not to sing.

The strangest lines of all, these two. How do you not sing
while singing? Perhaps you just sang more quietly, a lesser
melody.

The question that he frames in all but words
Is what to make of a diminished thing.

Binstock sits back, the poem before him. It is as if he's just created it instead of simply copying it out to get it straight in his head. Everybody seemed to be writing this poem, singing this song these days. He remembered Tarloff, the company's third president in two years, taking him to lunch to say good-bye.

"It's not just that we're facing hard times here at the firm or even here in America."

"No?"

"We're looking at a worldwide diminution of assets." Tarloff's gnarled hands shaped — what? An apple? A melon?

"Just imagine, Lee, that this whole globe we live on was of a certain diameter, worth a certain amount — something so large, of course, no computer could even figure it out. And now, it's just — shrunk." His hands collapsed to a smaller apple or melon. "The value of the whole world as we know it. Permanently. It was worth X in total. Now it's worth V. Simple as that."

Binstock had not asked if that was why they'd had to let him go. It was a lofty reason, very classy; but he was afraid it might come down to something not quite so elegant. It was perhaps not that the dollar value of the planet earth had shrunk; more like the fact it was November, his end of the year bonus would have been substantial and Tarloff needed every penny to keep the place afloat. Or because he had worked closely with Sorkin and was afraid Binstock might be implicated in that mess. The firm didn't need one more arrest on the business pages of *The New York Times*. But instead of asking he'd just laughed nervously. And Tarloff had asked if Binstock had understood what he was saying and Binstock had said oh, yes, he understood it quite well.

He walked back to the bedroom to the edge of the bed. Eugenia slept, lightly snoring, her sweet mouth pushed open and closed by the push and pull of breathe. Binstock stood by the bed waiting, watching her breathe, anxious and grateful. When she woke he would tell her, "I saw Jenny Maslow this afternoon. I tried to find the poem in the library and I couldn't. Sorkin mixed up Sandburg and Frost and I figured Jenny would know."

She would say, "Oh?", noncommittal as usual in these matters. He was the one who was jealous of ex-husbands, ex-lovers. Eugenia lacked the jealous gene. For her love and sex were one and entirely in the present.

He remembered their first sexual play, one, two, three times until one night she asked, why always three, one good is better than three any which way. But forced or natural, he mourned the energy of youth which could play the games it wished — could push to the edge, foolish bravado or not.

Gone now was their Italian driving all night on impulse in the warm rain, stopping in a hilltop town at midnight, the piazzas mysterious in the moonlight, the ubiquitous cats lurking around silent fountains, the pensiones all full or shut, the first one no, the second one no, the third pensione seedy but offering a room, the walls damp, the bed not made up, one towel for both of them, too exhausted for anything more interesting than sleep but holding each other anyway, almost too tired to make love so love made them, falling asleep on scratchy sheets the instant after. Later, of course, came the careful planning of travel, the well-planned reservations with the precisely specified rooms.

Eugenia rolled to her side; her eyelids fluttered. When she saw him standing there she called out his name. Binstock sat down next to her. Eugenia laid her head on his chest and she suddenly shook with tears. He didn't know what to do except hold her and stupidly say, "What is it, what is it?"

She spoke between sobs as children do, hard to hear at first, almost a whisper, then louder and louder. "I thought there would be more time . . . I thought we would have a child, maybe two by now . . . I wanted to start a real magazine one day . . . *Partisan Review*, *Vanity Fair* I don't know what but not just a newletter that tells everybody — stuff . . . I majored in literature not journalism . . . When my sister died so young

I knew I would always feel less than before . . . everything *is* less than before . . . we make love less . . . we probably waited too long to start children and now maybe we can't . . . "

She lifted her head from his chest, blinking at Binstock.

"Do you know," she said, "I had to start holding my head at a funny angle because I couldn't hear clearly with my left ear, do you know that was when I was only fourteen? I didn't tell you when we got married because I was ashamed to be losing such serious things still so young. I don't know which is a worse diminished thing—the body or the way the mind dreams and then gives up dreaming. For God's sake I'm thirty-eight. Isn't that too young for all this?"

She sobbed lightly, exhausted by her own emotions.

"I knew about that," he lied. "I just ignored it."

Binstock forgot about telling her he'd seen Jenny, forgot about selling the clarinet, a dumb idea whose joy was just as dumb, just as temporary. Instead he held Eugenia tightly, miserable at hearing so many unspoken regrets.

After a few moments he got up and went to the end table and got the round metal ashtray which had not been used since he'd given up cigars two years ago—now as useless an object as his clarinet. He crumpled up the piece of paper on which he'd written the Frost poem and found his old lighter in a bureau drawer. It was mysterious, a morning flame inside their bedroom. Eugenia pulled herself up on one elbow and watched the poem burn into black and white and then into crumbs of black.

She murmured, "What are you doing?"

When he told her, she nodded. Binstock watched her watching the embers. It was as if his wife had been his partner in writing the poem down in order to figure out what to make of it, as if copying and then burning poems was an ordinary event. She'd woken up, weeping variations on the same theme. The Oven Bird was a tough teacher. Sorkin had learned the hard way. Now it was their turn. Subtraction was the law and the sentence. Everything else was just a plea bargain.

Afterwards, Binstock was starved, the way you are sometimes after a funeral or after making love. He and Eugenia covered the kitchen table with smoked salmon, cream cheese, breads, jams and had a feast.

"You know," she said, trying not to spill her coffee, her mouth full of sweet strawberry jam. "The important part, the part we sort of missed, is 'what to *make* of a diminished thing.' The ball, as we say when we play tennis, is in our court."

"Yes," Binstock said. "That's what the bird *wants* you to think."

Primo Levi
The Art of Fiction CXL

Born in Turin in 1919 of middle-class parents whose ancestors fled the Spanish Inquisition, Primo Levi was subjected in the thirties first to Italian racial laws that threatened his academic studies, and then to German racial edicts that threatened his life. Because of a sympathetic professor who agreed to be his dissertation advisor, he finished his studies at the University of Turin, where he was granted a Ph.D. in chemistry that eventually saved him. Early in 1943, Levi left Turin with a group of ten friends and fled to the mountains with the intention of joining Giustizia e Liberta, *the Italian resistance movement. These plans were aborted when Levi was arrested in December of that year by the Fascists, to whom he admitted being a Jew. By February 1944, he was imprisoned in Auschwitz. There, working in a chemical laboratory but expecting death at any moment, he knew he was living what he called "the fundamental experience" of his life.*

After the war's end, he returned to Turin where he resumed his profession of chemist. In 1948, the year after his first book, Survival in Auschwitz, *was published (if hardly noticed) he was made manager of a laboratory in a paint factory, the position he held until he retired in 1977. In 1975 he published* The Periodic Table, *in which, among other things, he acknowledged his debt to his scientific profession. Widely recognized by this time as one of Italy's most important writers, he continued to produce poetry, memoirs, fiction and essays.*

Levi committed suicide in 1987 — hurling himself over the railing of the marble staircase outside his fourth-floor apartment. It was the same apartment in which he was born in 1919, where he and his wife raised their children and where this interview took place in July 1985. When we met, Levi led me into his study, where we sat on a leather couch and drank coffee served by the Levi's maid. A computer sat on the desk, and Levi mentioned how useful it was to him in composing his fiction. Like Levi himself, the room, whose windows looked out on the Corso Re Umberto, was extremely neat and well ordered.

In his person as in his writing, Primo Levi was a master of the understated. Speaking gently but animatedly and with the wry sense of humor that became increasingly evident in his later work, he ranged over topics as diverse as Tzvetan Todorov's theory of language, Italy's socio-economic structure and the need to have all scientists study ethics in the university as part of their training.

Patient, soft-spoken, diffident, Primo Levi was nevertheless capable of intense passion. Relating the fundamental concerns of life to science, particularly its concision and precision, Primo Levi was able to perfect his art. The Periodic Table, *a history of his family as well as of his time, is also a history of his own evolution from a scientist to a writer, which he relates metaphorically in the story of the carbon atom. In "Carbon," the last chapter of the book, Levi presents one of his major themes: the representation of matter as the universal thread that not only connects one life to another, not only to all life itself, but also to the very matter from which life is derived. Thus, that infinitesimal trace of matter, that particle of carbon, takes on symbolic significance of cosmological proportions.*

The year before he jumped to his death, Levi published The Drowned and the Saved *in which he spoke of the pain he suffered from having been a prisoner at Auschwitz, the shame that continued to torment him, the revulsion he still felt not only towards those who participated in the brutality but also towards those who could have but did not speak out against it. He believed, as he mentioned during our meeting, that all people have a responsibilty to each other as well as to other living things, not only because of our moral and ethical tradition, but also because, whether ape or apple, we are all made up of the same material.*

INTERVIEWER

Could you say something about your education?

PRIMO LEVI

I had a classical education. Training in writing was serious. Oddly enough, I wasn't fond of the Italian literature program. I was fond of chemistry, so I refused the humanistic teaching of literature, but as matters go it entered me through the skin without my knowing. I engaged in a sort of polemic against my teachers because they insisted on proper construction of the phrases and so on. I was very cross with them because to me it was a waste of time when what I was looking for was a comprehension of the universal meanings—of the stars, the moon, microbes, animals, plants, chemistry and so on. All the rest—history, philosophy and so on—was simply a barrier to be crossed so I could get my diploma and enter the university.

INTERVIEWER

Your books suggest a deep as well as a very broad reading —
American, Italian, German literature.

LEVI

Yes, my father was fond of reading. And so, although he
was not very rich, he was generous in giving me books. It
was different then. Today, it's easier to find foreign books
everywhere — translated or not. You just go to a bookshop,
and everything is there. At that time, it was not easy because
the Fascists were very keen about distinguishing: this book —
yes, this book — no. They allowed, for instance, translated English or American books if they were critical of English or
American society. The books of D.H. Lawrence about life in
the coal mines were not only published in Italy but distributed
widely because they were so critical of the condition of miners
in England. The implication was that Italian miners' lives were
not like this. Lawrence mistook Fascism for a romantic adventure, one reason more for translating him. Yes. The Fascist
censors were intelligent, in their way. Admitting something,
and excluding something else. Like Hemingway, for instance.
Hemingway had been a quasi-pseudo-communist in Spain.
His books in translation came into Italy only after the War.
My father let me read Freud, for instance, at twelve.

INTERVIEWER

Really!

LEVI

Illegally. Freud was not admitted. But my father managed
to have a translation of *The Introduction to Psychoanalysis*.
I didn't understand it.

INTERVIEWER

What about other American writers? Mark Twain? Walt
Whitman?

LEVI

Mark Twain was politically neutral. Who else? John Dos Passos. Translated. Sholem Asch. Translated. Well, Italy was not completely cut off from abroad. Melville was translated by Pavese. *Moby-Dick* was a discovery; it had no political implications. I read it at twenty. I was not a boy anymore, but I was fascinated by him. Cesare Pavese was one of the great translators though hardly orthodox. He distorted it, fit it into the Italian language. He wasn't a seaman — Pavese — he hated the sea. So, he had to prepare himself. I knew him. I met him twice before he committed suicide. In 1950, at full literary success, he killed himself in a room in the Hotel Bologna — for mysterious reasons, but then every suicide is mysterious. He had sex difficulties, apparently, without really being impotent. A sort of sexual timidity. Moreover, he was a very complicated man. He was never satisfied with his work as a writer. Political difficulties too — because he was a follower of communism during the war, but hadn't the courage to go in to the resistance. And so after the war, he had a sort of guilt complex for not having fought the Germans. These are some reasons for his suicide. But I don't think I have exhausted them.

INTERVIEWER

In *The Periodic Table*, you talk of the difference between the spirit and matter, suggesting that only through matter can we understand the universe and its components.

LEVI

The Fascist philosophy insisted a lot upon spirit. The slogan was: "It is the spirit that masters matter." For instance, the Italian Army was badly equipped but if its spirits dominated matter, so we could win a war even without the equipment. The idea was that if you had the spirit, you'd be able to win. It was foolish, but it dominated the mood of the school. In the language taught us in philosophy hours, the word spirit had a very ambiguous meaning. Most of my comrades accepted it. I was cross with this insisting upon spirit. What is spirit? Spirit isn't soul. I was not a believer; I am not a believer. Spirit is something you can't touch. At that time it seemed to me an official lie insisting upon something you can't experience with your eyes, your ears, with your fingers.

INTERVIEWER

There's a danger in the spirit . . . that it can control reason.

LEVI

Mind you, spirit is instinct not reason. In fact, reason was discouraged because it was the tool of criticism. In their language, spirit was something very indefinite. A good citizen has to be tuned . . . You know Orwell? Do you remember the afterword of *1984* about Newspeak? It was copied from totalitarianism. The fact was many things in Fascist Italy didn't work at all. But teaching did. They were careful about having anti-Fascist teachers discarded, thrown away, or punishing them, and having enthusiastic teachers instead of them. So Fascist ideas painlessly penetrated, one of them this preeminence of spirit and not matter — the very reason I chose to be a chemist, to have something under my fingers which could be verified as true or false.

INTERVIEWER

The spirit can never be proven except by those who believe.

LEVI

Yes. The same problems discussed by Plato are still discussed. There is no end to the discussion about what it means to be, to exist, if the soul is immortal or not. To the contrary, with the natural sciences any idea can be proved or disproved. Thus it was a relief for me to shift from indefinite discussions to something concrete, to what can be tested in the laboratory, in the test tube. You see it, you feel it.

INTERVIEWER

The question of science and ethics or morality comes to mind as one reads your work. Is the scientist expected to be more ethical than other professionals?

LEVI

I expect everyone to be ethical. But I don't think scientific training as one is taught in Italy or America brings you to an especially ethical consciousness. It should. In my opinion a young man or woman entering the university in natural science departments should be told sufficiently and heavily: remember you are entering a profession where morality is important. There is a difference between a chemist working in a paint factory like me or in a poison gas factory. You should be conscious of your impact in real life. You should be able to refuse some jobs, some employments.

INTERVIEWER

What you are saying comes through in your writing. So does what is allied to loyalty, love of a friend. Sandro, for

Primo Levi in a chemistry laboratory in 1985.

instance, in *The Periodic Table*. It's a very touching part of
the text when you say, "Nothing of him remains—nothing
but words, precisely." But you've made him live again through
the words.

LEVI

Yes, for the reader. Not for me. It was the best approxima-
tion I could reach on the printed page. There is always a
difference between a portrait and a living individual.

INTERVIEWER

He would regard your tribute to him with pleasure.

LEVI

Sandro would laugh. Oddly enough, I had not a quarrel,
but a conflict with his family, because they did not recognize
him. It is always like this. If you attempt to put any individual
who's alive onto a printed page, you put him at unease, even
if you have the best intentions to improve his or her qualities.
Everybody has an image of himself. It's very rare that your
personal image of yourself coincides with the one described
by an observer. Even if the image in the book is more beautiful,
it's not the same. It's as if you go to a mirror and find a face
nicer than yours, but not yours. I wonder if you remember
in *The Periodic Table* the story about phosphorous?

INTERVIEWER

Oh yes.

LEVI

The young lady in it is a friend of mine. After I wrote the
chapter about her, I went to Milan where she lives and gave
her the manuscript. I told her, "I've written a story about
you and me, slightly clouded up. I would like to have your
permission to print it." She gave her permission, but because
she is married, I read on her face a slight sense of uneasiness,
embarrassment. In fact, I had changed her person for obvious

reasons not to have her recognizable. "Well," she said, "Okay, I'm glad, I'm happy, I'm satisfied . . . " but she wasn't.

INTERVIEWER

How about the man who created the college reunion in *The Periodic Table*?

LEVI

Well, he's an artifact. When your character is not first-rate — stupid or clumsy — it's good politics to reconstruct him from different parts. I took a forehead from one man, the chin from another, the tics from a third and so on. Despite all that . . .

INTERVIEWER

They all say, "That's me!"

LEVI

I met the one who had the trembling hands. He didn't tell me anything, but he didn't praise the book. He was cold with me.

INTERVIEWER

I suppose that's the penalty one pays. *The Periodic Table* is different from your other books in language and style. What is your awareness of what some call the new fiction or Neorealism? Italo Calvino is considered to be a writer who belongs to that group.

LEVI

That's a difficult question. Calvino began in the wake of Neorealism, but he minted a style and a personality so personal that you can't classify him in any way. I am often asked to which current I belong. I don't know. It doesn't interest me at all. Of course, in Calvino's writing — we have been friends for a long time — or in my writings you can find traces of dozens of writers: recent, classical, Dante, Virgil and so on. They are all packed together. My background as a chemist weighs much more than what I've read. In fact, it does. It brings me new raw material. For Calvino, it was his travels, his stay in Paris, his coming in touch with important French intellectuals. All of this had a very heavy impact on his writing. Whether he's aware of it or not, I don't know.

INTERVIEWER

Wasn't he also trained as a scientist?

LEVI

Not exactly. His father and mother were keepers of a botanical garden, first in Cuba and then in San Remo, Italy. And so his childhood was spent in botanical gardens with plants, animals, beasts. He's very attentive to new conquests of science, astronomy and chemistry.

INTERVIEWER

Your career as a scientist also broadened your knowledge of languages. Is that how you learned English and German?

LEVI

I used to speak English when I was a chemist in the factory and talked to customers. But shoptalk is easier. The first time I went to the U.S. and appeared before an audience was the first time I spoke English continuously for more than ten minutes. Before an audience I was clumsy. People asked questions from far in the back, sometimes with different or blurred accents so that I had to ask somebody to translate from English into English! My difficulty is not in talking; my difficulty is in understanding. I have studied very little English methodically, but I do read a lot of books. My lexicon is rich. Many times I know a word but not its pronunciation.

INTERVIEWER

What about your knowledge of the German language?

LEVI

I learned German in a concentration camp. My English is incomplete but civil, polite. My German is not, wasn't. Not very polite. It was barracks German. I learned it in Auschwitz for reasons of survival. It was, in that life, necessary to understand in order to live. In fact, many comrades of mine died for lack of understanding. They were suddenly parachuted, dropped into a world speaking German or Yiddish or Polish. Almost no Italian speakers — it is unusual in Italy to study German and, of course, nothing of Polish or Yiddish. So it was a world of utter incomprehension. It was maddening, it drove me crazy. In fact, I remember with horror the first days, when luckily I knew some German from chemistry — because at that time chemistry was a German art. Many texts were in German, and I had studied some German to follow them. So I was not completely blank. But I hurried to friends, comrades from Alsace-Lorraine who were bilingual. "Please give me lessons quickly to understand what this shouting means." The Germans used to shout orders, very rough . . . in their style like a dog barking. Well, I managed to learn some German, but in the camp it was sort of pidgin German, mixed with Polish, with Yiddish words. It was not polite German. After some years, in 1951, I went to a town near Cologne on business. After discussing matters, one of the Germans said, "Look, it is very strange for an Italian to speak German. But your German is a weird one. Where did you learn to speak this way?" And I purposely told him abruptly, "Yes sir. It was in a concentration camp. Auschwitz." And then it was like a curtain fell. I used to do the same with other people. I don't resent it, but it was like a . . . litmus test with whom I was speaking. The way he or she behaved was a sign — if he was a Nazi, as most of them were, or if he worked in a concentration camp.

After that, of course, I tried to polish up my German to civilize it, to make it presentable — especially the accent. I have no conditioned reflex towards the language. I don't resent speaking German or hearing German. I think German is a noble language — the language of Goethe, of Gotthold Lessing. The language itself has nothing to do with the Nazis;

it was distorted by the Nazis. Enough about German! Today's
Germany is not a Nazi Germany anymore.

INTERVIEWER

So you don't feel uncomfortable going there today?

LEVI

Generally not. It's different with Poland and Russia. In
Poland I was in Auschwitz twice for memorial services. I found
a far different Poland: A country profoundly divided, very
lively, a concentration of tensions, of interests, of mixed feeling toward Russians, toward Germans, toward Jews.

INTERVIEWER

Are they still strongly anti-Semitic in Poland today?

LEVI

They're not any more. For lack of material! Only about
five thousand Jews left. Half of them in the government — as
functionaries. And half of them in Solidarity.

INTERVIEWER

When you were a prisoner, did you expect to receive more
humane treatment from scientists who recognized your own
scientific background?

LEVI

I didn't expect it. My story was an exception. Because they
discovered my background as a chemist, I worked in a chemical
laboratory. We were three out of ten thousand prisoners. My
personal position was extremely exceptional, like the position
or situation of every survivor. A normal prisoner died. That
was his escape. After passing an examination in chemistry, I
expected something more from my bosses. But the only one
who had a trace of human comprehension towards me was
Dr. Müller, my supervisor at the laboratory. We discussed it
after the war in our letters. He was an average man, not a

hero and not a barbarian. He had no inkling of our condition. He had been transferred to Auschwitz a few days before. So he was confused. They told him: Yes, in our laboratories, in our factories we employ prisoners. They are fiends, they are adversaries of our government. We put them to work to exploit them, but you are not supposed to talk with them. They are dangerous, they are communists, they are murderers. So put them to work but don't keep in touch with them. This man Müller was a clumsy man, not very clever. He was not a Nazi. He had some traces of humanity. He noticed I was unshaven and asked me why. Look, I told him, we haven't any razor, we haven't even a handkerchief. We are completely naked. Deprived of everything. He gave me a requisition that I must be shaven twice a week, which wasn't really a help, but a sign. Moreover, he noticed I had wooden clogs. Noisy and uncomfortable. He asked me why. I told him our shoes were taken away the first day. These are our uniform, standard. He made me have leather shoes. This was an advantage because wooden clogs were a torture. I still have the scars made by the clogs. If you are not used to them, after a half-mile walking, your feet are bleeding and encrusted with dirt and so on, and they become infected. To have leather shoes was an important advantage. So I contracted a sort of gratefulness to this man. He was not very courageous. He was afraid of the SS, like me. He was interested in my work being useful, not in persecuting me. He had nothing against Jews, against prisoners. He just expected us to be effective workers. This story about him in *The Periodic Table* is completely real. I never got a chance to meet him after the war. He died a few days before our appointment to meet. He phoned from a spa in Germany where he was recovering his health. As far as I know, his death was natural. But I don't know. I purposely left it undecided in *The Periodic Table* . . . to leave the reader in doubt, as I was.

INTERVIEWER

Tell me about Lorenzo, the man who gave you food.

LEVI

It was a different thing for Lorenzo. He was a sensitive man, almost illiterate but really sort of a saint. After the war, when I met him in Italy, he told me that he didn't help only me. He helped three or four prisoners without telling one he was helping another one. Mind you, we almost never spoke. He was a very silent man. He refused my thanks. He almost didn't reply to my words. He just shrugged. "Take the bread. Take the sugar. Keep silent, you don't need to speak."

Afterward, when I tried to rescue him, he was difficult to reach, to talk to him. He was . . . very ignorant, almost illiterate, hardly able to write. He was not religious; he didn't know the gospel, but instinctively he tried to rescue people, not for pride, not for glory, but out of a good heart and for human comprehension. He asked me once in very laconic words: "Why are we in the world if not to help each other?" Stop. Period. But he was afraid of the world. Having seen people die like flies at Auschwitz, he wasn't happy anymore. He was not a Jew, not a prisoner himself. But he was very sensitive. After he returned home, he took to drinking. I went to him — he lived not far from Turin — to persuade him to stop drinking. He had abandoned his job as a bricklayer and used to buy and sell scrap iron because he was an alcoholic. He drank every lira he earned. I asked him why and he told me outspokenly: "I don't like to live any more. I am fed up with life. . . . After seeing this menace of the atom bomb . . . I think I have seen everything. . . ." He had understood many things, but he did not even realize where he had been: Instead of "Auschwitz," he used to say "Au-Schwiss" like Switzerland. He was confused in his geography. He couldn't follow a timetable. He would get drunk and sleep in the snow, completely drunk with wine. He got tuberculosis. I sent him to be cured in the hospital. But they did not give him wine, so he escaped. He died of tuberculosis and of alcohol. Yes. It was really suicide.

INTERVIEWER

When you worked in a paint factory you had a superior who appreciated your literary ambitions.

LEVI

He was a very clever, an intelligent man but at the same time there was a tacit understanding between us. You, Primo Levi, are supposed to be a writer in your spare time but not in the factory. He was proud to have a writer as a chemical director, but he never spoke about that, though I knew he did boast to other people. Afterwards, when I got a pension, we became friends. We invited each other to lunch.

INTERVIEWER

You didn't do that before?

LEVI

No. I wasn't that rich to be able to invite him to a fashionable restaurant. It would have been a transgression. He knew how much I earned. And I didn't earn anything by writing at that time. I lived out of my salary.

INTERVIEWER

You couldn't invite him to your home for dinner?

LEVI

He never came here. Sometimes I went to his house when there was a party, but the revenue difference was so high— he was a millionaire and I was his dependent. So it was a very sharp division. Now it is not like this anymore.

INTERVIEWER

Heinrich Böll has been quoted as saying that one of the reasons the Germans allowed the holocaust to take place was that they were too law-abiding; they listened to the law. One of the things you say about the Italians is that they are not law-abiding.

LEVI

Yes. That's the main difference between the Italian Fascism and the German kind, the Nazis. We used to say that Fascism

is a tyranny made milder on account of our general disregard
of the laws. And it was like this. Many, many Italian Jews
were rescued on account of that. When laws are bad, disre-
garding laws is a good thing. Generally speaking, there is no
xenophobia in Italy. Having seen something of the world, in
Europe and elsewhere, I'm not unhappy being Italian. Of
course, I know our defects very well. We have never been able
to express a political class worthy of the name. Our government
is weak, not solid; we have corruption. In my opinion, our
most serious diseases are the schools and the health policy,
which is terrible. The teaching class is made of men and women
in their forties who took part the upheaval of 1968, and many
of them didn't study at all, didn't specialize in anything. How
can you teach without having been taught? They refused culture for activism, adventure, quarrels, politics and so on. Now,
they are a majority of the teaching class. Their pupils resent
it. Their textbooks are terrible.

INTERVIEWER

I notice in your work, and even as we talk, that in spite of
the things that have happened to you, you show no animosity,
no hatred.

LEVI

It's a question of natural hormones. In situations where I
should get angry, with my children, for instance, when they
were young and it would have been better to have a fit of
anger to impress them, well, I was never able to. It's not a
virtue, it's a defect. I have many times been praised for my
lack of animosity towards the Germans. It's not a philosophical
virtue. It's a habit of having my second reactions before the
first. So before heating myself to a fit of anger, I begin reason-
ing. And generally the reason prevails. That doesn't mean
I'm prepared to forgive the Germans, I'm not. And I would
prefer — although I am Italian — the law to prevail over personal resentment. I was happy when Eichmann was captured

and brought before a tribunal and executed — although I am opposed to the death penalty. In this case it was all right. I had no doubt about that. But if I told you I hated Eichmann, I would be lying. My first reaction was to try to understand him. Two months ago I was asked by my publisher to write the preface to a book by Rudolph Hess. Do you know him? The commander of Auschwitz. It is a first-class book in my opinion. I wrote more or less like this: Generally, when a writer is asked for the preface of a book it is because he loves this book, because he thinks this book is beautiful. Well, dear reader, this book is not beautiful. I don't love it, I hate it. But it is very important because it teaches you how a normal man can be distorted by a regime into becoming a murderer of millions. Hess had in fact a difficult youth . . . put to fighting the *fedayeen* in Iraq during the First World War. Anyway, he was not made out of other stuff than you and me. The human stuff he had. He was not born a criminal. He was not a freak. He was of standard human matter. But entering into this channel of nationalism and after that of Nazi education, his training made him into a *Jasager* — the one who always says Yes. Law-abiding. Böll was right, Hess was the typical German. He didn't mind in that epoch if the law coincided with the words of Hitler and Himmler. He said quite sincerely that it would have been impossible for him and his fellow Germans to disregard an order by Himmler. It was not to be thought of. They were trained to follow punctually every kind of order — not to judge the content of the order. Just to obey.

INTERVIEWER

Matter is honest and irreproachable. Spirit, since to understand is irrelevant, can bring destruction and deceit. That's why I think you say Mendeleyev's periodic table becomes poetry.

LEVI

It's a joke in fact. Have you ever seen the periodic table?

I've seen it in chemistry classes.

LEVI

It reads like a poem because you have lines, every one ending with a kind of element, like a rhyme. It's a very stretched simile. It is admitted in the text, told as a paradox to Sandro: "Look, it's like a poem. As you have rhymes, you have rhymes here too." But, of course, there is something hidden behind this paradox. In fact, I think there is something really poetic about science and chemistry in understanding matter. In my opinion, Galileo was one of the most important writers in Italy, although he is not considered as such; his texts, which I have, are wonderful for precision and concision. And he had something to say. In my opinion, for a writer having something to say is very important. If a writer is convinced that he is honest, has something fundamental to say, then it is very difficult for him to be a bad writer. He is obliged to carry, to convey his ideas in a clear way. On the other hand, if a writer hasn't anything to tell, even if he possesses the tools of writing, he's second rate.

INTERVIEWER

The Periodic Table has got a quality to it that shows that if you had not been a prisoner at Auschwitz you would still have been a writer.

LEVI

The question I am most often asked: If you hadn't been an inmate, what would you have become? I am not able to reply. I am so ingrained, so intertwined with my condition of a chemist and of an Auschwitz inmate that I can't distinguish anymore my other personality from that one. In fact, when at the *liceo* — the *liceo* is the high school, I was very weak in Italian. They taught me to imitate the top writers, to imitate Dante. I didn't feel like this. I didn't feel like imitating any-

body. But I did imitate many of them unconsciously. I resented
being invited to model myself on these writers. And so I was
a very poor student in Italian, in fact I almost flunked. I was
in despair. The top mark is ten; my mark was three. Three
of us had threes and two of us are now writers. The second
one is Fernanda Pivano, a friend of Pavese and Hemingway.
She is a critic of American literature. Well, two out of three
became writers. Although I was suspicious toward literature,
I have always been fascinated by the history of languages. As
a child, at eleven, I asked my father to give me a book on
etymologies. And I kept it as a treasure. Well, I do remember
that when in concentration camp, although as you know, the
conditions were of hunger, cold and so on, I was fascinated
by the language and by the similarity between German and
English. In the few hours of respite, I pondered the similarities
and dissimilarities. Why German had developed such a complicated grammar and English such a simplified one. I never
studied systematically languages, theory.

INTERVIEWER

You had contact with Greek Jews?

LEVI

Yes, we managed to understand each other because they
spoke Ladino and I spoke Italian. They were very hard-boiled
because there were very few survivors of the deportation from
Salonika, which took place two years before. The survivors
were sly. They were without scruples. To be a survivor it's
useful not to be too kind, too mild. They weren't mild at all.
They were cooks or woodworkers. So, not very reliable people,
but we had something in common. Not being able to speak
Yiddish. So there was a trace of solidarity among us. Have
you read my book, *The Reawakening*? You remember Mordo
Nahum? I had mixed feelings toward him. I admired him as
a man fit for every situation. But of course he was very cruel
to me. He despised me because I was not able to manage. I

had no shoes. He told me: "Remember, when there is war, the first thing is shoes, and second is eating. Because if you have shoes, then you can run and steal. But you must have shoes." Yes, I told him, well you are right but there is not war any more. And he told me: *"Guerra es siempre."* There is always war.

— **Gabriel Motola**

A.R. Ammons

Picking up Equations

Not smart to be out under trees with the wind still this
high: billowing & breaking bring down stob ends

of last year's drought-wood that died way up in the branches,
and a thwack on the noggin could drop you, no one around

to see after you or call the physician, or you could just be
dazzled and wander off down the road, wild: still, don't

you like picking up storm cast, swatches of leaves snapped
off, bark rippings, to weigh the wind's reach each thing

gave to, how high they held or hung, what angle brought
them down: one thing's certain, fall shadows the wind,
ellipses, sprung, noding downwind to the arc including
   everything.

Two Poems by Linda Stern Zisquit

Unopened Letters

An unopened letter is like
an uninterpreted dream.
                — The Talmud

My brother's eye was painted
clear in family portraits.
At ten I saw the cloudy
cataract he was born with,
and in that paint my mother's
denial of deviance.
He stole cars parked out front, and
I'd watch from the second floor
master bedroom. He managed
card games, smoky secret clubs
in our basement. I was his
sidekick until mother screamed
'criminals!' We chased after
everything she denied us,
caught in our magic vision,
family blindness and doom.

Body Shop

Wherever else I seek
hasn't his grip or gear.

Always withdrawn into his own
mechanics, there I find him

puttering around, there
a place reserved for my

repair. Come at the wrong
time, it's bound to be

disaster. Tap lightly
at the edge, a sound does

reach him. I know because
I've witnessed his reception.

Having lost worlds once,
I won't think round again,

or whole. It's another way
of seeing, in pieces, in

parts. Anyhow it's all
a rendering, so why not

entrust the old reliable
to his garage, try this one

on for size, test if it
fits, see how it goes.

Peter Gizzi

A World Entire

At sunset the mill workers convene at the tavern
talking of their children and how they bathed them in a cistern.
One man compared the evening sunset to his boy's letter
which he carried everywhere and kept on his person.
He recalled the patterned light display during the ceremony
of his only child's interment by the shadow of a lantern.

At their home they light that same funerary lantern
as he walks each evening home from the tavern
by its light remembering a brighter day — the ceremony
of his son's name day, he held so small above the cistern.
That day filled with joy and the promise of a person.
Yes it is a world entire for him contained in a letter.

It was their ritual to listen to the man read from his letter.
On the way home the workers gather under the lantern
while the man reads to all the words from this person
he keeps in his vest pocket. The congregation of the tavern
is respectful of the man. And by the waters of the cistern
in the yard under the lantern they conduct their small
    ceremony.

It is a world entire for them each night in that ceremony.
Listening to the distant words inscribed in the letter.
The workers refresh themselves with the waters of the cistern
and wash their tears as they recline beneath that lantern.
It is a world unto itself that convenes each night at the tavern
where the scales of all measure are in relation to each person.

It is the person they uphold and venerate. Yes the person
they take into their arms at the center of their ceremony.
He forever younger than the youngest man who lists at the tavern

as the night rebounds; and doubling the signals of the letter, words echo the patterned light of memory cast by a lantern. Then they are awakened by sprays from the sweet water cistern

and awakening they discover themselves. This very cistern has been percolating since the town's beginning and the person who built its basin is the founder. Above his grave a lantern stood. Today visitors gather to celebrate his story in a ceremony where a man reads a dedication from a child in the form of a letter.
This story, it's been said, was painted on the walls of the tavern.

The tavern is gone, a few stones are what's left of the cistern. Only six words survive the letter, deciphered by a person studying the ceremony, and the varied uses of the lantern.

Four Poems by Billy Collins

My Heart

It has a bronze covering inlaid with silver,
originally gilt;
the sides are decorated with openwork zoomorphic
panels depicting events in the history
of an unknown religion.
The convoluted top-piece shows a high
level of relief articulation
as do the interworked spirals at the edges.

It was presumably carried in the house-shaped
reliquary alongside it, an object of exceptional
ornament, one of the few such pieces extant.
The handle, worn smooth, indicates its use
in long-forgotten rituals, perhaps
of a sacrificial nature.

It is engirdled with an inventive example
of gold interlacing, no doubt of Celtic influence.
Previously thought to be a pre-Carolingian work,
it is now considered to be of more recent provenance,
perhaps the early nineteen-forties.

The ball at the center, visible
through the interstices of the lead webbing,
is composed possibly of jelly
or an early version of water,
certainly a liquid, remarkably suspended
within the encasement of such intricate craftsmanship.

Sunday Morning with the Sensational Nightingales

It was not the Five Mississippi Blind Boys
who hoisted me off the ground
that morning as I drove down
to get the Sunday paper, some oranges and bread.
Nor was it the Dixie Hummingbirds
or the Soul Stirrers, despite their quickening name,
or even the Swan Silvertones
who inspired me to cast my eyes
above the commotion of trees
into the open vault of the sky.

No, it was the Sensational Nightingales
who were singing on the gospel radio
station early that Sunday morning
and must be credited with the bumping up
of my spirit, the arousal of the mice within.

I always loved this harmony,
like four, sometimes five trains running
side by side over a contoured landscape —
make that a shimmering red-dirt landscape
with wildflowers growing along the silver tracks,
lace tablecloths covering the hills,
and men and women in white shirts and dresses
walking toward a tall steeple:
Sunday morning in a perfect Georgia.

But I am not here to describe the sound
(the tenor whine, sepulchral bass,
the alto and baritone fitted in between)
only to witness my own minor elevation

that morning as they sang, so parallel,
about the usual themes,
the garden of suffering,
the beads of blood on the forehead,
the stone before the tomb,
and the ancient rolling waters
we would all have to cross some day.

God bless the Sensational Nightingales,
I thought as I turned up the volume,
God bless their children and their powder-blue suits.
They are a far cry from the quiet kneeling
I was raised with,
a far, hand-clapping cry from the candles
that glowed in the alcoves
and the eyes of the saints that fixed me
from their pedestals.

O, my cap was on straight that morning
and I was fine keeping the car on the road.
No one would ever have guessed
I was being lifted into the air by the beaks
of nightingales, unfurled like a long banner
curling across the empty blue sky,
announcing some highly cheerful tidings.

Workshop

I might as well begin by saying how much I like the title.
It gets me right away because I'm in a workshop now
so immediately the poem has my attention
like the ancient mariner grabbing me by the shirt.

And I like the first few stanzas,
the way they establish this mode of self-pointing
that runs through the whole poem
and tells us the words are food thrown down
on the ground for other words to eat.
I can almost taste the tail of the snake
in its own mouth,
if you know what I mean.

But what I'm not sure about is the voice
which sounds in places very casual, very blue jeans,
but other times seems very standoffish,
professorial in the worst sense of the word,
like the poem was going to be on the final.
But maybe that's just me.

What I did find engaging were the middle stanzas,
especially the fourth.
I like the image of clouds flying like lozenges,
which gives me a very clear picture.
And I really like how this drawbridge operator
just appears out of the blue
with his feet up on the iron railing
and his fishing pole jigging—I like jigging—
a hook in the slow industrial canal below.
I love slow industrial canal below. All the l's.

Maybe it's just me,
but the next stanza is where I start to have a problem.
I mean how can the evening bump into the stars?
And what's an obbligato of snow?
Also, I roam the decaffeinated streets.
At that point I'm lost. I need help.

The other thing that throws me off,
and maybe this is just me,
is the way the scene keeps shifting around.
First, we're in what seems like an aerodrome
and the speaker is inspecting a row of dirigibles,
which makes me think this could be a dream.
Then he takes us into his garden,
the part with the dahlias and the coiling hose,
though that's nice, the coiling hose,
and then I'm not sure where we're supposed to be.
The rain and the mint-green light,
that makes it feel outdoors, but what about the wallpaper?
Or is it a kind of indoor cemetery?
There's something about death going on here.

In fact, I start to wonder if what we have now
is really two poems, or three, or four,
or possibly none.

But then there's that last stanza, my favorite.
This is where the poem wins me back,
especially the lines that are spoken in the voice of the mouse.
I mean we've seen these images in cartoons before,
but I still love the details he uses
when he's describing where he lives.
The tiny arch of an entrance in the white baseboard,
his bed made out of a rolled-back sardine can,
the spool of thread for a table.
I start thinking about how hard the mouse had to work
night after night to steal all those things

while the people in the house were fast asleep,
and that gives me a very strong feeling,
a very powerful sense of something.
But I don't know if anyone else was feeling that.
Maybe that's just me.
Maybe that's just the way I read it.

Aristotle

This is the beginning.
Almost anything can happen.
This is where you find
the creation of light, a fish wriggling onto land,
the first word of *Paradise Lost* on an empty page.
Think of an egg, the letter A,
a woman ironing on a bare stage
as the heavy curtain rises.
This is the very beginning.
The first-person narrator introduces himself,
tells us about his lineage.
The mezzo-soprano stands in the wings.
Here the climbers are studying a map
or pulling on their long woolen socks.
This is early on, years before the Ark, dawn.
The profile of an animal is being smeared
on the wall of a cave,
and you have not yet learned to crawl.
This is the opening, the gambit,
a pawn moving forward an inch.
This is your first night with her,
your first night without her.
This is the first part
where the wheels begin to turn,
where the elevator begins its ascent,
before the doors lurch apart.

This is the middle.
Things have had time to get complicated,
messy, really. Nothing is simple anymore.
Cities have sprouted up along the rivers
teeming with people at cross purposes —
a million schemes, a million wild looks.
Disappointment unshoulders his knapsack
here and pitches his ragged tent.
This is the sticky part where the plot congeals,
where the action suddenly reverses
or swerves off in an outrageous direction.
Here the narrator devotes a long paragraph
to why Miriam does not want Edward's child.
Someone hides a letter under a pillow.
Here the aria rises to a pitch,
a song of betrayal, salted with revenge.
And the climbing party is stuck on a ledge
halfway up the mountain.
This is the bridge, the painful modulation.
This is the thick of things.
So much is crowded into the middle —
the guitars of Spain, piles of ripe avocados,
Russian uniforms, noisy parties,
lakeside kisses, arguments heard through a wall —
too much to name, too much to think about.

And this is the end,
the car running out of road,
the river losing its name in an ocean,
the long nose of the photographed horse
touching the white electronic line.
This is the colophon, the last elephant in the parade,
the empty wheelchair,
and pigeons floating down in the evening.
Here the stage is littered with bodies,
the narrator leads the characters to their cells,
and the climbers are in their graves.

It is me hitting the period
and you closing the book.
It is Sylvia Plath in the kitchen
and St. Clement with an anchor around his neck.
This is the final bit
thinning away to nothing,
This is the end, according to Aristotle,
what we have all been waiting for,
what everything comes down to,
the destination we cannot help imagining,
a streak of light in the sky,
a hat on a peg, and outside the cabin, falling leaves.

Judith Hall

Hats, A Chiaroscuro Madrigal

A cloche in plum,
In lion marigold,
Or mannish toques; a Borsalino. Bring
The pillbox ocelots
And marabou;

A monkey ear
Atrocity or hounds
Of washed vanilla silk; though leashed with leather,
Muzzled, on display,
A pack of fangs.

A ladies' laugh,
Sufficient in her eyes.
Another weapon, shrunk to millinery
Trifles; ridicule,
Will it expire?

A brim the span
Of swans; all diffident,
Marmoreal, the goal; the inner band
Will smell of rosemary,
A signature

Adrift. A hat
To hide in, further, feathers
Dyed cassis; a gathered arsenal
On mousseline. Remote,
Protected ghosts.

Pam A. Parker

Transgress, Transdress

— Marjorie Garber, *Vested Interests*

One can, she says, rewrite the story so it
becomes a progress-tale, a *Bildungsroman,*
at the end of which our protagonist,
having suffered indecision, sloughs
herself (or him, whichever might be wrong),
shrugs out from under the coating shell,
the trousers (or skirt, whichever) to stand
finished, a whole woman (or man). Done
with struggle, or rehearsal or pretense
(whichever), she (or again, he) is free,
being, now, purged of opposites, single,
unitary, one (or the other) thing.

One can, she says; it's a mistake, misses
the point, the possibility offered:
neither man nor woman, some third, new, thing.

Creating its own space this third creates
displacement, shoving balance off, it hacks
the former axis, splits the center point
to make new lines, triangulates between
a trinity of possibilities;
replaces two with three, and supercedes
the play of doubles, swapping back and forth
between two poles, with half again as many
choices, roles, positions, points where light
can shine, expand the mind's delight, and play
a newly tempered scale of human notes.

Top Ten Philosophical Hits

Tibor Fischer

One of the best books I never wrote was one to cash in on the millennium. I did get as far as the title: *The Two Meets the Three Zeros* (Uptown).

So delighted with that, I took a year off before purchasing and designating an exercise book to imprison my thoughts on the subject. Ten years on, I flicked through to light upon three terse entries, a squashed ant and an address I had wanted so badly at one point I had completely emptied my study in a frenzy to locate it. Two of the entries were illegible and the third was an attempt at a biography to go on a dust jacket of another book I didn't write.

I am working on the assumption that my lifelong sloth hasn't been that, but a well-disguised storage of creative vim for the killer opus to leave known civilization gasping. One book and out. I'm taking it all down. The trivialities. The ramblings. The drearies. The trites. I'm taking no chances. Rounding up all the usual suspects, and all the unusual ones, picking them off as they emerge one by one.

The only frank and remotely pleasant exchange I ever had with the Master of my college was very short, after one of my slips. "I'm flabbergasted," he perorated, "that you have managed to make a career as a philosopher."

"Not, I assure you," I replied, "as gobsmacked as I am."

People have said to me: "Eddie you're a loafer." People who don't like me very much and who have assessed my progress uncharitably have said: lush, compulsive gambler, zero, drug-dealer, fraud, disaster, slob. People who like me have said much the same.

For the record, I am well aware that I didn't execute any of the chores, that as a pro, as an official thought trafficant I should have done. I didn't write any papers or books. I didn't do so much teaching, though this made me rather popular. People were eager to be supervised by me since when they didn't turn up I didn't remonstrate because I wasn't there either.

I did go to conferences though, if someone else paid. And I was very hot on subscribing to journals. I did the same lecture, year after year, without yielding to the temptation to make changes.

I blame the authorities. In a half-reasonable world I would have been fired a long time ago. In a sixth-reasonable world I would have been booted out sooner. Even in a hundredth-reasonable world I wouldn't have got far.

I did everything wrong. I got a first at university. I didn't mean to (perhaps the secret). By the time of my finals I had chosen to go into banking and I knew that without any effort I could pick up enough degree for that. For the last paper, I almost didn't go. It was only because it would have offended Wilber, my director of studies, who had taken much stick in my defence, that I trudged along. Perhaps the first was a subtle, rigged, way of encouraging me to stay on, as Wilber had been persuading me to do.

No, I left (though I didn't get far). Nick, who had been on the substitutes' bench took the slot for zetting young philos-opher, but then topped himself. I was expelled from the towers of high finance and parachuted back into Cambridge, months after vowing never to return.

I made my speciality the Ionians. Very few people realise

that you can read the entire extant oeuvre of the Ionians, slowly and carefully, in an hour. Most of them come in handy packets of adages. Extremely important, the first caught having a go with their reason, the inventors of paid thought and science — anything you'll find in a university — and blissfully curt.

Years ago I had noticed some domains in which no one had done any work, but the thing about these areas in which no one has done any work is (a) there's nothing to be done or (b) it's extremely difficult to do something or (c) the work's been done but you didn't know about it because you were too sloppy when you checked the first time. In addition, as a specialist in the history of philosophy, I can assure you that there isn't a thought that the Greeks didn't copyright; they corralled all the concepts long before Christ. That's a position you could defend comfortably. And any cranial creations that you might maintain weren't spotted by them have certainly been mopped up by the French, German and British crews.

Take my favorite researcher, the brilliant John Smith, (try checking up on that name) whose hermit-like existence rapidly achieved legendary status. A legendary hermit-like existence that was necessarily legendary and hermit-like because John Smith didn't exist.

People have read and, allegedly, enjoyed his work. They've seen his documentation. He had a room in college (arranged by me and praised by the cleaners for its tidiness). People had distinct memories of him. They discussed the meetings he didn't attend, lunches he mysteriously cancelled at the last minute via bizarre forms of indirect communication. And even if he was, in essence, a figment pigmented by my wit, where did it say on the application form you had to be able to make a bed creak?

And there were naturally bona fide zettists too (eletromagnetically discernible to others) who got the peel of the financial fruits. There will be those who will say I was blocking those with talent from furthering the cause of the biz. Good, I'm glad, as the politicians say, that you mentioned that. That's exactly what I was doing. Three years at university doing philosophy is enough for any healthy individual.

It occurs to me that with the demands that are made on our leisure time, a wallet-sized, handbag-fitting Top Ten Philosophical Hits might be a profitable venture. I scrawled down some of the most salient prosifications:

1. *"Hoc Zenon dixit.": tu quid?* — Seneca
2. *On ne saurait rien imaginer de si étranger et si peu croyable, qu'il n'ait été dit par quelqu'un des philosophes.*
   — Descartes
3. . . . . . . και παντ ειναι αληθη — Protagoras
4. *Stupid bin ich immer gewesen.* — Hamann
5. Σκεπτομαι — Sextus Empiricus
6. Themistocles driving in quadriga pulled by four harlots through the agora in Athens at the height of business.
7. *Wenn ich nicht das Alchemisten-Kunstück erfinde, auch aus diesem-Kothe Gold zu machen, so bin ich verloren.*
   — Nietzsche
8. I dine, I play a game of backgammon, I converse and am merry with my friends; and when after three or four hours' amusement, I would return to these speculations, they appear so cold and strained and ridiculous, that I cannot find it in my heart to enter into them any further.
   — Hume
9. *Infirmi animi est pati non posse divitas.* — Seneca
10. For how few of our past actions are there any of which we have memory? — Hume
11. God knows all. — Ibn Khaldûn.
12. *Secundum naturam vivere.* — Seneca
13. *Si fallor, sum.* — St. Augustine
14. *La lecture de tous les bon livres est comme une conversation avec les plus honnête gens des siècles passés.*
    — Descartes
15. *Impera et dic, guod memoriae tradatur.* — Seneca

So there's the squad I have to whittle down. It's interesting that Seneca charts so often. Zero as a thinker, a failure on the

new grey juice front, one has to own up that as a commentator
and ideal salesman, he's unbeatable.

1. This is arguably the top sentence in the biz. The maximum
   maxim. "This is what Zeno said, but what about you?"
   You might have some trouble deciding which Zeno Seneca was referring to, but this question unquestionably
   captures the gist; it's not the enlightenment that counts,
   but the taking part. The great heavyweights of antiquity
   are not there to be admired but to be lifted, to be tested
   against your brain's brawn. The prosifications of the greats
   are no more use than dumbells under the bed if you don't
   pump them.

4. Stupidly, that's me: Hamann doing his Socrates number
   (as well as issuing a reminder that no amount of intelligence can save you from stupidity), and unless you're
   lucky enough to be portering a massive arrogance, a quo-
   tidian sensation, one neatly glorified by St. Augustine in
   (13) (If I'm in bed with a hippopotamus, I am), then
   covered more successfully by René, producing one of the
   greatest one-liners. You've got to get the monostich right.
   Posterity won't bear anything that can't be fitted on a
   beer mat. You need the catchphrase. For the T-shirts.

12. Live according to nature. This is an evergreen one. You
    get this everywhere: the problem is making up your mind
    what nature is. Get someone to tell you and give them
    your money. Great all-purpose line massive with con men
    and fakes of all nations. Also this Senecaism encapsulates
    the old style phil which promises to make a real man of
    you, to deagonize your life, to give you a tonic, as opposed
    to Ludwig's light for hire and what you see is what you
    get clarification.

11. God knows all. Always a popular cop-out, and a good
    one to stick in to avoid lapidation, burning at the stake,
    being machine-gunned and so on, unless you're living in
    a society where the clerics have gone in for social work.
    This should be squired by: *"audacter deum roga"* — Sen-
    eca. Call boldly on God, a move hardly limited to prac-

titioners of the biz, the only recourse most of us have. The striking thing about the biz is that despite the wielding of rationality, the brouhaha over proof, the bravado of the *nous*, you can't turn the history of philosophy without tripping over mysticism, spectre-spectaculars and bleatings for celestial authorities to sort out our riddle-riddled universe.

6. Themistocles zooming around the agora in a tart-powered chariot. Nothing to do with philosophy of course. But what an idea!

I rererererereturned[10] to Cambridge from London one Monday to find a letter enclosing a contract for me to write a history of thought. Perplexed, I surmised I had impressed someone at a party. It was a period when I spent a lot of time blathering at parties. Money, a zam-zum-mim of an advance for a signature? That seemed a good deal, a bonus for being rat-arsed. However, it soon transpired that more was required from my pen than my mark but a quick tour of philosophical bloodshed through the ages? A doodle.

The advance for the book was unnaturally large and caused pleasing amounts of resentment amongst my colleagues, with Featherstone in the lead. I bought a case of Chateau Lafite '61 and put it down for two days (the irony is that I don't even like Chateau Lafite, I'm not sure anyone does). I consumed it in one sitting and lying on the floor. I pissed the money away — mostly through my best suit. I was a middle-aged home for the world's griefs, homing in on me.

Why do you drink? I have been asked. Because (a) I like to and (b) it's hard to stop. When you've got the hole, you can't go to the corner shop and ask for a couple of pounds of meaning, a packet of panacea, a can of resolution. A solution for one's plight is hard to find, but solutions aren't. You can't go a hundred yards without a pick-up point for zymurgic solutions: off-licences, pubs, supermarkets, restaurants. Civilization is a careful construction for the production and distribution of alcohol.

The publishers eventually tracked me down and asked me

about the book, how it was, where it could be found? I coun-
tered by asking for more money, simply so I had something
to say apart from, I can't find the typewriter and even if I
could find it, it doesn't have a ribbon, and the a and the z
don't work.

I don't know whether I have unwittingly the knack to sound
charming, or whether I had latched onto a singularly profligate
publisher, but more money was sent.

I bought ten crates of tequila, true brainwash, which would
have cleansed the life out of me if a cohort of crack barflies
hadn't volunteered to spend the weekend with me at a cottage
near South Zeal. It's not a fact that has been widely marketed,
but that weekend we created, over three hundred square feet,
for several hours, intergalactic euphoric eternal fraternal just
benevolence.

The thing about signing a contract is that it can mislead
people into thinking something has been agreed. In reply to
their missives, I snarled for more money, more rudely. I trusted
that they would get tired of me, but no, the cheques came
unabated.

To an extent, I did bring it on myself. I did weaken and
send in an outline (knocked out for me by a most junior
research fellow). They responded by sending me their catalogue, announcing my forthcoming title. The arrival of the
catalogue became an annual event. There is a part of me that
likes to make people happy so when they asked if the book
would be ready I said yes, granting them an epoch of content-
ment.

Alternating with the catalogues were telephone calls from
distraught females, some bursting into tears, some threatening
me with that hushed, knotted hatred that proceeds fevered
stabbing with a good quality kitchen knife. My guilt was such
that after four years I went to the university library and copied
out a few pages of a nineteenth-century work on medieval
thought by a Reverend, updating a number of the verbs.

Then one day I got a call from a Scottish voice introducing
herself as my new caseworker. "Why don't we have a drink?"

A woman who knows how to handle crabby philosophers, I thought.

Hence I arrived at the offices to be the target of those regards that only someone who is seven years late with delivery of book and who has been the beneficiary of small, but accumulatively obscene and ruinous advances gets. My arrival at the publishers and holding a glass of zinfandel was my last usuable memory for some time. I misplaced quite a bit of time mnemonically. I have a hazy thought on why planes have to be too hot or too cold, and more distant sensations of discomfort and disorientation.

Of cold and discomfort, more reports were submitted by my body and as my consciousness gave them serious consideration, my senses gave me an image of myself handcuffed to a radiator in a bare, white-walled cottagey building. The handcuffs seemed an official philosopher-restraining device, so I assumed I was in some backward, hard-up clink. I wondered how the nearest British Consulate would react to me.

Then the young lady who was my current editor walked in.

Certainly, in an attaching-a-philosopher-to-a-radiator situation, the handcuffs win; they are the supreme rhetorical device for attaining juxtaposition. If you must do this, I do endorse an attractive young woman as a kidnapperess, though preferably one that doesn't want you to write a book.

So, I was bereft of booze, captured in a cottage, devoid of hyperspace liquid that could gain me access to ticketless travel.

"Dr. Coffin, you are lazy . . . thoughtless . . . crapulent . . . contemptible." I was biding my time until something came up to which I could object, but nothing surfaced in her disdain that I could really contest. "You're on Barra. You're miles from the nearest off-licence, even if you could decuff yourself. You have a problem: me. And I have a problem: you. We can unproblem ourselves. I enjoy working in publishing, but you are impeding, indeed threatening my career. No one has ever been so reluctant to blacken paper as you, no one has ever been so absorbent of funds. Now I have the task of getting a book out of you. I didn't ask for it, but my job depends on it. I've tried being friendly, I've tried being stern, I've tried leaving you alone, I've tried pestering you . . . "

"I can remember the being left alone, but I can't place the pestering or . . . "

"Your memory is extremely selective."

"All memory is extremely selective," I said attempting a wriggle, "otherwise we'd be in a mess; that's what memory's there for, to not remember, otherwise we'd be weighed down with telephone numbers, tooth brushings, zouk, nose blowings, ceilings, furniture, shopping, waiting for public transport, our work . . . " I petered out, being poorly and unable to mount a rhetorical blitz from the floor.

"At the risk of wearying your memory, let me reiterate the salient facts. You've had seven years and the largest advance we've ever given. We've had thirty badly typed, treble-spaced pages, which don't make much sense."

"Let's hire someone to hunt down some nice illustrations . . . to fatten it up a bit."

"Dr. Coffin, we, but particularly I, need a book. Books start at four times the length you've submitted."

"We could be different."

"No, we can sit down and write. Ten pages a meal. When you've done two hundred you can say goodbye to the radiator."

I have my faults (there aren't many I don't have) but in many ways I'm reasonable and unflappable. With good humour I had been conducting a colloquy from a cold floor, abducted and manacled to a radiator. Perhaps my personality hadn't been switched on; but suddenly my ego bounded out of its kennel and barked. I went berserk and had a good zob.

Do you know who I am?

This is I risky ploy. Akin to parachuting, you've got to be sure it's going to work, otherwise all you're doing is outrageously multiplying your discomfort. It was the only time I made a claim to importance; my play for dignity only resulted in pure indignity.

Still, if you're going to lose all dignity, look utterly ridiculous and be stripped of all cultivated attributes and blub pathetically, there are a few places better than a cottage in Barra with an audience of one to get it out of the way.

I frothed for four minutes. Then I was too knackered to rant, so I did enough sulking for a small town in five minutes. However, being a pro, I couldn't delude myself about the rapidly approaching craving for a drink. I had a go at negotiation. It didn't work.

"I haven't kidnapped you, Dr. Coffin. No one could believe that a slip of a lass like me could force a beachmaster of erudition such as yourself, a man with a history of violence, to do anything. There are plenty of witnesses to your travelling up here zealously, bottle of malt in hand. I can't make you write, but I warn you I'm on holiday for two weeks and that's a long time for a man in your position."

I weighed things up: fuming and refusing and enduring, or capitulating and scribbling? Perhaps this was the induced birth of a mighty opus.

"Forget the food," I said in heroic stoic, "get me a drink."

We had a new contract. I remained on the inclement floor and with a volume of the Shorter Oxford English Dictionary (Marl-Z) as a desk, tried to write, the bottle of whiskey opposite me across the room, onerous when you feel as if you are under thirty feet of water.

Using big words and big letters and a deal of repetition, I had reached the furthest reach of page ten when she reentered.

"That's the Renaissance," I said, sullenly indicating the papers, "bottle please."

While I badgered, she scrutinized the sheets. "I can't read this," she pronounced, "I can't read a word of this, apart from one that looks like *geranium* and that can't be right." I reminded her, whilst thrashing about on the floor and worming down to new depths of abasement, that she hadn't asked for ten legible pages. She fetched a typewriter and a low table.

I threw another zam-zum-mim of a tantrum because typing out the pages wasn't appealing, and I had an even more harrowing moment when I realized I couldn't read my own writing either. I sprinted across the pages, because whatever you do, the desire for a drink remains patiently.

"Do you do this for a living? Am I mistaken in thinking
that you are a specialist in the history of philosophy?"

By then the residue of dignity had gone, and I simply
slumped on myself in the way you see people do in disaster
areas when they know that they will never enjoy themselves
again. Darkness came and I was given a bowl of porridge and a
banana. I smouldered through the night like a harshly-treated
primate, having come to terms with perishing on Barra. But
the next morning when she turned up with some toast, she
handed me a chapter.

"What do you think?"

"It's very lucid," I commented.

"Fine," she said unlocking me. "I take it you have no objec-
tion to me writing your book for you?"

"I cannot agree to such subterfuge, unless you give me a
cast-iron guarantee that I will get all the royalties."

A Studio Visit with
Mia Westerlund Roosen

Mia Westerlund Roosen's 1994 exhibition at the Storm King Art Center brought together some of her key works of the last fifteen years, a diverse group of sculptures united by their resonant organic forms and their sexual charge. They ranged from singular flaring "columns" evocative of limbs, horns and phalloi, to serial pieces such as American Beauties, *a row of swelling discs suggestive of, among other things, sea creatures and breasts. Most recent were the large outdoor sculptures that literally penetrated the landscape: fragile-seeming carapaces — actually papery sheets of special concrete — arching out of a steel-lined "grave," a riffle of concrete leaves or a portly mass, all striving to escape their excavated "containers." The most spectacular of the new works,* Adam's Fault — *a title rich with alternative readings — was a hundred-foot long trench with robust man-made "boulders" punctuating its walls. At once wound, archaeological site, fortification, assertion of will and phenomenon, the piece changed dramatically as you moved along it and peered into its recesses, your viewpoint subtly altered by shifts in the terrain. Assertive and mysterious, the earth pieces are among her most provocative sculptures to date.*

Not long ago, Roosen moved into a light-filled studio near the Holland Tunnel. It is already filled with new works, radiat-

ing sculptures that she refers to as "hair pieces." On a long window sill, like miniature variations on the works she showed at Storm King, is a series of low earth mounds.

INTERVIEWER

How did the Storm King exhibition affect you?

WESTERLUND ROOSEN

Being asked to do that show was a big impetus to do something outdoors, obviously. In the late 1980s, I started feeling that I wanted to so some pieces that made larger gestures in an interior space than I had been doing, but were still discrete objects. I did *American Beauties* and *Olympia*, which were inside at Storm King. They were my first pieces that were about really trying to fill a space. They were the predecessors of the pieces in the ground. I work like a turtle, going from one thing to another, very slowly. I don't think I could have made that big leap to the Storm King pieces without having done some pieces like *American Beauties* in the last four years.

INTERVIEWER

Would you call the earth pieces installations?

WESTERLUND ROOSEN

When I started figuring out how to do the pieces for Storm King, one of the obvious things was that the place is so much about welded steel — the macho guys like Mark de Suvero — pushing up into space very aggressively. And I thought that the only way to respond would be to go down into the earth. The fact that the pieces are actually placed in holes in the ground gives them a hyper-real sense of place, and the seriality of the pieces gives a flexibility of installation. However, the clustering of the parts also contributes to the creation of a kind of monolith.

INTERVIEWER

Had you thought about going into the ground before the Storm King show was proposed? I remember a series of sculptures like tables with troughs in them and elements inserted the way you inserted elements into the excavations.

WESTERLUND ROOSEN

I made them after I started thinking about Storm King.

INTERVIEWER

So the tables were surrogates for the earth?

WESTERLUND ROOSEN

I had already done two of the earth pieces, *Crib* and *Legion*, before I did the tables. The tables were like drawings for the pieces in the ground, but they ended up having a very different feeling because a table is a real object. One of the things that occurred to me when I was doing these pieces is that the relationship between the volume and the surface, which was emphasized by the skin or the sheathing with encaustic or lead in the indoor sculptures, changes in the earth pieces. You get the tension between the volume and the earth. The volume is pushing through the earth and that's where the main energy of these pieces comes from.

INTERVIEWER

You had masses and "leaves" pushing through the table tops in the trough pieces, so what was underneath became important. It was fascinating. Here was this utterly familiar object, doing something wholly unexpected.

WESTERLUND ROOSEN

It's the first time that a drawing or a maquette of mine has taken on a life of its own and such a different meaning. They have a much more surreal aspect than the earth pieces. Most models translate sculpture or even architecture into solely acts of seeing, looking or gazing. The body is absent. The use of

the table form encourages the body's presence literally and
metaphorically. The table is a kind of horizon, but also a
domestic object. That's why, when I showed them, I decided to
emphasize their domesticity, to contrast with the earth pieces.

INTERVIEWER

The domesticity of the tables gives them female connotations, but there's always a very strong feeling of the body—
male and female—in your work.

WESTERLUND ROOSEN

Having been the only female sculptor at Leo Castelli's gallery
for the fourteen years I showed with him, I certainly was very
aware of maleness! The earlier pieces that I showed with Leo
were in direct response to this. I was always struggling to carve
out an identity within this group, which led me to working
with these connotations that you allude to. At the time, it
was surprising to me that the women's movement hadn't particularly embraced me.

INTERVIEWER

I would suspect that was because your work hasn't been
solely about "women's issues"—which I think has been part
of its strength.

WESTERLUND ROOSEN

It's never been particularly narrative. I've always felt that
overt autobiography and narrative get in the way of seeing
the aesthetic of a piece. The earth pieces were like—this is
true about a lot of my pieces—like a big bang in my head.
Much of my work is very intuitive and instinctual and just
sort of comes. What makes it difficult to work that way is that
you commit yourself to an idea and a process and a scale, but
you don't really know whether it's going to work until it's
actually all done.

INTERVIEWER

There certainly were big changes in the pieces at Storm King as the summer progressed, from when the edges were still raw earth to when the grass had grown, just as there was a difference between the pieces where the walls of the cut were lined with steel and *Adam's Fault*, with its raw earth walls.

WESTERLUND ROOSEN

I am having a very hard time trying to figure out how to make *Adam's Fault* a permanent thing instead of hundred foot trench in the ground, but it's very hard to go back to a wall that isn't made of earth. I am thinking of stone or of making concrete look like earth, but nothing will be as satisfying as the real earth. I've just recently heard of some California technology that involves tamped earth that seems promising.

INTERVIEWER

Permanence is a whole other issue. I know a French conservator specializing in contemporary art who says that old master art is easy, because conservators know what goes wrong with it and they know what they can do. But with contemporary art, it's not only the materials that drive them crazy, but all kinds of other issues. If something is made from its conception out of materials that are, by their very nature, ephemeral, is it a violation to preserve it or to remake it?

WESTERLUND ROOSEN

I think it makes more sense to remake. I think most artists would feel that way.

INTERVIEWER

A painter I know, who uses a lot of very questionable materials, has a theory that if something is good and it starts to fall apart, then someone will figure out a way of fixing it.

WESTERLUND ROOSEN

I think that's true.

INTERVIEWER

What will become of the pieces at Storm King now that the show is over? If they were "traditional" earth works — the kind where the whole meaning of the piece was simply making a mark on the landscape, or I should say, in the landscape — then they could gradually disappear. But your sculptures aren't like that.

WESTERLUND ROOSEN

The pieces will be de-installed in order to have them reappear in another context in another landscape. This malleability interests me greatly. A truth or an experience is not fixed — it is fluid. I keep coming back to the need for ambiguity in the work. I think it is a reaction to dogma, a need to allow for more participation by the viewer rather than less. Dogma and the fixed sign defeat this.

— Karen Wilkin

Works

Mia Westerlund Roosen

Crib

Bethlehem Slouch

Legion

Adam's Fault

Eudora Welty

Two Encounters

INTERVIEWER
Do writers ever come down here to see you?

EUDORA WELTY
Yes. Henry Miller came one time. My mother said he'd never enter my house. We had him for three days. I got two or three boyfriends to help me with him and drive the car and protect me from God only knew what my mother thought. They were going to give him a glass automobile, from which he could see out and they could see in. He didn't come in a glass automobile, but he came anyway.

INTERVIEWER
I've never even seen a glass automobile, have you?

WELTY
No.

INTERVIEWER
What a shame that Doubleday didn't build one for him.

WELTY
Well, I wish they had.

INTERVIEWER
Did you like Mr. Miller?

WELTY

Not much, he was so dull. He never looked at anything.
I guess he was bored by being in Mississippi. That day they
were going to move the hospital for the insane down on North
State Street to the next county, to a bigger place. The patients
were helping move themselves. I thought that that would be
a funny sight for Mr. Miller, especially since the superintendent was named Love. Superintendent Love, moving the insane hospital patients from Jackson to across the river. It meant
absolutely nothing to him.

INTERVIEWER

That's hard to believe.

WELTY

I thought so too. It's not every day there's something like
that in Jackson to offer anyone. These poor old crazy people
carrying their own beds out, and putting them in a truck and
driving away. Don't you like that?

INTERVIEWER

It's wonderful. Did you ever write about that yourself?

WELTY

No. But I thought it was a gift that I could offer as a hostess.

INTERVIEWER

I think you said that he always wore a hat.

WELTY

He never took his hat off.

INTERVIEWER

Even indoors?

WELTY

Oh, he didn't come in much when he visited Jackson. He
had written a letter suggesting I write pornography. He really

was doing it out of kindness. He thought it was a way to make a little extra money. I guess he had different people he knew that were doing this. Some of his friends. I was so astonished that I told my mother about it when I read the letter, and she was shocked. She said, That man can never enter my house. I think he was planning to do so. We took him out to dine. There was only one good restaurant in Jackson then. We took him to it every night. There were different entrances. Afterwards, he said, "How is it that a hole like Jackson, Mississippi has three good restaurants?" We didn't ever tell him it was just one.

INTERVIEWER

What about William Faulkner? It must have been rather difficult, I would have thought, writing in the same state as this extraordinary figure, this mountain of a man in Oxford.

WELTY

Well, that's it, he *was* a mountain man. And everything else was the plains. He was lovely. I liked him very much. I had friends in Oxford that I used to go up and spend the weekend with. They were longtime friends of the Faulkners. I met him the best way, at a dinner party for about six people.

INTERVIEWER

Did he know your work?

WELTY

He wrote me a letter once. I framed it. I don't know where it is. But it said: "You're doing all right, you're doing all right." I was so thrilled that he had ever even read anything I'd written. Wasn't that nice of him? At Oxford they sort of made a pet of him and watched over him and took him fishing. I went sailboating with him.

INTERVIEWER

Where did you go sailboating with him?

WELTY

He invited me and a friend from here. He invited us to go out in the sailboat. We just sailed.

INTERVIEWER

He never said anything at all?

WELTY

I don't remember that he did. And I didn't neither because I wasn't going to open the conversation. I didn't know how. Well, that was his way.

INTERVIEWER

A quiet cruise. How long were you out there in the boat?

WELTY

It seemed a long time, I don't know exactly. He'd made the boat along with a couple of cronies. He never did say anything the whole trip.

INTERVIEWER

What is his genius, Faulkner's?

WELTY

I first think to say knowledge, he knew so much. And what he knew was right. He really learned about his part of the world and, of course, responded to it in every way. All those marvelous details in his stories and everything, spring out of fact. It makes it so powerful, you don't have to know it's out of fact. But when he wrote it he knew it was out of fact. I believe everything Faulkner said. I know a funny tale about him, but it may involve somebody still alive, I don't know. I'll tell you anyway. Somebody who lived around Oxford, somewhere in north Mississippi, decided she was going to give a party for all the writers in Mississippi. Her name was Cile White—like the second half of Lucile. She had a printing shop. She made calling cards for herself. Cile White, the

South's Most Lovable Love Story Girl. She wrote love stories.
So she decided to give a party on the dam for all the Mississippi
writers. She printed invitations saying: Present Card at Dam.
Most anybody counts as a writer in Mississippi. Everybody
writes something down here. I didn't go to it. She decided
she was going to be a writer, and the way to do it was to get
all of us organized. That's typical of Mississippi. She invited
Mr. Faulkner, but he didn't come.

INTERVIEWER

But there is one lovely story you told about a writer who
wrote to Mr. Faulkner wanting some advice on how to do a
romantic scene.

WELTY

Someone sent him a manuscript, and the author of it told
me that he wrote back a real nice letter. He said, "I read your
story. Honey, it's not the way I'd have done it, but you go
right ahead." That was kind.

— George Plimpton
Jackson, Mississippi
October 14, 1994

Jacqueline Osherow

My Cousin Abe, Paul Antschel and Paul Celan

O one, o none, o no one, o you
Where did the way lead when it led nowhere?

Perhaps, like everything, it has its flow and ebb,
The way nowhere, I mean, your brutal question.
Not that you were asking me. You asked no one
But I once eavesdropped on the conversation.
Regards, by the way, from my cousin, Abe;
I'm hoping they will serve as introduction.

Do you remember him? For twelve years your classmate?
A Yiddish speaker, religious, quick at math?
I was telling about his great *landsmann*-poet
And he identified you by your death:
He killed himself? In Paris? In the Seine?
His name is Antschel, Paul Antschel, not Celan.

He even has a picture of your graduation
(You were both dark-haired dreamy-eyed young men).
It's a wonder that the photograph survived.
My cousin must have brought it to Japan,
A surprising place to go, once the war began,
But, for a while, his uncle's business thrived,

Import-export, I think it was, coral, pearls.
My mother has a strand of heavy beads
That Abe's wife, Beka, brought to her years later,
Like setting suns erased by wisps of clouds.
Abe must have meant them for his mother or sister
Or perhaps even the shiest of the girls

In matching fur-trimmed muffs and collars and hems
Whom you'd watch dawdling on their way to *shul*
While you were working on your weekly themes.

Abe said no one else could win the prize,
That everything you wrote was something beautiful
And he's a hard man, of little praise.

When I asked him more questions, he grew fierce:
Nice? Sure. We were all nice. Nice. Quiet.
Yes. I saw him daily for twelve years
But what do you ever know about a person?
I would speak in Yiddish, he spoke German;
My family was religious, his was not.

He pointed out some others in the picture:
The one who got to Venezuela to manufacture
Was it textiles? The one who managed to hide,
The one who teaches chemistry in Austria;
He didn't bother to say the rest had died
With his mother, his sister, your parents, in Transnistria . . .

As a child, I never dreamed it was a place,
It seemed to me some sort of fatal curse,
The heaviest among the floating words
I'd always heard but couldn't precisely trace.
Transnistria, it was only uttered in whispers
That lingered, unresolved, like bungled chords.

I later learned that Beka's mother had died
In Transnistria, my grandma's brother's wife.
They'd written back and forth, a charming girl,
So gracefully she'd filled sheaf after sheaf:
How they went out picking berries, mushrooms, sorrel . . .
Perhaps she met your parents on the ride.

How she must've made my grandma long for home
When she described her soups of sorrel and mushrooms,
The brandy she would coax from new, ripe plums,
From raspberries, the syrup to sweeten soda;
From gooseberries, the compote, sponge cake, jam;
I suppose you could call Transnistria their coda,

Certainly no more letters ever came
And there was no more anything to long for;
Longing was, itself, a strange taboo
But you couldn't quite help yourself, could you?
All you wanted was one untroubled hour
In the cinema, perhaps, or in a dream

Or wandering, aimless, down adopted boulevards
Oblivious to storefronts, noises, faces,
Trying to piece together shards of words
Scattered over Europe like the scattered beads
Of a thousand trunks of undelivered necklaces,
Bent on mapping out where nowhere leads.

Wherever it is, the way is rich in colors,
Loosely strung with dark-pink coral beads,
Littered with fur-trimmed muffs and matching collars,
Crumbs from airy cakes, gooseberry seeds,
Ink stains from a schoolboy's dreaming pen
And pale confetti floating on the Seine

And here is Abe, as he interrupts his wife
Who's describing making brandy out of plums,
To no one in particular he's quoting psalms,
Mumbling about the holiness of life.
What could have happened? He is bruised, distraught,
What could have made him do a thing like that?

Four Poems by John McKernan

The Shadow Beneath My Corpse Is Always

In training   He loves pretending he is
A layer of skin   Peeled from Death's moonburnt

Shoulders   Tonight he is resting under
Me   As I write these words
As I lie here on this bank

I tell him   Beware   I am
Breeding a Herd of Fireflies   I am
Weaving a net to skim the starlight
Off the surface of any river

His silence becomes a species of laughter
He thinks the only noise here is
The scraping of my pencil   He doesn't know
That I am sharpening the tips of each syllable
To impale him   Him and his little brother Fear

When the Ghost of Weldon Kees Visited

Our high school in Omaha
None of us knew it was Weldon Kees

We were all looking
For Natalie Wood
And coupons for red nylon jackets

We didn't really have any idea
At all   That we were part of a conspiracy
By our parents   Against us
That our incoherence was programmatic

We should have   We should have had
Weldon Kees trading cards
That way we might have guessed
That our pain was not yet an art form
But an inarticulate move in the right direction

Waiter   I Would Like a Dish of Feebly

Please   Waitress   More feebly please!   This is
The orangest feebly I have eaten   In a long time

I think this brand of feebly has a nice light
Airy texture   Even though it tastes somewhat
Like the flame inside unlit altar candles

I have never used such a tiny spoon   Nor seen
Such gigantic portions of lemon feebly   Almost

As large as that grain of salt we watched dissolve
Last month   Every time I taste another spoonful

Of lime feebly   It seems twenty years pass   Sometimes
When the sunlight smacks hard   On the marble
Then ricochets into the lilac   I wish I could take
One more breath   Or walk up   One more step
Even if it were feebly   Even if it were the last

I Abused My Father

Almost every chance
I could get   As a child

I discovered new uses
For most parts of my body
Lip   Eye   Shoulder   Foot   Etc

I experimented and developed
A new theory of silence
Polishing   Shining   Buffing
Until my absence sparkled like a shiv

Even today
I won't ever leave him alone   In my dreams
I continually plot   To crack
Open his coffin   I have a need to shake him
To tell him   OK   Yes   I am sorry

Vickie Karp

The Juniper Bonsai

It rests on tiny roots, a vision of angles,
And lives long.

It has no passion for gossip and little need for the usual,
Yet craves aftermath.

Likes to drink simply. Holds up its arms as directed
Yet does not harvest bitterness.

Is increasingly valuable with age.
Would not pay so much for itself.

Teaches quality through the distilled masterwork
Of each leaf, through its accurately expressed trunk.

Is beyond the concept of seasons as loss.
Measures in minutes and sees years as a form of belief.

Prefers suggestion: humidity for rain, admiration for
    ownership,
A firm pot instead of the earth itself.

Contains a noise of emotion in its resistance
Rather than in its growing.

Does not like to be touched without motive.
Does not ask which sorrow will fell us,

Will shrink us into a single gesture
So that one or two may deny that we are gone at all

By using our very lumber to make man-made shapes
Of our original unarticulated selves,

Even as we stand,
Even as we live.

Three Poems by John Burt

Charles Capers

St. Helena Island, South Carolina, 1815

Impatient at the ferry slip, he hoped
He'd long be out of Beaufort when they heard
The fool he'd been, the fools he'd made of them,
Who, with their greetings neatly written out,
And their proffer of the finest house in town,
Had rushed to Charleston, puzzled, but "prepared
To show what grace St. Helena can show
For one whose name alone made kingdoms fall."

St. Helena, it seemed, was somewhere else.
A heron beat across the steaming marsh.
He heard each rush of wings, so still the air,
And saw, where willows bent, the blur of white,
And saw the flash of hoes among the fields
Where all the bolls were bursting like small bombs.

Ice Storm

A fragile ringing all round suddenly
Awaking me, thought-stupid, elsewhere, chill,
My eyes on nothing but my road, my mind
On nothing but that same old thought again,
Then joy, all joy, as if I'd never been
What I would later be. And there they were,
The living branches radiant in ice,
Their sound like motion in the sky, alert,
Their trembling light uncertain in that wind.
It was their life I had again, and would
No matter what, hold hard to me as breath.
Oh, black branches! We are not made for death.

Mary's Gift

Pale, bone tired, she raised herself on one elbow,
Brushed her damp hair back with uncertain fingers.
There he was. They wiped off the wrinkled body
    Steaming in lamplight.

"Bring him to me." Fitfully twitching, silent,
How he lay, bewildered, his eyes unfocused,
Fumbling till she steered his blue mouth to nipple.
    "Oh, but he's lovely."

In the forest, shivering, one tree waited,
Secret, patient, keeping watch, still a sapling.
Yet the woman, singing to God in nonsense,
    Taught him what love is.

Tom Andrews

Cinèma Vérité: A Map Is Not a Territory

in memoriam Paul Celan

Blackout—in the theater as well as on screen. From a distance we hear Steve Reich's "Music for 18 Musicians." It almost sounds like a train approaching. Now we hear voices: by turns hushed and strident, interrupting each other, impossible to know how many . . .

Voice: In Czernowitz where I was born
Voice: In Chernovtsy where I was born
Voice: In Czernowitz, Bukovina, where I was born
Voice: Even the words Bukovina, Romania
Voice: In Romania where I was born
Voice: Even the words
Voice: Romania, Bukovina
Voice: Much has been said
Voice: Even the words in the language
Voice: In Czernowitz
Voice: Bukovina Bukovina
Voice: I hear the sounds
Voice: Even the words
Voice: I do not want to describe my memories for you
Voice: Where I was born
Voice: Czernowitz
Voice: Much has been said
Voice: What the land was like
Voice: I do not want to
Voice: Ukrainians of course Romanians Jews
Voice: I hear the sounds
Voice: Where I was born
Voice: Where I was born
Voice: Romanians Jews

Voice: I hear the sounds
Voice: What the land was like
Voice: Even the words
Voice: I hear the sounds

Silence.

Aerial shot rushing over the mountain ranges near Chernovtsy:
dense pine, spruce and beech trees for miles and miles.

Blinding light.

Susan Fox

Cro-Magnon

1. Bear

I make this line
my beast
of claw of tooth
who struck
and did not slay
whose blood
healed mine
whose pelt
my ease my ease my winter life
I draw now
where I killed him
mark here
the darkest meat
my children ever knew.

2. Stag

These lines are stag
wary, lithe,
my fear my feast my fair design.

3. Wounded Man

Here the brave one
crying horndeath
my kin my chief my mother's son
here we bore him
to his silence
here I keep my mother's son
for his sons and for mine.

4. Spotted Horses

Horses shatter sunlight
stain my eyes.
Why do I love
a running beast
so swift so changing so unknown.
If horse would heed
if horse would love —
but horse and hope and love
are nothing
and I love
my running beast
of broken sunlight
and I make it here.

5. Hand

The hand that made these lines
I print in ash
my lines my wall my hand.

Daniel Stern

Excommunication

And still there is no season's story told
by words, expressive, eager to explain;
no winter's tale will pass from mouth to mind;
only the sleepy, sensual touch is shared—and pain.

Perhaps some other language can be found;
our lexicon from birth is vague and thin:
the metaphor, the smile or bitter scowl—
these are not sharp enough to break the skin.

Though gaze or gesture, silences or song
cling to the memory like a summer cold,
they cannot tell us love is right or wrong.
Desire and blindness guide us: we are old.

What Remains

Robert Menasse

*Whenever we believe that
we recognize something,
we are especially forgetful.*
—Franz Josef Czernin

1.

I want only you. PAUSE
Who is she?
Some girl. We don't find out her name.
She seems to be afraid. The way she sits on the bed, her legs drawn up, and the way the blanket covers them and is pulled up to her throat. And look at her face, it seems . . .
It seems distorted. But that could be from having it on pause. That always causes some distortion.
Did he film everyone with whom he . . .
He didn't film everyone, yet he's the one who filmed everything.
Where was it filmed?

In a hotel somewhere in Brazil. But let's look at it again from the start. REW.

2.

Back in São Paulo. She immediately called a friend and told her about the hotel, the beaches and the departure schedule, her voice bubbling with the enthusiasm of a travel agent. Meanwhile, he was angry that he hadn't stayed home. Lying in his room or perhaps outside in the hammock, he would rather be reading a novel undisturbed or simply closing his eyes. But he always fell for the same thing. Again and again she dragged him off to foreign scenes that, when all went well, looked exactly like the pictures in the brochures that had enticed her. He asked himself why people took such pleasure in recognizing something, even though it was the first time they saw it. Or why they believed that the sun in a different place was a different sun, or was it that when they encountered surroundings different than those at home they needed to stay on guard. But in fact, he didn't ask himself any of this. How had this vacation come about? He said that he asked himself this later, after the return home.

The way she screamed. There is an expression, "screaming for joy," as if such a thing existed. He heard the way her steps slapped the parquet, he heard the slam of bedroom doors and closet doors, heard the hard rush of water from the faucet hitting the sink, he even heard how she opened her suitcase in the next room, the two quick, bright snaps when the locks sprang open. He knew he would only feel at home when she was again at work. He picked up a book that lay on his desk, holding it up to his face, and blew a sharp puff to see if any dust swirled up from it. No dust. He let the book fall open to a page. He read: *Stupidity, I contend, is nothing more than blind agreement with the outward appearance of the world*, and already he wished to read no further. In his room, tacked up on the wall, there hung a large map of the city of São Paulo. He stood before it and observed the shadow that lay on the map, a thin, meaningless, contoured shadow. He

had to shake his head a couple of times before he was certain
that it was the shadow of his own head. Then he drew away,
went into the bathroom and looked at himself in the mirror
for a long while, staring as if at a photograph. Finally, he
took a shower, washing himself in an odd manner such that
he avoided all contact with himself. Still wet, he lay on the
bed, and after a while got up again, dressed, and for three
hours played with his camcorder. He filmed every room in his
small house with slow pans and carefully considered zooms,
then the garden behind the house, the orchids, the hammock
that he had tied between two coconut trees and finally also
the street on which he lived. He placed the camcorder on top
of the television, looked at the film that was running on the
screen, then he taped it onto a cassette, which he later placed
next to the others on the bookshelf.

3.

PLAY. *Give me your most seductive pose.*

I think that's awful. Why does he have to do that? That
must be agony for the girl.

I don't know. On the other hand, she's going along with
it.

There's a lot of flirting involved.

You think so?

Yes.

Someone might see. Someone might be looking.

But we're alone. No one can see.

*But maybe later. Anything that's filmed can be played, and
someone can watch. I don't want that to happen.*

Come on, pull away the blanket, I want to see you.

*Turn the camera away. You can see me, you can see every-
thing, but turn the camera away. Do you have to tape everything?*

A pan of the room. It is mainly decorated in red, the plush
headboard of the bed, the curtains, while so much red produces a red tint to the film, a red shimmering, a chair covered

in red velvet over which clothing is draped, next to a reddish
brown chest on which there sits a purse.

Why do you need this camera?

Say: I want only you.

I want only you.

Again. More convincing.

I want only you. Can you turn the camera away now?

Zoom in on the red high heels in front of the chair. STOP.

I think that's disgusting. Can we turn it off? Maybe we can
find a tape on which he's filmed himself.

He's not on any of the tapes. He was always behind the
camera. PLAY.

Suddenly the camera wheels much too quickly. The girl
stands next to the bed, once more pressing the blanket to her
body, then she lets it fall.

She isn't naked!

What made you think that she was naked?

Then the girl runs towards the camera and away, no longer
in the picture, pure motion, then nothing, then the girl from
behind, blurry and out of focus, the camera not having enough
time to focus precisely on the girl before she is in the bathroom,
the girl already standing in the tub with the shower curtain
drawn. Pink plastic. The camera focuses on the shower curtain,
nothing discernible, no shadow to be seen behind it, until
suddenly a T-shirt sails over the curtain, a bra, jeans, panties,
the camera retreating as it films the pieces of clothing that lie
on the floor. The splashing of water can be heard. Pan to a
bath towel that hangs on a chrome rod between the tub and
sink, then zoom in at the same time that a laugh can be heard.
PAUSE. The towel fills the picture. Beneath the inscription
HOTEL REI MOMO the figure of an unusually fat man is embroi-
dered, wearing an odd hat that is not immediately recognizable because of the distortion caused by freezing the picture.

The fat man on the hand towel looks like a Buddha with
a fool's cap.

That is King Momo, the king of the carnival.

Do you know the hotel?

No. It could be any small hotel in Rio.

4.

He had often heard (and every time it's told the same way)
that things happen so fast that the one who is surprised has
no time to react. Then why had it gone so slowly, such that
he could observe it and even react in defense? Perhaps the
initial grip was clumsy, which can easily occur when the partici-
pants, both the criminal and victim, find themselves in motion
together.

Suddenly two young hoodlums were there, one hit him in
the shoulder, the other grabbed his throat. They did it suddenly, very much a rash assault, but it seemed at the same
time so slow and drawn out, as if they didn't really want to
grab him and hit him, but rather they were trying to release
themselves from a tough, sticky substance that held them from
behind. There was enough time to raise his arms in defense,
the movement of his arms strangely slow as they hovered before
the attackers, and so awkward that he would have preferred to
scream instead. But it happened without a sound. Soundless,
whirling movements that seemed so tranquil, and which presented their whirling like snowflakes in one of those globes
that, when shaken, depicts a scene in winter. It was all he
could think of despite the tropical heat.

Why had he in fact put up a fight? He would not have
resisted if they had tried to take the watch from his wrist or
the money from his wallet. But the gold necklace with the little
gold heart attached, he didn't want to give that up without a
fight. As far back as he could remember he had owned this
necklace and had always worn it; it was older than his own
memory, something from the time before one even begins to
forget.

The boys fled; had they abandoned him? He didn't see
them anymore; he saw before him nothing but the darkness
of the street. It wasn't black, wasn't simply nothingness; the
darkness was porous, illuminated by streetlights, lit with a
painful light that swelled and then shrank on its own, a stabbing pain at the back of his head, now complete blackness,

finally nothing, at last a dreamless sleep. It was only strange
that he knew that: at last a dreamless sleep.

Suddenly he saw something white, and he knew nothing
more. A shimmering white plain, a broad crack, a hole in the
blackness that stood around him like a wall. He wanted to
step through it into the shining brightness. He pressed his
head into this passage, pressing inward where it was soft and
warm, but why was he pushed back? He tried it again, but
something pushed him back, though he didn't give up, gasping as he bore into the warm whiteness, though not gasping
alone, for there was a ring of people, and he heard a voice,
words that he didn't understand at first. Was it the voice that
repeated the words continually, or did he repeat them himself
inside his head for so long that he eventually grasped their
sense? *Wake up! Everything's okay. Everything's okay. Wake
up!* He felt pressure from behind and he returned the pressure,
let himself sink back, and as he lay gasping on his back he
saw a white enameled metal tube, above him a gallows — a
gallows? next to him a woman, a nurse, who scrupulously ran
her hands over her white apron, smoothing it out with quick
rubbing motions. *Everything's okay. I'll get the doctor now.*

The doctor gave the impression of being a happy man. With
a beaming smile he said his name, appearing deeply satisfied
that the patient had already regained consciousness, saying
more than once, *You were lucky!* consulting a radiologist's
report, *Nothing serious!* he said and laughed. Now all one
had to do was *get everything down.* He asked him what his
name was, but he didn't know what his name was, where he
lived, he didn't know how he had gotten the head wound,
he didn't know it. The doctor, who had said his name in such
a friendly way at the start, became angry with the patient,
who seemed to be persistently keeping something to himself,
and he tried once more. Again and again he asked him what
his name was. He didn't know it.

5.

Then he was walking through the city again; it was no longer
night, but also it wasn't daylight, rather the dusk of semi-

consciousness. The streets were busy, he walked and walked, the hurried, purposeful movements of everyone else creating lines and rows, a thick net through which he slipped as if he were bodiless. Again and again he gripped his throat with his hand, knowing not why. What was he doing here? Who was he? It was unknown. It occurred to him to look through his pockets in order to look for a clue. He found a handkerchief with flecks of blood on it, some money, a half-full pack of cigarettes, a match book from a hotel, a key ring. What was this key for? He didn't know. Where did the flecks of blood on the handkerchief come from? Had he had a nose bleed? He shoved his index finger up each of his nostrils to see if they were crusted with blood. Children came up to him and laughed. Was he a smoker? He lit a cigarette. He experienced nothing more than the fact that it felt good to smoke. Then he took off his Sakko and checked the inscribed label. The Sakko was from Paris. Was he in Paris?

He looked around and recognized nothing. He was a stranger. But where? And from where? He closed his eyes, as if wanting to separate the night he experienced inside himself from the night that was beginning to fall over the city. Someone jostled against him. He heard someone talking so close to him that he thought he could smell their breath. He heard someone else laughing. Why? Why didn't he know? Why did he know nothing? If he could at least know that. He opened his eyes again and saw a man who was hawking newspapers. *Diario da Noite! Diario da Noite*! To his ears it sounded like *Diaranoi*. He repeated it softly, Diaranoi, then repeated it a few more times, then louder: *Diaranoi*. He chuckled with satisfaction, as if he had suddenly learned the language of this city. Out of gratitude he bought a paper from the man. Where was this paper published? In São Paulo. He was in São Paulo. But why? And from where had he come? He understood what he read in this paper, but at the same time he knew it was not his mother tongue. In what language did he think? At the very moment he asked this, he no longer knew in what language he had thought the question, and then no more words occurred to him, only the words that he saw on the front page of the paper. He opened the newspaper. Body of a young woman found in hotel room. A grisly murder. *Hotel Rei Momo*. The woman must have been *systematically tortured, mutilated, the entire room red with blood, the identity of the murderer unknown, not a clue*. Within his thoughts something was set in motion, perhaps an image, a visual memory that was trying to reach him. But it exhausted itself in having to cross such a distance and was only barely familiar. He could make out hardly anything more than a shapeless, reddish glimmer of light in which there was an incomprehensible whirling of colors that wavered, blended together, and were lost.

He folded the newspaper under his arm and lit another cigarette. His glance then fell upon the writing on the matchbook that he held in his hand. He was startled, stuck it quickly into his pocket, and felt the handkerchief with his hand.

The glimmer of light he had felt earlier now tried to reach the surface of his consciousness, and he squeezed his eyes shut with a feeling of utter panic, tried to suppress it. Back down into the darkness. He groaned aloud and crumpled up the handkerchief in his pocket. Someone was asking him whether he was all right, meanwhile the handkerchief grew bigger and thicker in his hand. He yanked it out of his pocket, balled it with both his hands, wanting to make it very small, squeezing it, wanting to make it disappear.

What's the matter? Then the light was there.

6.

He knelt in bed and rubbed the blanket until he was surprised to find himself awake. Little by little he was getting used to the light as he began to not only see the things in his bedroom, but also to recognize them.

She had turned on the light. Wake up, what's the matter? she said once more.

I was dreaming. I was dreaming something awful.

With hesitation he began to tell her the dream. He began with the attack. Two boys had tried to rip the necklace from

his throat. He reached for his throat; there was the chain. He
searched for the pendant until he could feel it between his
fingers. Look how misshapen the pendant is, one can hardly
tell that it was a little heart. I must have chewed on it as a
child.

He breathed deeply, gasping for air, his chest heaving. He
was still upset enough that he could hardly speak and breathe
at the same time. With my baby teeth, he said, still gasping
for air with a rattle in his throat. She sat there motionless with
her legs crossed next to him in bed and listened. He asked
himself why she made no attempt to quietly caress him, for
couldn't she see how bad off he was? Then it hit him, everything that had been lost from his memory. Waking up in the
hospital without knowing who he was, later running around
in the city as a stranger, feeling so absolutely alien that he
no longer knew anything at all. She yawned.

And then what happened?

He looked at her and became furious, because it was obvious
from the way she looked that she had to make a real effort,
that she felt obligated to listen to him in order to settle him
down. And what did she do to try and quiet him? Not a
single gesture of tenderness, not even a soothing word—just
a question to prod him on! She sat there wooden, holding
herself erect in a taut, disturbing pose that only demonstrated
to him all the more how she tormented him by posing a question only so that he might finish all the more quickly and she
could go back to sleep. He impatiently cleared his throat a
couple of times and nodded his head as an indication that it
really wouldn't last that much longer.

Why did you wrap the blanket around yourself that way, as
if you were angry with the blanket, what were you think- . . .

I don't know. Maybe I was hot. The sweat of pure fear. I'm
really exhausted. Would you make me some warm milk with
honey?

She went into the kitchen and came back a brief moment
later with a glass of water.

Her whining voice. That the floor in the kitchen was too
cold. That she didn't want to stand there barefoot for so long.

That during the night the cockroaches always came out. That she was afraid of them.

And then, as she saw how he looked at her: Drink a little water; that will help to settle you.

He had the urge to throw the water in her face, to tell her to wake up. He took a sip from the glass and thought that it would be impossible to wake her. For people like her there was no such thing as a good shock. If he should leave her, she would no doubt be telling someone in her whining voice how sympathetic and tender she had been, even when he was so rude or mean, even though when he had bad dreams she was nonetheless patient and — was she crazy? It was sugar water! She had been so kind as to bring him sugar water in order to soothe him, always so kind and always doing everything, patiently listening, while he on the other hand . . . That's the way she would tell it, and she was also firmly convinced that it was so. Still on the verge of spitting at her, he put the glass down, thanking her. She gave him a pained smile. He saw that her weariness pained her, yet she seemed self-righteous in her suffering, proving yet again that she would stay with him through thick and thin. At the same time, infantile as she was, she did not understand why things couldn't be easier, for she loved being in Rio again for a weekend, having a couple of days on the beach at Barra de Una; she loved all that, loved all situations in which he asked himself what there was to do but kill time, watch it go by and begin to sweat, while for her it was sheer happiness, and when it was perfect, when she was happy, that was when he had no nightmares, no bouts of irritation, no strange ideas which she did not understand, asking him why he was so restless, my dear, why are you so upset, it is really so beautiful here.

Was that the entire dream?

No, he said, although he had no more desire to relate the rest of his dream. Certainly he didn't want to say anything about buying the newspaper with the article about the murder. A murder in the hotel which they had only recently checked into — in Rio. She felt herself capable of suddenly screaming from within the emptiness of her obligation to listen to him,

and only because she could imagine herself doing that, she
suddenly began to try to think of a reason why he was upset.
It was almost impossible. Sometimes people ate too late and
too heavily, then they had bad dreams, though that seemed
not to be the answer, or at least not an answer that explained
everything. Right now what he really wanted was—what?

And what happened then? Did your memory return?

Did my memory return, he thought dumbfounded, did
your memory return, how dumb she really was. Since when
have nightmares had a happy end? Yes, he said, it came back;
listen, this is what happened.

As I was saying, I ran around without knowing who I was
and where I was. Then I walked by a sidewalk café and decided
to have a bite to eat and methodically try to remember.

In any case, I ordered a cup of tea and one of those little
cakes that are dry as sand and which they had in the display
case. I felt a jolt and suddenly a singular euphoria burst inside
me.

I saw a gray house and its facade. I saw it as a piece of
scenery from the theater. Then I saw in my imagination a
small addition on the back of this house, which caused me
to think of a sentence that said it was erected for my parents,
and along with the house the entire city was erected, as well
as the square, the square into which someone sent me before
lunch, the street, the church. The sentences that occurred to
me conveyed the feeling of something certain, yet something
that really didn't connect up with the images, sentences such
as *clear and observable the city and the gardens rise from my
cup of tea*. And then I saw clearly and precisely the apartment
in which I had lived as a student, seeing it in all of its particular-
ity, and I saw myself sitting there within it and reading, a
young student in Vienna who was eager and excited to devour
the great novels of the world and to spend all night discussing
these books with friends, and—

He stopped short. He saw all of it clearly before him, and
also his grandmother's house in the country where he had
always spent his summer vacation.

And?

And nothing, that was all, he said in irritation. As a result
of the sudden appearance of remembered images, within
which the mechanism for revealing their meaning was buried— I know, no, I *knew* once more who I was and from where
I came.

Then he said nothing more and stared at her, waiting for
a reaction. He had stared in this same way as a child, on a
bleak and rainy holiday, stares at a test tube into which he
had poured two fluids from his chemistry set in order to see
what would happen. As he thought about this, he no longer
saw her, but rather himself and his odd, cold, childish mixture
of curiosity and fear. Nothing had happened; his chemistry
set was one that was safe for children.

7.

In the German bookstores and used bookshops he bought
countless books that he arranged on the shelf at home and
left unread. He had already read them. He would also have
liked to buy the children's books that he could remember
having read. He wanted to stand before the shelf in order to
receive signals from the spines of the books about what in fact
was inside his head.

Instead, what was gathered together in this house appeared
to be covered with a layer of dense varnish that deflected his
gaze. Not once did anything surprising reveal itself.

The distant noise of the city expressway that he had accepted
as acoustic proof of his urban existence. The odors that blew
in through the open window, a mixture of dead leaves, exhaust
fumes and the smells of cooking, which were also exhaust
fumes. Most of all, odors. The smell of alcohol in his living
room and study. The cleaning lady wiped everything down
with alcohol. The smell of propane in the kitchen. The musti-
ness of the bedroom, a result of the dampness in the air, which
would permeate the robe that hung in the closet, even if it
were not worn, so that it had to be washed regularly, otherwise
it would become mildewed. São Paulo meant certain odors
to him. Or a quality of light. Above all, it meant a wavering

haziness, blinding and dusky at the same time. A light that lay upon the city like cellophane. He found it impossible to capture with his camcorder.

8.

In a valley next to very clear water I once saw a dead stag. He had been shot, a bullet hit him in the side, and he had tried to get to fresh water in order to cool his pain. But he had died at the shore. He lay there with his head resting on the sand and his front hooves stretched out into the pure water. Not a single living creature could be seen anywhere around. PAUSE.

What's that supposed to mean. What's he talking about?

I don't know. Perhaps he's fantasizing, maybe he's quoting from something.

But there's nothing to be seen in the picture.

It's not exactly nothing. There is something. But it's hard to recognize. Perhaps a shadow or a spot. PLAY.

I was so taken by the animal; I admired its beauty and felt an enormous sense of compassion for it. His eyes were just barely open.

The image on the screen began to move, the camera pulled back, widening the perspective, making it possible to recognize that . . .

Yes, it's sand, a sandy beach. The spot is a depression, a shape in the sand. Something evidently had been lying here.

Or someone. But certainly not a stag.

Can you make it out?

The camera now moved slowly around the body's shape in the sand. The sea washed softly to the edge and back again, leaving a glittering trail.

It glistened with a painful brilliance and made it seem as if his countenance, which almost appeared to be speaking, was also a reproach to his murderer.

Then the camera turned swiftly upwards, soon people in bathing suits appeared within it, then, for a moment, the sun just above the horizon, an explosion of light, a white-gray shimmering, and suddenly the frame is black.

What's wrong?

I don't know. Perhaps he's . . .

The stag that I saw has always hovered before my eyes. He was a noble, fallen hero and a pure being. STOP.

**— translated from the German
by Peter Filkins**

Jumping from Bridges

M.F.K. Fisher

Now I am thinking about jumping from the Golden Gate Bridge, and about other places where people have jumped to their deaths for many years. I think I should find out more about this, for I have an idea that there is some sort of collection of spirit strength or power or love in them that says *no*, or *yes*, or *now*.

I feel very strongly that this is true about the Golden Gate Bridge. Today, I heard that people are trying once more to build a kind of suicide-prevention railing along its side, which would keep us from seeing the bay and the beautiful view of the city. I haven't read much about suicide lately, but I believe that almost 98 percent of such deaths leave more evil than good after them. Even my husband Dillwyn's death, which I still feel was justified, left many of us with some bad things. And when my brother died, about a year after Timmy did, my mother asked me very seriously if I felt that Timmy's death had influenced David to commit his own suicide, which to me remains a selfish one, compared to the first. I said, "Of course, yes! I do think so, Mother." And I *did* think then that Timmy's doing away with himself helped my young brother

David to kill himself, a year later. But there was *really* no connection; we don't know what the limit of tolerance is in any human being.

I do think, though, that there *has* to be a place where one can jump to one's death. There have always been such places. There is one in Japan that is quite famous. I believe it has something to do with beautiful Mount Fuji, which I saw in a strange breathtaking view from far away one day when Norah and I were in Japan in 1978. We had gone out with our chauffeur to meet some people for lunch, and suddenly the driver stopped the car abruptly. He said in an odd voice, "Look! Look!" And there, rising above a most dramatic Japanese-carved bank of mist and dark and light and lavender and white, was Fujiyama.

Even from a distance I could feel some of its enormous magic, and my hair prickled on my head. It was so beautiful! It was exactly like all the bad pictures I had seen on calendars and cans of beer. But it was *there*, and it was beautiful beyond the face of any god. It was all-powerful, and I felt like dying.

I have always known there are some people who must jump, but I never really knew about it myself until I was almost overcome once by a need to go off the Golden Gate Bridge. I feel quite impersonal about it now, just as I did the day Arnold Gingrich came out and dedicated one whole day to me.

He said, "Please, let's make a list of everything you like to plan but never really do." It was all very touristy: we went to the Cliff House first, and then we drove to the San Francisco end of the Golden Gate Bridge where I thought we would walk halfway across and then walk back. I never did tell Arnold about what happened, but about a quarter of a mile onto the bridge I realized that the whizzing cars on one side, and the beautiful peaceful bay on the other, were splitting me in two. The stronger half looked toward the city, the beautiful tranquil city, and I was almost overcome with the terrible need to jump off and be more peaceful.

I know it wasn't the sound of the traffic. It was a kind of force that was almost as strong as I, and I felt sick at the effort to resist it. I remember I took Arnold's arm and said, very coolly, "Let's go back now. Let's not go any further." And without any question we turned around, and I stayed on the inside track, near the bridge rail, and as long as I kept my hand firmly on Arnold's arm, I knew I would not do anything foolish. But I know too that I have never had such a strong feeling of forces outside myself, except once in Stonehenge—

No, now that is not exactly true; there *were* two or three other times. One, I remember, was on the steps of the cathedral in Dôle, a miserable little dim rainy city on the edge of Burgundy. I was standing on the steps of the cathedral when suddenly I was overcome by a feeling of evil. And instead of running into the church for holy reassurance, I ran away. I had to get away from the church, not into it. Maybe I could trace this back somehow to Carmina Burana and those secular plays that were given on the steps of the old cathedrals, like Dôle's. I don't know, but for a minute I was almost overcome by older spirits than mine.

And one time I felt a wave of horror, when Al and I were living in a room in Dijon above a pastry shop on the rue Monge. I didn't know it then, but the little square where I went to get water in big pitchers for our cooking and washing and so on had been an execution spot during the French Revolution. The guillotine had been set up in that little *place*, and many fine Burgundians had had their heads roll there.

I remember our apartment was charming—one large room with three windows looking down onto the old *place*. It was big and airy with a red tiled floor and a little old fireplace; it had been a parlor, I'm sure, in a modest townhouse. There was an alcove with a bed in it, and Al slept on the outside of the bed and I was on the inside, and one night I jumped right over him and stood in the middle of the room, overcome by a sense of horror and fear. I felt filthy. Al woke up and asked me what was wrong. I said, "Nothing! Nothing!" But I felt absolutely clammy and horror-stricken by something I did not understand.

Such times have made me believe that there are congregations of evil and that they are stronger than any of us. This is why people who are perhaps weak to begin with jump to their deaths at times. Perhaps many of them, like me, do not want to jump off into the deep water far, far below, but something says: Get out! Jump!

This is why I have often said, in a rather casual way, that I don't think there should be a fence on the Golden Gate Bridge. Some people are going to jump. And if they can't join the waters deep below, and be swept out to sea — or, very rarely, picked up and made to survive the ordeal of hitting that surface so far below — I think there should be someplace else for them. But that place, and others like it, have always been chosen not by the citizens of San Francisco or elsewhere, and not by the people who built the bridge, but by something much stronger than we know about.

Perhaps there is something about water, or anything bridging a body of water, that seems to attract people to jump off out down into it. Very few people jump down into a pit of manure, except by accident, but there is something about a bridge over clear water, no matter how far down (perhaps the farther the better), that does pull people down into it, toward it. I know this pull well, and I have no feeling of impatience or anything but tolerance for the people who jump. There *must* be those places. There are those places.

I have not said that the Golden Gate itself had a feeling of evil when I almost jumped off it. Rather, I felt an urging toward oblivion, I suppose, toward peace. I do not believe it was bad. I do feel the Golden Gate Bridge is a place of great beauty, where many people merge with that beauty into a kind of serenity, a compulsion to get out of this world and into a better one. And that is not evil at all. But I do know that there are many evil things that lurk in the minds of all people who are left after the suicide of somebody they love.

— Glen Ellen, California, 1986

M.F.K. Fisher

Why Again

At first, in the immediate impact of grief,
The body lay criss-cross.
The arms were spread out, and the legs stretched.
Gradually the immediate impact of grief grew less.
The legs came up, and crossed at ankles.
Arms folded softly across the wracked chest cage,
And the abandoned heart softened and came alive again.
The body grew quiescent, receptive,
A chrysalis, not dead
But reviving, curling into a further acceptance of the same
    process, the same physical position.

Within, there was still protest.
Why again, asked the vigorous spirit.
This time is surely enough, to be stretched out and pinned,
Pickled in the brine of the spirit.
No, said the spirit.
But the legs straightened and then pulled up,
The wracked arms crossed with gentle resignation over the
    breasts,
And the life began to slow to the waiting throb in the
    ever-hollowed still soft bosom.

Everything was ready for more.

—St. Helena, California, 1965

NOTES ON CONTRIBUTORS

FICTION

Tibor Fischer was born in 1959 and brought up in London where he now lives. He won a Betty Trask Award for his first novel, *Under the Frog*. The story in this issue is adapted from his novel *The Thought Gang*, forthcoming from The New Press.

Marcia Guthridge's first published story, "Bones", which appeared in the fortieth-anniversary issue of *The Paris Review*, won her the 1993 *Paris Review* Discovery Prize. She lives in Chicago, Illinois.

Robert Menasse lives in Vienna, where he was born in 1954. He has taught at the University of São Paolo in Brazil, and is the author of two volumes of essays on Austrian culture and three novels, most recently, *Schubumkehr*. His translator, **Peter Filkins**, has held a Fulbright grant to study in Vienna and is a graduate of Columbia University. His translation of Ingeborg Bachmann's complete poems, *Songs in Flight*, is available from Marsilio Publishers.

Helen Schulman teaches in the Graduate Writing Division of Columbia University's School of Fine Arts. She is the author of *Not a Free Show*, a collection of short stories, and a novel entitled *Out of Time*.

Daniel Stern is the author of nine novels and two collections of short stories. He is a professor of English in the University of Houston's creative writing program. Mr. Stern's poetry also appears in this issue.

POETRY

A.R. Ammons is the author of *Garbage*, which won the National Book Award in 1993. He resides in Ithaca, New York.

Tom Andrews's second book of poems, *The Hemophiliac's Motorcycle*, won the 1993 Iowa Poetry Prize. His first book, *The Brother's Country*, was a National Poetry Series selection in 1989. He teaches at Ohio University.

Rick Barot lives in Oakland, California. His poetry has appeared in *The Georgia Review* and *The Gettysburg Review*.

Molly Bendall is the author of a collection of poems entitled *After Estrangement*, published by Peregrine Smith Books in 1992. She teaches at the University of Southern California.

Frank Bidart is completing a book titled *Desire*. He recently received a Writer's Award from the Lila Wallace–Reader's Digest Foundation.

George Bradley's most recent book is *Of the Knowledge of Good and Evil*. He lives in Connecticut.

David Breskin lives in San Francisco. His book *Inner Views: Filmmakers in Conversation* was published in 1992.

John Burt is the author of a book of poems, *The Way Down*, and a critical study, *Robert Penn Warren and American Idealism*. He teaches at Brandeis University.

Kevin Cantwell teaches writing and literature at Macon College in Georgia. His poems have appeared in *The New Republic*, *Southwest Review* and *Shenandoah*.

Billy Collins, whose latest collection, *Questions about Angels*, was selected by Edward Hirsch for the National Poetry Series, was a Guggenheim fellow for 1993 and 1994.

Fred Dings's first book of poetry, *After the Solstice*, was published in 1993 by Orchises Press.

Stephen Dunn teaches at Richard Stockton College. His most recent books are *Walking Light: Essays and Memoirs* and *New and Selected Poems*: 1974–1994.

Jane Flanders is the author of three poetry collections, most recently *Timepiece*. She lives in Pelham, New York and teaches poetry workshops in the Writing Institute at Sarah Lawrence College.

Susan Fox's poetry has appeared in *Poetry, Chicago Review* and *Boulevard*. *XXII*, a limited-edition fine-arts publication, includes her work along with etchings by Richard Ryan. Her forthcoming two-act libretto, *The Village*, premiered at Queens College in March, 1995.

Peter Gizzi's books include *Periplum; or, I the Blaze*, published by Avec Books, *Music for Films* from Paradigm Press, and *Hours of the Book* published by Zasterle Press. He is currently at work on *The Complete Letters* and *Lectures of Jack Spicer* to be published by Black Sparrow Press.

Jody Gladding's first book, *Stone Crop*, was published in the Yale Series of Younger Poets in 1993. She has taught at Cornell University and lives in East Calais, Vermont.

Rachel Hadas received an Ingram Merrill grant in 1994 and a Guggenheim prize for poetry in 1988. She is the author of *Other Worlds than This* and *Mirrors of Astonishment*, both published by Rutgers Press.

Robert Hahn has written three books of poetry, including *One More Time*, published by Cummington Press.

Judith Hall's first book, *To Put the Mouth To*, was selected for the National Poetry Series. She lives in Pasadena, California.

Barbara Hamby is the winner of the 1994 Vassar Miller Prize from the University of North Texas Press, which will publish her collection, *The Ovary Tattoo*, in 1995.

Joseph Harrison is a resident of Baltimore. His poetry has appeared in *The Missouri Review* and *Western Humanities Review*.

Scott Hightower lives in New York City. His poems have appeared in *Salmagundi*, *Southwest Review* and *The Minnesota Review*.

Vickie Karp is a senior writer for Thirteen/WNET and a recipient of a 1994 NEA grant for poetry. Her work is forthcoming in *The New Yorker, The New Republic* and *The Yale Review*.

Sue Kwock Kim is the co-author of the play *Private Party*, which was produced in New York and Edinburgh. She is currently living in New York City.

Carolyn Kizer won the Pulitzer Prize in 1985 for *Yin: New Poems*. She has just been made a chancellor of the Academy of American Poets.

James Longenbach is the Joseph H. Gilmore Professor of English at the University of Rochester. His poems have appeared in *The Southwest Review* and *The Yale Review*.

John McKernan teaches at Marshall University. He is the author of *The Writers Handbook, Walking along the Missouri River* and *Erasing the Blackboard*.

Susan Mitchell has been awarded fellowships from the Guggenheim and Lannan Foundations. She received the first Kingsley Tufts Award in 1993 for her book *Rapture*.

Joan Murray is author of *The Same Water*, published by Wesleyan in 1990. She received a New York State Writer in Residence Grant in 1994.

Jacqueline Osherow's most recent book is titled *Conversations with Survivors*. She has been awarded the Witter Bynner Prize by the American Academy of Arts and Letters and an Ingram Merrill Foundation grant.

Pam A. Parker works on Wall Street as a computer programmer. From 1986 to 1989 she served as an editor for *Conditions* magazine.

S.X. Rosenstock's poetry first appeared in *The Paris Review* and is forthcoming in *The Western Humanities Review*.

Phillip Sterling is a professor of English at Ferris State University in Big Rapids, Michigan. He is the recipient of an NEA fellowship in poetry, the PEN Syndicated Fiction Award and a Senior Fulbright Lectureship to Belgium and Luxembourg.

Daniel Stern's short story, "The Oven Bird by Robert Frost," is also featured in this edition of *The Paris Review*.

Greg Williamson teaches in the Writing Seminars at Johns Hopkins University. He is the recipient of the 1994 Nicholas Roerich Poetry Prize, and Story Line Press will publish his first book this spring.

Max Winter's poems have appeared in *The Quarterly* and *The St. Mark's Poetry Project Newsletter*. He lives in St. Louis, Missouri.

Linda Stern Zisquit was born in Buffalo, New York. Since 1978 she has lived in Jerusalem, Israel where she teaches and translates. She is the literary editor for *Tikkun*.

INTERVIEWS

Drue Heinz (Ted Hughes interview) is the publisher of *The Paris Review*.

Gabriel Motola (Primo Levi interview) is an adjunct professor of English at Bronx Community College and at New York University's School of Continuing Education. He is a novelist and has published essays on Primo Levi and other victims of the Holocaust.

FEATURES

M.F.K. Fisher (1908–1992) was the author of over sixteen volumes of essays and reminiscences.

Donald Keene's most recent book is *Modern Japanese Diaries*.

George Plimpton spoke with Eudora Welty at her home in Jackson, Mississippi in October of last year.

ART

Rhett Arens is a freelance photographer and writer living in St. Paul, Minnesota.

Burhan Dogançay was born in 1929, in Istanbul, and received a doctorate in law from the University of Paris. His work is included in many museum collections internationally, including the Museum of Modern Art and the Solomon R. Guggenheim Museum as well as the Nicolas Alexander Gallery in New York.

Tony Fitzpatrick's etchings appear courtesy of the Bridgewater/Lustberg Gallery in New York City. His work can be found in the collections of the Museum of Modern Art, the Art Institute of Chicago and the National Museum of Art in Washington, D.C.

Mia Westerlund Roosen received a fellowship from the John Simon Guggenheim Foundation in 1993. She lives in Buskirk, New York and New York City. The photographs of her work appear courtesy of Lennon, Weinberg, Inc.

Karen Wilkin is an art critic for *The New Criterion* and *Partisan Review*.

The Paris Review
Booksellers Advisory Board

THE PARIS REVIEW BOOKSELLERS ADVISORY BOARD is a group of owners and managers of independent bookstores from around the world who have agreed to share with us their knowledge and expertise.

ANDREAS BROWN, *Gotham Bookmart, New York, NY*
TIMOTHY CARRIER, *Odegard Books, St. Paul, MN*
CHAPMAN, DRESCHER & PETERSON,
  Bloomsbury Bookstore, Ashland, OR
ROBERT CONTANT, *St. Mark's Bookstore, New York, NY*
JOSEPH GABLE, *Borders Bookshop, Ann Arbor, MI*
MARGIE GHIZ, *Midnight Special, Santa Monica, CA*
THOMAS GLADYSZ, *The Booksmith, San Francisco, CA*
GLEN GOLDMAN, *Booksoup, West Hollywood, CA*
JAMES HARRIS, *Prairie Lights Bookstore, Iowa City, IA*
ODILE HELLIER, *Village Voice, Paris, France*
RICHARD HOWORTH, *Square Books, Oxford, MS*
KARL KILIAN, *Brazos Bookstore, Houston, TX*
KRIS KLEINDIENST, *Left Bank Books, St. Louis, MO*
FRANK KRAMER, *Harvard Bookstore, Cambridge, MA*
RUPERT LeCRAW, *Oxford Books, Atlanta, GA*
TERRI MERZ AND ROBIN DIENER, *Chapters, Washington, DC*
MICHAEL POWELL, *Powell's Bookstore, Portland, OR*
DONALD PRETARI, *Black Oak Books, Berkeley, CA*
ENCARNITA QUINLAN, *Endicott Booksellers, New York, NY*
JACQUES RIEUX, *Stone Lion Bookstore, Fort Collins, CO*
ANDREW ROSS, *Cody's, Berkeley, CA*
JEANETTE WATSON SANGER, *Books & Co., New York, NY*
HENRY SCHWAB, *Bookhaven, New Haven, CT*
RICK SIMONSON, *Eliot Bay, Seattle, WA*
LOUISA SOLANO, *Grolier Bookshop, Cambridge, MA*
DAVID UNOWSKY, *Hungry Mind Bookstore, St. Paul, MN*

LIZARD FEVER

Poems Lyric, Satiric, Sardonic, Elegiac

EUGENE WALTER

LIVINGSTON UNIVERSITY PRESS, ALABAMA

Since 1936 this poet's work has been
published in America, Europe, the
Antipodes. Set to music by many
famous composers, these lyrics have been
performed in Carnegie Hall, in Paris,
Brussels, New Zealand, Japan, etc.
Now they are collected in a volume
with many poems never before in print.

LU PRESS
tation 22
Livingston University
Livingston, Alabama 34570

$12.95 plus $1.50 Postage & Handling